Katerina's Wish

Katerina's Wish

Jeannie Mobley

MARGARET K. MCELDERRY BOOKS
New York   London   Toronto   Sydney   New Delhi

MARGARET K. McELDERRY BOOKS
An imprint of Simon & Schuster Children's Publishing Division
1230 Avenue of the Americas, New York, New York 10020

MARGARET K. McELDERRY BOOKS is a trademark of Simon & Schuster, Inc.

For information about special discounts for bulk purchases,
please contact Simon & Schuster Special Sales at 1-866-506-1949 or
business@simonandschuster.com.

The Simon & Schuster Speakers Bureau can bring authors to your
live event. For more information or to book an event, contact the
Simon & Schuster Speakers Bureau at 1-866-248-3049 or visit
our website at www.simonspeakers.com.

Book design by Debra Sfetsios-Conover
The text for this book is set in Cochin LT Std.
Manufactured in the United States of America
0113 FFG
10 9 8 7 6 5 4 3 2
Library of Congress Cataloging-in-Publication Data
Mobley, Jeannie.
Katerina's wish / Jeannie Mobley.
p. cm.
Summary: Thirteen-year-old Trina's family left Bohemia for a Colorado coal
town to earn money to buy a farm, but by 1901 she doubts that either hard
work or hoping will be enough, even after a strange fish seems to grant her
sisters' wishes.
ISBN 978-1-4424-3343-4 (hardcover)
ISBN 978-1-4424-3345-8 (eBook)
[1. Family life—Colorado—Fiction. 2. Coal mines and mining—Fiction.
3. Immigrants—Fiction. 4. Czech Americans—Fiction. 5. Colorado—
History—1876-1950—Fiction.] I. Title.
PZ7.M71275Kat 2012
[Fic]—dc23
2011044392

In memory of my father, whose dreams took us
so many places,

And to my mother, whose belief in me helped make
this wish come true.

Chapter 1

MY PAPA'S DREAM brought us to America. Momma said only a fool believed in dreams, but she knew Papa, so she packed our trunks. And whether she believed or not, that dream swept us out of Bohemia and across the ocean. We'd arrived, in the autumn of 1900 in "a new land for the new century," as Papa put it. By May of 1901, neither the dream nor the country felt new. They both felt old and worn out. As I stood behind our house, staring at a dozen bundles of filthy laundry, I couldn't help but think Momma had been right.

Papa had dreamed of a thriving farm where we would live well. He had imagined acres of green fields, not the dry, barren hills of southern Colorado. He had imagined fresh air and sunshine, the bounty of the fertile land filling our larder and our pockets. Instead, he spent long days underground, toiling in the unwholesome air of a coal mine. And even with all this laundry Momma took on, our pockets stayed empty and our larder was never full. Now that my sisters and I were out of school for the summer, Momma had determined to take on as much washing as we could from the bachelors in town. But it still wasn't likely to mean much money.

"This is too much wash to do in the kitchen," Momma observed from the back door.

"It's too much to do at all," I grumbled.

"If you want to be going back to school in the fall, you'll be needing a new dress," she said. "And the money's got to come from somewhere."

The new term would not start until October, when the schoolmaster returned from one of the other coal camps in the area. But saving money wasn't easy. When we left Bohemia, Papa had thought a year in the coal mines would earn us enough for a farm. We had been here nine months already and had saved almost nothing.

"At least Trina will get a new dress," Aneshka said. She was sitting on the back step, kicking at the dust. "I'll just get her old dress cut down to my size, and Holena will get mine that used to be hers."

"I don't mind," Holena said quietly from her seat beside Aneshka. She would be starting school for the first time in the fall.

"Mind or not, it can't be helped," Momma said, her mouth setting into a thin, tight line. It was almost the only expression she had worn since coming to America. "And you do have to go to school." School was important. Momma had had few chances to learn English. She relied on my sisters and me to translate for her.

Momma sighed, looking again at the big piles of coal-blackened laundry. "We'll take this load down by the creek. That way we don't have to haul water. Trina, you carry it there, and we'll all join you when chores here are done."

I began hauling tubs and bundles of filthy clothes across camp and down the steep slope to the little creek to the west. It took me four trips back and forth across the shabby town, and each time I returned to the house it seemed Aneshka was working slower and slower at her easy jobs. Holena, who was too little to help carry anyway, was watching Momma knead the week's bread dough. I glared at Aneshka as I gathered the bundles, but she ignored me.

In the creek bottom, I found a wide, grassy spot and built a fire, then arranged stones to balance a tub over the flames. Then I filled the tub with water from the creek. By the time I was done, my sweat-soaked dress clung to my shoulders. My mother and sisters had still not arrived. I wiped the sweat from my forehead with the corner of my apron. Was this all there was to my father's dreams—sweat and coal dust and endless hours of work?

I stretched and looked around. If I was going to spend the day scrubbing filthy clothes, I wasn't going to stay here while I waited for the water to boil. I deserved these few minutes to myself. I wandered along the water's edge, listening to the birds chirp in the low bushes and trying to forget the drudgery of the day ahead.

A short distance downstream, the valley narrowed and turned. The slopes of the valley became steeper, blocking the view of anything around the bend. I had never gone there. For months, I had come only to the creek to draw water. My pace quickened as a flutter of adventure stirred in my heart. I glanced back toward the laundry. My mother and sisters still weren't there. I had time to see what lay beyond the shoulder of land.

Around the bend, I stopped in amazement. The creek spread out into a still pool. At its edge, an ancient cottonwood tree leaned out, its massive branches reaching across until they shaded the creek bottom from slope to slope. For a moment I thought I might be dreaming. I had never seen this tree before.

As I approached the tree, the high slopes of the valley shut out all sounds from the mine. For the first time in months, I couldn't hear the clank and screech of the cables in the hoist. The only sounds were the gurgle of the stream as it entered the pool and the sighing breath of breezes in the leaves overhead. Unexpectedly, tears filled my eyes. How often I had taken those sounds for granted in Bohemia. How foolishly we had left that behind to come here.

I pressed my hand against the rough bark to assure myself the tree was real. The trunk was so thick, I could not have reached even halfway around it if I'd tried. Two massive roots, each as thick as a mule's haunch, ran from the trunk to the water's edge, enclosing a triangle of soft grass between water and tree. I stepped over the closer root and sat down, my back against the massive trunk. The roots encircled me like my father's arms had when I was a child, making me feel safe. In the stillness, the constant ache for our home in Bohemia welled up inside me.

I watched a small leaf spinning lazily across the surface of the water, feeling like I was in a secret place. The mine, the washing, the endless chores had disappeared. There was only me, and the soothing stillness of this place. But as the leaf drifted out over the deepest part of the pool, I realized that I was not alone. A movement beneath the surface created a ripple that caught the leaf and spun it faster. I sat up to see better. With a flash of silver, the thing disappeared under the bank. I crawled forward and leaned out over the pool. The water was clear, and I could see the pebbles on the bottom in the shifting green light beneath the tree. I lay still and watched. After a long moment, a fish emerged from beneath the bank. It was not a large fish, but

4

larger than I had expected in a creek that size. It watched me, just as I watched it.

A story stirred in my memory. Back in Bohemia, my grandmother had told stories as we helped her stuff sausages. One had been about a fish—but I couldn't quite remember.

The fish began to rise toward me with slow sweeps of its tail. I leaned closer, until my face almost touched the water. I could clearly see its flat, broad head and the whiskerlike feelers protruding from either side of its mouth and chin. It was a carp, a fish we had considered lucky back in Bohemia. Only a few inches and the surface of the water separated us as it watched me with one shiny black eye. I held my breath, waiting to see what it would do.

"Katerina!"

A shout from upstream shattered the moment. I jerked my head up and the fish darted away. Aneshka was standing at the bend, her hands cupped around her mouth, getting ready to yell again. I scrambled quickly to my feet and stepped out from the shade.

"Coming!" I called, and hurried toward her. I didn't want Aneshka here. This place felt special—magical—in a way Aneshka couldn't understand. She was too much like our mother.

"Where have you been?" she said, her hands going to her hips.

"Nowhere," I said, and brushed past her without another word. She was five years younger than me; I didn't have to answer to her. But as I approached the washtubs, I knew I would have to answer to Momma.

"Where have you been, Katerina! I sent you down here to start the washing."

"The water was heating; it wasn't ready," I protested. I hadn't been gone very long.

"But it isn't hot, because while you went off daydreaming, the fire went out."

I looked at the washtub. Weak wisps of smoke and bits of half-burned wood were all that remained of the fire I had started. No steam rose off the water.

"I'm sorry." I began stuffing fresh wood beneath the tub. Soon the fire was lit again, but Momma wasn't satisfied.

"Trina, the family needs your help, not your daydreams. You are thirteen, practically a woman, but you act like a child. Honestly, Holena is more help than you some days."

"I am sorry, Momma," I said again. What else could I say? I couldn't talk back to her. And there was no point in saying how I ached with homesickness, not just for what we had left behind, but for what we were supposed to have here in America. That was not the sort of thing I could say to my mother.

I wasn't sorry I had left the laundry and found that peaceful place beneath the tree, either. It had been worth a scolding to feel still and secure for those few moments.

We boiled and scrubbed laundry until dusk that day, stopping only briefly to eat a lunch of bread and pickles while a fresh tub of water heated. In the afternoon, Momma left us to finish while she returned to the house to form the week's bread into loaves and begin preparing our supper.

"You are in charge, Trina, so don't go wandering off again," she said before she left, proving she hadn't forgotten my mistake. I hadn't forgotten either. I had worked extra hard to make it up to her, but I was still thinking about the fish and trying to remember the story.

As soon as Momma left, Aneshka started complaining, but I wasn't listening. Every time I bent over the boiling tub, I saw the fish in my mind, just beneath the surface. As I scrubbed the

6

clothes on the washboard, I searched my memory for the story that I couldn't quite recall.

We carried load after load of heavy, wet laundry to the house, and hung it to dry. When we finally heaped the last pile into the washtub and struggled up the slope into camp, the whistle had blown at the mine and the shift was changing. Aneshka and I were still hanging shirts on the lines when my father arrived, trudging silently, his shoulders slumped by exhaustion. In Bohemia, he had always whistled or sung when he walked. Here, he was just too tired.

I was relieved when Momma said nothing over dinner about my absence that morning. I didn't want to tell them about the tree or the fish. It would sound childish, like something out of a fairy tale. Besides, my mother's accusation of daydreaming still stung. I hadn't been daydreaming. What I had seen was strange, but real.

When supper was over, Papa went out to sit on the porch in the cool evening, and Momma took out her mending basket and sat with him. Before she went, she turned to me.

"Trina, you will wash the dishes tonight. Holena and Aneshka may do as they like."

I opened my mouth to protest, but closed it again when my mother gave me a sharp look. "They worked all day without complaint—you ran off and left your work undone, which slowed us all down. So this evening, you will make it up to them by doing the dishes alone."

I bit back my reply as I stacked the plates and carried them to the counter. Couldn't she tell that Aneshka had dallied at her morning chores while I did the hard work? And, she had done nothing but complain after Momma left us at the creek. Still, I couldn't talk back to my mother. Soon I was alone in the kitchen, scrubbing plates while my sisters giggled and played outside.

Our neighbor Old Jan arrived just as I finished. Like us, he was Czechy, or "Bohemian," as we were called in this country. He and his two sons had lived in the coal camp longer than we had, but had fallen on hard times shortly after our arrival. Old Jan's leg had been crushed in a cave-in at the mine and had been amputated just below the knee. The old man had not worked since, nor would he again. As they were our neighbors and our countrymen, we had stuck by them, and they had become like family to us. His younger son, Marek, was a year and a half older than me and had gone to school with me at first. After his father's accident, however, he had lied about his age to get a job in the mine.

Since both sons worked the night shift, Old Jan was alone in the evening, so my parents welcomed him, no matter how tired they were. Momma got out of her chair and scooted it forward for Old Jan, while Papa filled a pipe with tobacco for him.

"Trina," Momma said, "go put the coffee on for our guest."

I turned back into the hot kitchen and set the pot on the stove to heat. By the time I returned, Old Jan was comfortably settled. Holena and Aneshka were sitting cross-legged on the porch in front of him, begging for a story. In Bohemia, Papa or our grandfather had often told us stories after supper, but since starting work at the mine, Papa was always too tired. My sisters had discovered, however, that Old Jan was more obliging.

"Come on, Trina." Aneshka patted the porch beside her. "Old Jan is going to tell a story."

I was too angry to sit by Aneshka. I gave cups of coffee to my parents and their guest and sat down on the porch steps a few feet away.

"What story would you like?" Old Jan asked.

"A story about a princess!" Aneshka cried.

"And what kind of story would you like, Holena?" Old Jan asked, leaning forward and patting her round cheek lightly with his gnarled fingers.

"I would like a story about animals," Holena said quietly.

"Animals and a princess, eh?" Old Jan said with a chuckle. "And what about you, Trina? What story would you like to hear?"

"My grandmother told a story about a fish. I've been trying to remember it all day."

"A fish. Hmmm." He considered for a long moment. "Was it 'The Magic Carp,' perhaps?"

I sat up straighter, feeling the same tug of excitement I had felt that morning when I saw the tree. "Yes, that's it! Can you tell it? Please?"

He smiled. "That is a good story, and it has animals. Very well, then. 'The Magic Carp.'"

Aneshka scowled at me, but Old Jan didn't seem to notice as he began the tale.

"There was once an old fisherman and his wife, so poor they had only fish broth for supper and went to bed hungry. One day the old man had caught nothing all day long. He was about to give up when he saw a flash of movement in the deepest pool in the river, so he cast his line one more time. When he did, he hooked a carp with whiskers on its chin. This carp was hardly big enough to eat, but it was all the old fisherman had, so he prepared to kill it.

"'Stop!' the little fish pleaded." Old Jan spoke in a high-pitched voice that made Aneshka and Holena giggle. "'If you let me go, I shall grant you three wishes.'

"'Three wishes?' the fisherman asked, amazed.

"'Three wishes,' the fish assured him. 'Spare me and your dreams could come true!'

"Well, the fisherman couldn't believe his luck! Dreaming of what he might wish for, he unhooked the fish and let the little fish slip back into the water before he knew what he was doing. He thought he had lost his chance, but the carp poked its head up above the surface of the pool. It twitched its whiskers three times and said, 'Three wishes are yours, before the summer's end.' Then, with a slippery white flash, it disappeared into the depths of the pool.

"The fisherman hurried home to his wife and told her of the wishes, but she merely grumbled that he was a fool to fall for the trick. She gave him his bowl of fish broth, even thinner than usual. The fisherman looked into the bowl, and with a sigh he said, 'I wish just once I had a nice, fat sausage for my supper.'

"And what do you know, just like that, a nice fat sausage appeared on his plate. Well, the old couple was amazed, but immediately the old woman began scolding, 'Now look what you've done! You could have had anything and you've wasted a wish on a silly sausage!'

"The old man tried to calm his wife, but she kept scolding until he got angry. 'Quiet, woman!' he shouted. 'I've heard enough about this sausage! I wish it were stuck to your nose!'"

Old Jan paused while Aneshka giggled. Holena clapped her hand over her nose, her eyes wide. "Sure enough, that sausage stuck itself to the old woman's nose. Well, they tugged and pulled, and pulled and tugged, but they couldn't get that sausage off! So in the end, they had to use their last wish to wish the sausage away, and they ended up no better off than they were before." Old Jan paused and turned to me. "Is that the story your grandmother told?"

"Yes. Grandmother always asked us what we'd wish for if we had three wishes." I ached remembering how we would laugh at our wishes as we worked.

Papa smiled. "So she did. Very well, my girls, what do you wish for?"

"All the plum dumplings I could ever eat!" Aneshka cried, clapping her hands in delight.

"I would wish for blue hair ribbons," Holena said dreamily.

I couldn't believe what I was hearing. Hadn't they learned anything at all from the story? Holena was only five, but Aneshka was old enough to understand the moral.

"You're as foolish as the fisherman and his wife," I said. "You would waste your wishes on simple things!"

"Well then, wise Katerina, what would you wish for?" Papa asked, smiling.

I frowned, wishing I hadn't started the game. "There's no such thing as wishes."

"You sound like the fisherman's wife," Aneshka said. Then she giggled and added, "Trina's going to end up with a sausage stuck to her nose!"

"It's only a game, Trina. What would you wish for?" Old Jan asked.

"It's a stupid game," I insisted.

"Just say what it is you want, Trina. Please?" Holena asked, but even her sweetness couldn't soothe my annoyance.

"I want to go back to Bohemia!" I said, bitterness sharpening my words more than I intended. I could see in my father's eyes that my words hurt him, but before I could take them back, he gave an answer I hadn't expected.

"And I would wish us right back to America and onto a farm. So you see, Trina, your wish would be wasted too."

"But why?" I asked. "It's horrible here!"

"Perhaps for now it is, but here in America, we will have a better future," he said.

"That's right," Old Jan said. "In America, our children's dreams can come true."

"Dreams don't come true! Especially not here!" I knew better than to talk back to my elders, but now that I had given voice to my anger, I couldn't seem to stop it.

"They do if you know what to wish for," Old Jan said. "And if you find a magic carp."

I opened my mouth to answer, but I couldn't. *Had I found a magic carp?* I was staring at him with my mouth open when my mother stood abruptly. "Enough of this nonsense. It is time the children were off to bed," she said.

Aneshka protested, but I did not. Old Jan's words had made me uncomfortable, and besides, I was tired from a day of scrubbing clothes. I thanked Old Jan for the story. Taking Holena's hand, I retreated into the house. I helped her into her nightdress before changing into my own, and the three of us lay down on the mattress we shared. Through the thin walls, I could hear my mother apologizing for my outburst to Old Jan, and my cheeks burned.

"Never mind, Mrs. Prochazkova," Old Jan said in his kindly way. "She is just homesick. She's very young yet, after all."

"She is old enough to know better," Momma said.

"But she is still a child inside," Old Jan replied.

His tone had been kind, but I squeezed my eyes shut in shame and turned toward the wall so I could not hear what else they might say. I did not want to be talked about as a child—I didn't want to be talked about at all. I wanted to go to sleep and forget the day, and, slowly, I did.

I woke in the cool moonlight, lying on the thick cottonwood root, leaning out over the water. A flash of white deep in the pool caught my attention. I leaned farther, watching and waiting, my nose almost against the surface of the dark water. The gleaming carp slipped out into the moonlight and rose to the surface. It thrust its flat head up through the glassy surface and its whiskers twitched — one, two, three times.

"Three wishes before the summer's end," it said in a voice that bubbled like washwater. "Wise Katerina, what do you wish for?"

Suddenly I was aware of Aneshka beside me. "Plum dumplings!" she squealed, clapping her hands. "I wish for all the plum dumplings I can eat!"

"And blue hair ribbons!" added shy little Holena from my other side.

"Stop! Stop!" I cried, leaping to my feet. "You're wasting my wishes!" But it was too late; the dumplings and ribbons had already appeared.

Only one wish was left! I had to formulate it carefully. Before I could speak, Momma appeared from over the hill with bundles of laundry, calling my name and scolding me for dreaming.

I woke with a start, my heart thumping in my throat. I was back on the thin mattress, Aneshka and Holena pressed up against me, breathing evenly. It had only been a dream, but it had seemed so real — just as being beneath the cottonwood that morning had seemed like a dream. Momma was right; I was too old to believe in fairy tales. But if there really was a magic carp in the creek by the coal camp . . . I smiled to myself and snuggled deeper under the covers, comforted by the idea. Soon I had fallen back into a dreamless, forgetful sleep.

Chapter 2

I HAD NEARLY forgotten the dream the next morning, but I had not forgotten my mother's disappointment in me, or my own embarrassment at being thought of as a child. I determined to do my chores quickly and allow nothing to distract me. When the kitchen was clean, I heated the irons on the stove and carried in the mounds of stiff, wrinkled clothes that had dried on the lines overnight.

Ironing was hot, tedious work, with the stove burning all day. The piles of clothing never seemed to get any smaller, and by midmorning, I could not keep the cool, shady pool of the creek out of my mind. I tried to push it away, but it lapped back in, and I found myself ironing the same spot on a shirt long after the iron had cooled. I jerked my attention back to my work with a guilty glance toward Momma. She hadn't noticed, so I folded the shirt and quickly took the next one from the pile, trying harder to keep my mind on my work.

The ironing took all day, Momma and I pressing clothes

while Aneshka and Holena carried each neatly folded pile back to the house of its owner. The men were all at work in the mine, of course, but no one locked their doors in camp.

It was late afternoon when we folded the last shirt and sent Aneshka off with the last pile. Momma poured herself a cup of coffee from the pot on the back of the stove and slumped into a chair at the table. She mopped her brow with her sleeve.

"It'll be time to be getting your papa's supper soon," she said. She nodded toward the tobacco can on the shelf behind the stove. "I need you to run to the store, Trina. Take the money from the washing."

I took the can down from the shelf, my heart sinking. Momma often sent me on this chore, since I had learned enough English to speak with the storekeeper, Mr. Johnson. I didn't mind the chore so much, but I hated the idea of spending the money we had just worked so hard to earn. We would never save money at this rate.

"Shouldn't we save some for new dresses?" I asked.

Momma shook her head. "Shame on you, Trina. Think of your papa. Think of how hard he works! He needs a few good meals a week."

That was true enough, but I left a little in the money can anyway, hoping I had enough. If I didn't, I would just have to put it on credit. Mr. Johnson kept a ledger book under his counter for such occasions, and was happy to let us use it if we needed to.

I was glad to be outside at last. I was grateful for the breeze that dried the sweat along my hairline. The street we lived on — in fact, the whole camp — ran in rows of drab houses up a hill, with the mine at the top. At the bottom stood the only fine buildings in the town, a few two-story houses with picket fences and neat yards for the mine officials, a school, and a community meeting house that served as Saturday night dance hall and Sunday morning church. The largest building in the group, a long, low building with a covered porch, housed the store and company offices.

I had never been in those offices, but I came to the store at least once a week. It was jammed with an assortment of goods, from buckets and brooms to coffee, flour, and fresh meat two days each week. As I approached, I noticed a team of horses and a wagon tied up at the rail beside the steps. The front door was open and I could hear voices inside, but it wasn't until I had stepped through the doorway that I realized the voices were raised in anger.

I paused uncertainly. Mr. Johnson was behind his counter, and facing him from my side was a tall, dark-haired man I didn't recognize. He was holding a piece of paper under Mr. Johnson's nose. Beside him on the floor were two wooden crates. A third crate was open on the counter.

"But you ordered them!" the dark-haired stranger was saying. He had an Italian accent, but his English was better than my own. He gave the paper a little shake. "It says so right here on the invoice. Twenty crates. Right here on the invoice."

"That's not my invoice," Mr. Johnson said without looking at it.

"It's your company. It came from the head office in Pueblo, like always."

Mr. Johnson pushed the paper away from his face impatiently. "Well, I didn't order them, I can't sell them, and I won't take them!"

The man with the invoice clenched his free hand. I backed out of the doorway, afraid a fight was about to start. My movement caught Mr. Johnson's eye.

"Now, look, you're scaring my customers," he said. He turned his gaze to me and smiled. "Come in, missy, and tell me what I can do for you."

Both men's eyes were on me then, and I felt foolish as I stepped forward into the store once again. I swallowed hard and spoke, just wanting to get my purchase and get out before their argument resumed. "I need a pound of coffee and four chops, if they aren't too much."

Mr. Johnson turned back to the other man. "'If they aren't too much.' You see what I'm dealing with here? Miserly Greeks and tight-fisted Irishmen, all day long."

Anger warmed my cheeks, but I held my tongue. The Italian man was still looking my way. His mouth turned downward into a frown under his bushy mustache. "She's just a kid, Johnson."

Mr. Johnson was wrapping the chops in paper. "Yeah, well, kid or not, they won't buy that lot around here, so you might as well haul it back out to your wagon."

The Italian's frown deepened, and he turned back toward Mr. Johnson. But before he could say anything, Mr. Johnson slapped the chops onto the counter beside a tin of coffee and looked back at me, still rooted beside the doorway.

"Well, come on, missy. You can't very well pay for these from over there, can you? Torentino here won't bite."

I hurried to the counter, pulling the handful of coins from my pocket. "How much?"

"Seventy cents for the coffee and two fifty for the chops." He gave a sudden, insincere smile and reached into the open crate on the counter. "Say, missy, how about a special treat for your family, huh? A nickel a can."

I looked at the can. Across the top it read EMPSON'S FANCY. Below that was a picture of ripe, purple plums on a branch. It would have been a treat, he was right. I thought briefly about Aneshka and her love of plum dumplings, but I only had enough money for the coffee and meat. "No, thank you, sir," I said, and handed him the money for my order.

"Don't you like plums, miss?" Mr. Torentino said.

"Yes, sir, but I have no more money."

"You can put them on credit on your father's account," Mr. Johnson said, reaching under the counter for his credit ledger.

I shook my head. "No, thank you."

Mr. Johnson tossed the can of plums back into the crate. "You see, Torentino? I can't sell them, and I won't take them. Send them back. Tell the head office they made a mistake."

"I can't send them back; I'll lose too much money. The order —"

"Damn the order — get those crates out of my store!" Mr. Johnson said.

More uncomfortable than ever, I scooped up my packages and hurried for the door. Behind me I heard the scrape of the crates being picked up and the heavy step of Mr. Torentino as he lugged them toward the door. Though I longed to escape, he was coming behind me, so I held the door for him. He carried the crates out onto the porch and set them down.

"Thank you, miss," he said. "Do you buy all your food from Johnson?"

"Yes, sir," I said. "There's nowhere else to buy it."

Mr. Torentino glanced over my shoulder, back through the open doorway toward Mr. Johnson's counter. "And he's getting plenty fat off you folks at those prices. Send back all twenty crates! We'll see about that!"

He seemed to be talking more to himself than to me. I tried to go around his crates and down the stairs, but he called out to me, plenty loud enough for Mr. Johnson to hear him.

"Hold up there a minute, miss."

I paused.

"You say you like plums, and I'd guess you got a family from that package of chops."

I nodded, edging a little closer to the steps. I could see Mr. Johnson watching suspiciously through the open door.

"Here," Mr. Torentino said. He took a can from the top crate and held it out to me. I shook my head.

"Take it, it's free. Here, take a couple more, too."

"Free?" I said. I couldn't believe it—it had to be a trick.

"If he won't take them, I have to do something with them. Take these for free and tell everyone you see that I'll be selling the rest for a penny a can."

"Hey!" Mr. Johnson yelled from inside the store. "Hey, you can't do that!"

Mr. Torentino put the three cans in my arms and grinned. "You'd best run along now."

I was happy to oblige. I went down the stairs two at a time. Behind me I heard Mr. Johnson burst out onto the porch, shouting at Mr. Torentino.

I kept my head down and ran! I was panting by the time I burst into the kitchen. Momma looked up in alarm, but her expression shifted quickly to annoyance when she saw me cradling the cans of plums.

"Trina! We don't have money for such things!" she scolded. As soon as I could catch my breath, the whole story tumbled out of me.

"He said he'd be selling them for a penny a can, if Mr. Johnson hasn't run him off yet."

"A penny a can!" Momma exclaimed. "That's cheaper than anything else we can eat. Do you have any change left?"

"I left a little in the money can," I said. Momma reached for the can and got out the dime still there.

"Go back and get as many cans as you can carry. Aneshka, you can start mixing the dough. We'll have plum dumplings tonight after all."

Aneshka gave a little hop of delight and giggled. "Trina must have seen a magic carp in the washwater while she was daydreaming yesterday, Momma."

That's when I remembered my dream. It flooded back into my mind with brilliant clarity: Aneshka wishing for plum dumplings at the pool by the tree. And here they were, exactly as she had said, all the plum dumplings she could eat. The first wish. But it had only been a dream, I was sure of that. This was only a coincidence.

"Come on, Trina, don't just stand there," Momma prodded. "Go back and get more before they are all sold. Take Holena with you; she can help you carry."

I set out for the store again, Holena's hand in mine and the money in my pocket, and I pushed the dream out of my mind. As I passed neighbors and houses with their doors open, I called out Mr. Torentino's offer. Soon word was spreading and other women were hurrying down the hill with us. I was glad for their company, in case Mr. Johnson was still there, still shouting.

At my side, Holena trotted to keep up. "Did you really see a magic carp in the washwater, Trina?" she asked. "Really?"

"Of course not," I said. I was annoyed that Aneshka had made such a joke in front of Holena. And I was annoyed that it felt true, even though I was too old to believe it.

"But Aneshka got her dumplings," Holena said. "Do you think I will get my hair ribbons, too?" Her eyes were round and shining with hope. I hated telling her that her hope was for nothing, but how could I tell her otherwise? I turned my eyes back to the dusty road ahead of us.

"We had better hurry or there won't be any plums left for us," I said. I felt her hand slacken in mine and knew she was disappointed, but I didn't look at her. I just kept walking.

Mr. Torentino had moved his wagon across the street from Mr. Johnson's store. Though the storekeeper was standing on his porch, glaring at the growing crowd of women around the wagon, there seemed to be nothing he could do about it. Mr. Torentino was in the back of the wagon, prying open crates and handing the cans to the women who were holding money up to him. I tried to blend into the crowd, but Mr. Torentino noticed me.

"Well done, girl!" he called out over the heads of the gathering women. "Well done! And will you have more?"

"Yes, sir," I said and held up my dime. He took it and handed down ten cans of plums, which I cradled in my apron as I worked my way out of the crowd. I could not help noticing Mr. Johnson watching with narrowed eyes. He hadn't missed Mr. Torentino's words, I was sure of it.

"Papa will be surprised, won't he?" Holena said.

"He will," I agreed. Despite Mr. Johnson, I couldn't help smiling to myself. Plum dumplings! We hadn't had such a treat since arriving in America.

"You know what, Holena?"

"What?"

"We should make it a special night for Momma, too."

Holena's eyes glowed at the thought. "How?"

I thought for a moment, not sure how, but then I saw a patch of dandelions blooming alongside the road. "Flowers for the table?" I suggested.

Holena's smile nearly split her face. All the way home, she

skipped along the edge of the road and picked dandelions. They were only weeds, but they were bright and cheerful clenched in her little fist. When we got home, we put them in a can of water and onto the table while Momma's back was turned. When she saw them, she smiled—the first smile I could remember seeing on her face in a long time.

We busied ourselves in the kitchen, full of anticipation and excitement as we swept and washed and set the table with great care. Momma disappeared into the bedroom and came back holding a tablecloth, embroidered on the corners with flowers. She only brought it out on Christmas and Easter, so we were all surprised when she spread it on the table. She saw us watching and gave a little shrug.

"The Lord knows we have few enough things to celebrate here. We'd best use it while we can." She turned back to the stove, but I had seen the smile crinkling the corners of her eyes. I felt a pang, almost like homesickness. She had been quick to celebrate when I was little, but not since we had left Bohemia.

My thoughts were interrupted by the whistle at the mine. The shift was changing and Papa would be on the way home soon. I hurried to straighten the silverware Aneshka had laid on the table.

Papa always washed off the coal dust and dirt in a tub at the back door. It wasn't until he was drying his face that he stopped and sniffed the air.

"What is that smell?" he asked with a smile.

Holena tried to tell him, but Aneshka shushed her.

"It's supposed to be a surprise," she insisted.

Papa smiled at them both. "She doesn't have to tell me a thing, Aneshka," Papa said. "I know plum dumplings when I smell them. But how? Did your wish come true after all?"

"So it would seem," Momma said from the doorway behind me. "Now come inside. Supper's all ready."

Supper that night felt like a grand affair, although the food was much the same as always—gristly meat, boiled potatoes, and bread spread with salted lard. But the tablecloth, the flowers, and the plates of plum dumplings made it festive. I recounted for Papa all that had happened at the store. When I told him of Mr. Torentino's selling from his wagon while Mr. Johnson glared at him from the porch, he laughed.

"Serves the swindler right," Papa said.

Momma looked stricken. "Hush, Tomas! Don't say such things!"

"They can't hear us here, Ivana. Besides, this is America, isn't it? A man can say what he thinks here."

"They'll fire you for saying such things," she said.

"Not tonight," Papa said, unbothered by her warning. "Tonight we have plum dumplings and all the luck in the world, right, Aneshka?"

Momma frowned at Papa before rising from the table to fetch more of the dumplings still steaming on the stove. They were the best things I had tasted since we had left Bohemia. Aneshka ate so many we all thought she would be sick, and Momma made her stop.

We were still at the table when we heard the familiar clop of Old Jan's crutches on the porch steps. Papa went out to greet him while Momma dished up a bowl of plum dumplings and took it out to him. That left my sisters and me to tidy the kitchen.

For once Aneshka was cooperative and cheerful, and the job went quickly. I was soon stacking away the last plates on the shelf while Aneshka and Holena folded Momma's lovely tablecloth. Holena carried it into the bedroom to put away while Aneshka and I took coffee to the adults.

I had just settled myself comfortably on the porch steps when Holena appeared in the doorway. Rather than skipping out like usual, she seemed frozen, staring at us as if we were strangers. In her hand she held two long, sky-blue ribbons. Her eyes met mine.

"They were in the trunk," she said. "I found them."

Momma turned to look. "Why, so they were! I had forgotten I had such things; it's been so long!" she said.

"You wore them at our wedding, Ivana, remember?" Papa said.

Holena's face fell a little, but Momma smiled.

"So I did, but I have no use for such things now. And they are just the right color for your hair, Holena. Would you like to have them?"

Holena's little hand clenched the ribbons and she threw herself into Momma's arms with a dozen thank-yous.

Everyone was smiling. Everyone but me—I was still staring in disbelief. The second wish! My ears seemed to be buzzing with the shock of it.

What would you wish for, Wise Katerina?

I felt someone looking at me and glanced up into Old Jan's face. He, too, was smiling, but he was watching me. "You see, Trina, dreams can come true," he said.

I didn't know about dreams or about wishes—didn't know if they could come true or if they were even real. But maybe it was time I found out.

24

Chapter 3

I LAY AWAKE THAT NIGHT, feeling my sisters breathing in the bed beside me, as I tried to sort out what was real. In the months we had been in America, very little in our lives had been good. Momma and Papa worked to exhaustion every day. My sisters and I had gone to school, but we had so many chores to do to help Momma that we had little time for fun. We hadn't had money or time for anything new or nice until today. Today, there had been plums for dumplings, and hair ribbons—exactly what my sisters had wished for!

We had had so few truly happy days here in America, and none that I would have called lucky. It seemed lucky to have so much good happen in one day, but not impossible. It seemed impossible, though, that those things appeared the day after Aneshka and Holena had made wishes. How could an order have been mistakenly placed for plums and I *just happened* to be the one to discover it, and it *just happened* to be the day after my sister had made a wish for plum dumplings? Things didn't just happen like that. But if it wasn't just chance, that would mean I had discovered a magic fish in the creek by the coal camp and it had granted me three wishes. And it had spoken to me in a dream. It seemed that I was faced with choosing between a wish that had come true or an impossible coincidence. It was not a question of which was possible so much as which was less *im*possible.

Aneshka stirred and sighed, her breath still smelling of plums. A little smile curled at the corners of her mouth and I knew she was dreaming. I closed my eyes too, hoping to fall into a dream, but I could not. The day's events were too fresh in my mind, and I kept hearing that voice, prompting me for my wish.

My wish, of course, was to return to Bohemia, to the small village where my grandfather and uncle were still the clockmakers, and winter evenings were filled with family and laughter and the stories that had taught us to dream. I wanted to go back to how it had been before my papa's dreams had become too big for that village. Of course, I would not say that out loud again, not in front of my father. I didn't know why he would wish us back to America, but I knew that it was not a subject for discussion. Besides, we didn't have the money for the fare back to Europe. A wish was the only way we could return, and I'd have to make the wish in secret.

I caught myself. It was all nonsense. Fish did not grant wishes except in stories, and even in stories the wishes didn't fix people's lives, they only proved them foolish. I shifted in bed, trying to get comfortable enough to forget the day and go to sleep, but I only disturbed Aneshka, who muttered a complaint without waking. Eventually I must have drifted off, because the next thing I knew, Aneshka was poking me to wake me up. It was still dark out, but I could hear Momma in the kitchen frying the last chop for Papa's lunch bucket, and I could smell the coffee.

I rubbed the sleep from my eyes and sat up. Holena was still asleep, and I slipped out carefully so as not to wake her. In the kitchen, Papa was at the table, scooping oat porridge into his mouth as quickly as he could. In Bohemia he had taken his time over his breakfast, reading the papers and discussing politics with my grandfather, but here there was no time for that. If he was not in line to ride the hoist down into the mine when the shift whistle blew, he could miss a whole day's work—and a whole day's wages. So, I had learned to stay quiet and out of his way in the morning.

When he had eaten, he took the lunch bucket from Momma, kissed her cheek, and set off for the mine. Once he was gone, Momma filled a bowl of porridge for each of us and we sat down to our own breakfasts.

"I told Old Jan we would come give his floors a good scrub today," Momma said. "He can't do it himself with his leg as it is." She paused and looked at me, and I knew what she was waiting for.

"I'll do it, Momma," I said.

Her eyebrows raised a little. "There's a good girl." She was surprised. Though we had both known it was my duty to volunteer, she had not expected me to do so as quickly or cheerfully as I had. In truth, I was a little surprised myself—I had never liked cleaning for Old Jan and his sons. Marek and Karel worked the night shift at the mine, so they slept all morning. That meant I couldn't start cleaning until the afternoon, when the work was hotter and I was already tired. Today, though, I had been quick to volunteer because I wanted to talk to Old Jan. I was curious to know what he thought about dreams coming true.

The whistle blew at the mine, and a moment later Holena appeared in the doorway between our two rooms, still in her nightgown. Her hair was still messy from sleep, but she had tied the ribbons to the ends of her braids.

Momma smiled at her. "Perhaps we should save those for special days."

"Today is a special day," Holena said, her large eyes sparkling.

"Is it? What day is it, then?" Momma asked.

"Today we get our third wish," Holena said.

"What third wish?" Momma said.

"From the fish Trina saw in the washwater."

Aneshka giggled. I looked at her.

"Have you been filling her head with nonsense?" I asked accusingly.

"No." Aneshka's tone was defensive, but I could see the mischief in her eyes. "Wishes always come in threes. Everyone knows that. It's not nonsense."

"Of course it is," I said.

"It is," Momma said in a matter-of-fact tone that put the issue to rest. "And it is time we got dressed and started our chores. Trina, you get Holena her breakfast." She ushered Aneshka into the other room while I filled a bowl of oat porridge for Holena. I set the bowl on the table in front of her, but she didn't begin eating. Instead she looked up at me, her expression troubled.

"But you did see a magic fish, Trina. You must have."

"There's no such thing, Holena. Not really."

"But Aneshka and I both got our wishes," she insisted.

"That was just luck," I said. I could see she wasn't convinced, so I offered proof. "After all, I haven't gotten my wish, have I?"

"You didn't make your wish," Holena said.

I looked at her, confused. Had she had the same dream I had? We had all said our wishes after Old Jan's story. "Yes I did," I said.

She shook her head, her little brow still wrinkled. "You said it was a stupid game and that you didn't believe. You said what you wanted, but you didn't make it a wish. You have to say '*I wish.*'"

I thought about it. I couldn't exactly remember what I had said. I shrugged. "You should eat your porridge."

"You have to believe and make your wish. Then we can go back to Bohemia, just like you wanted."

Back to Bohemia! She said it with such conviction that it sounded almost possible. And it was the third wish, so Papa couldn't wish us back! I thought of our village, nestled among the dense forests I had loved, of the rolling hills, and of my grandmother's kitchen.

"Trina, go get dressed. Holena, get that porridge eaten; we have chores to do."

My mother's voice from the doorway jarred me out of my daydream, back to the bleak reality of our new life. I went into the bedroom, where Aneshka was braiding her hair, and I dressed quickly, still thinking of home and feeling a trickle of hope. That hope carried me through the morning chores. After lunch I gathered our buckets and rags and set out up the hill to do as I had promised and clean for Old Jan.

Old Jan was sitting out on his front porch, whittling a piece of wood with his pen knife. He paused and smiled up at me in greeting. "I'm afraid my boys are still sleeping," he said. "Would you sit here a bit with me while we wait for them?"

I sat down on the porch steps, happy enough to take a break

from work. I wanted to ask him about the night before, but I didn't know how. Every question I shaped in my mind felt foolish. So instead I asked him what he was making. He turned the block of wood over in his hands and considered it.

"I think it is going to be a horse," he said. "The horse is a noble creature. When I was a boy on my father's farm, we boasted the strongest team in all Bohemia. Those horses could pull a thousand pounds if they could pull one! And at the spring festival, we would tie ribbons and garlands on one of them. My mother would ride into the village, all dressed up, looking like a queen."

I nodded. "I miss the spring festival. There is nothing like that here, though. There's nothing but work here."

Old Jan looked up at me from the carving and smiled. "I've heard of a girl whose life was all work and never anything pretty. She was pretty, though, and her stepmother and stepsister were jealous, so they made her work very hard. But she was still pretty. So they tried to get rid of her."

I leaned back against the porch rail. I had heard the story before, but I was content to listen.

"'Marushka,' they said to her, for that was her name, 'Marushka, go up the mountain and pick us some violets.' It was the dead of winter and Marushka knew there would be no violets on the mountain, but they pushed her out of the house and forbid her to return without them. Crying bitterly, the poor girl set off up the mountain in search of the flowers.

"On the mountaintop she met the seasons of the year, sitting around a fire, and when she spoke kindly to them, they took pity on her. Spring rose up, waved his wand, and the violets sprung into bloom.

"Well, you can imagine the stepmother's surprise when she saw the violets. She wove them into her daughter's hair and thought, 'With Marushka's help, my daughter might become beautiful enough to marry a prince!' So she ordered Marushka back up the mountain for fresh strawberries to give the girl's complexion a rosy glow.

"Marushka went, more distraught than before, for where would she get strawberries in January? But once again, she met the seasons, and once again they took pity on her because she was good and gentle and wanted nothing for herself. So Summer rose up and waved his wand, and fields of strawberries glistened before her, plump and red and waiting to be picked.

"Marushka gathered all the strawberries she could carry and took them down the mountain. Well, of course, the stepmother was surprised and delighted. She and her daughter gobbled up every last strawberry, and the stepmother thought to herself, 'Now all my daughter needs are apples to polish her teeth, and she will be the most beautiful maid in the kingdom. So she ordered Marushka back up the mountain for apples.

"Marushka went, knowing there would be no apples but hoping against hope that there might be a way. Once again, the seasons saw how good and gentle she was, and when she told them she was looking for apples, Autumn rose up, waved his wand, and ripe, sweet apples burst forth on the trees.

"'Shake the tree once and take what it gives you,' Autumn told her. Two apples fell from the tree, and Marushka hurried home with them. Well, of course, the stepmother was amazed, but she was angry, too, because they were the best apples she had ever eaten, and she wanted more. She ordered Marushka back up the mountain, but her greedy daughter said, 'Marushka ate them all; that's why she only brought two. She's cheating us. This time we will go, Mother, and we will get everything we deserve!' And what do you think happened?"

"They got just what they deserved?" I guessed with a smile.

Old Jan nodded. "When they met the seasons, they were rude and selfish. So angry old Winter rose up and waved his wand, and a great blizzard blew over the mountain, and they were never seen again."

"And what became of Marushka?" I asked.

"The farm became hers from that day forward. The seasons blessed her with fine crops, and she made the house and everything around her beautiful. So you see, Trina, things can get better for a good, hard-working girl."

"It's a nice story," I said, "but I don't think anyone is going to rise up, wave a wand, and make the coal mine go away."

Old Jan laughed a wheezing, coughing laugh. "No, I suppose not. But if you are a good girl who works hard to help your mother, just maybe things will get better."

"Maybe," I said, "but it is harder for those of us without magic wands."

Old Jan smiled, his eyes twinkling. "Aneshka says she got her dumplings because you saw a magic carp. That is just as good as a wand."

I frowned. Aneshka must have told everyone her idea last night after dinner. At this rate she would have told everyone in the camp in no time. Everyone would be laughing at me. "I don't believe in such nonsense."

"Ah, but believing is never nonsense," Old Jan said. "You have to believe something can happen before it will, you know."

"Marushka didn't believe she would find her violets or strawberries or apples, though."

"So she didn't, but she tried to find them anyway, trusting for something to happen, even when she didn't know what it might be."

32

"My father's like that. That's how we ended up here. Momma says only a fool believes such things."

"Some would say Marushka was wise, and others that she was foolish, I suppose. You have to decide for yourself which you think she was."

Though I had heard the story before, I had never thought of it that way. I was still pondering Old Jan's story when Marek stepped out onto the porch, pulling his suspenders up over his shoulders as he came. When he saw me, he quickly combed down his rumpled hair with his fingers. He smiled at me. I smiled back and then quickly looked elsewhere to hide the discomfort I always felt in his presence.

"Good morning, Papa. Good morning, Trina."

"Good morning, Mark," I said, careful to pronounce his name the American way, which he had used since going to work in the mine. He said foreigners didn't have as good a chance as Americans at getting good jobs, so he no longer wanted a foreign-sounding name. Since his father's injury, getting and keeping a job had been his biggest concern.

"Good afternoon, you mean," Old Jan said.

"To you it's afternoon. To me it's morning," Mark said. He sat down beside me to put on his boots. I watched his hands as he laced and tied each one. When I had first arrived here and started attending school, I had shared a desk with him, and those same hands had guided me through lessons. They were entirely different hands now. He had lied about his age to work in the mine, since he hadn't been quite fifteen, and I had marveled that the coal company had believed he was sixteen. Now, looking at his hands, it seemed believable. When they had helped me at school, they had been like everyone else's in the schoolhouse. But now the fingernails and the creases at the knuckles bore the permanent stain of coal, and red scars and nicks showed where the chips of rock had cut them as he hammered and drilled underground.

Everything else about him seemed older too, and that's what made me so uncomfortable. He no longer joked and smiled like he had back then, no longer teased me or pulled on my braids for a lark. When his family spent time with mine, his concerns were all those of my father—wages, rumors of unions, paying off debts. It was like he had grown up and I hadn't, and I didn't know what to say around him that he would want to hear.

"I've come to clean. Is Karel up?" I asked.

Mark nodded. "He's just finishing his breakfast."

"Then Trina will want to be getting her work done," Old Jan said. "Be a good lad, Marek, and fetch Trina some water in her buckets."

"Glad to," he said, still grinning, and he picked up my buckets. "Will you come with me, Trina?"

"I should get started here," I said, jumping to my feet a little too eagerly. Mark looked disappointed as he set off with the buckets alone.

I got to work sweeping and beating the rugs. When Mark returned with the buckets filled, I scrubbed the counter and table in the kitchen, then scrubbed the floors, starting in the bedroom and working forward through the kitchen until I finished at the front door. I straightened, stretched my back, and heaved the buckets of now dirty water over the porch rail out into the yard. Old Jan and his sons were on the porch, and they invited me to sit down and rest with them, but I declined. I knew my mother would not be expecting me back right away, and there was something I wanted to do in the few free minutes I had.

"Let us pay you," Mark said, as he did every week, and as always, I shook my head no. My mother would not allow it, not when they were neighbors and friends and had been through hard times.

I said good-bye and hurried to the creek, where I set down my buckets on the bank. I walked downstream, but I paused as I neared the bend in the bank. Were the tree and the pool really there? It all felt too much like a dream, and I was suddenly nervous that it wasn't real. I stepped around the bend and breathed a sigh of relief. There stood the tree, its leaves moving gently in the breeze. Below it the shaded pool looked cool and inviting, just as before.

I paused in the shade of the tree and looked at the water, but I saw no sign of the fish. Suddenly I felt very silly. What had I been expecting to see? Had I really thought I could come make a wish and be back in Bohemia for supper?

I stepped over the tree's root, into the quiet space and sat down, my back against the tree. The shade was pleasantly cool and the soft sounds of the leaves and the water relaxed me. I leaned back and closed my eyes, thinking about magic fish and wishes, and about Marushka. She was wise, I decided. Certainly she had gone looking for something impossible, like my papa had done when he came to America. But she had been modest and good and sought nothing for herself, and so she had made friends instead of enemies. That was why she had received what she needed. In the stories with magic fish or fairies or rings that granted wishes, it was the selfish ones who were harmed rather than helped by their wishes. They were the fools. I smiled to myself at a new thought. If Marushka saw a magic carp, she would make the most of her wish.

What would you wish for, Wise Katerina?

My eyes flew open as I jerked upright, the voice ringing clearly in my mind. A perfect ring of ripples was widening in the pool before me. I leaned forward, my heart in my throat. There, just under the surface, I could see the carp, its tail waving slightly in the current. I was sure it could see me, too. Had it spoken, or had I been drifting off? What would I wish for, if I had a wish? My mind flashed to our village in Bohemia, but there was only one thing I could wish for if I were going to be Wise Katerina. I took a deep breath to quell the pang of homesickness at my heart, and I spoke.

"I wish for a farm where my family can be happy and live well—the farm my papa wants. I wish for a farm here in America."

Chapter 4

AS SOON AS THE wish was spoken, the fish darted off under the bank and disappeared. I waited. Nothing happened. Everything felt very ordinary, and once again I realized how foolish it was. I got to my feet, glad no one had seen me. I walked back to where I had left my buckets and I filled them, then climbed the slope and walked home. Nothing there was different either. Not one thing all evening. The feeling of foolishness grew, along with bitter disappointment. I had actually been hoping, I realized. Hoping to be saved by a magic fish! I was almost fourteen, too old for fairy tales or wishes. I could not stop myself from dreaming entirely, though. All that night, I found myself in fields of ripening wheat.

With the laundry behind us for the week, we had other chores, but we had a little free time in the afternoons, too. Out in the street, kids gathered for games of kick the can, hop-scotch, and skipping rope. I went along to watch my sisters, but I was too old to play. The girls my age gossiped over knitting or mending. I sometimes joined their conversations, but too often it turned to talk of boys. It made me think of Mark, and right away my feelings got tangled up inside me. I would send my thoughts off instead to the pool by the creek.

I felt strange, like a part of me was still waiting for something to happen, hoping it would. I suppose that part of me wanted to be like Marushka, or like my father, able to believe in the impossible. But as the week passed uneventfully, my hope dwindled. Even my sisters stopped talking about wishes, and things seemed to go back to normal.

Sundays were the only day of the week that the mine closed down and Papa stayed home. Momma, my sisters, and I got up quietly and went to church while Papa slept late. When we returned home on the Sunday after I made my wish, Papa was sitting on the porch reading the newspaper, his legs stretched out comfortably before him.

Momma sat down beside him with a contented sigh. "You girls can run along and play today," she said.

At once Aneshka was clamoring to go play in the creek.

"If Trina will go with you, to keep an eye on you," Momma said.

I agreed, so we changed out of our Sunday best and set off. Momma needn't have worried about the water. There were already several families spending the afternoon on the broad, grassy bank where we had done laundry. The creek was filled with laughing, splashing children, shouting in a mixture of languages, but playing together as if they understood one another.

I sat down on the grass and watched my sisters. Aneshka ran out into the middle at once so she could splash her classmates who were already there. Holena stayed close to the bank, looking for pretty pebbles and gathering them into her apron. Before long her quiet amusement was interrupted as a wild game of tag broke out. The older children, Aneshka among them, raced past her, splashing water and mud in all directions. A flailing arm caught Holena square in the back and she toppled forward, landing facedown in the icy water, soaked from head to toe.

I hurried to her, scolding the older children as I went. I helped her to her feet and up onto the grassy bank.

"Are you all right?" I asked her.

She nodded, but her teeth were chattering from the cold water and she was blinking back tears. I wrung the water from her skirt and invited her to sit with me in the sun to warm up. We watched the game continue for some time, Holena chewing her lip uncertainly. A big Welsh family had arrived, and the Welsh children were especially wild. We were always wary of the Welsh, who lived on the other side of camp. There were plenty of rumors that the careless Welsh miners had caused more than one deadly accident in the mine. Their children seemed just as troublesome as they went splashing and shouting into the creek. Aneshka wasn't bothered by them, and I knew she could hold her own. Holena, though, wasn't one for so much rough-and-tumble play. I stood and held my hand out to her.

"Let's take a walk," I said. "I know a quieter place I think you'll like better."

With a sudden, bright smile, she jumped up and took my hand. We set off downstream. I felt a little uncertain as we walked. I hadn't, until that moment, considered sharing my special place with anyone. I certainly didn't want to share it with Aneshka, but Holena was different. She appreciated quiet and beauty and wouldn't disrupt it with mindless prattle.

Holena was still holding my hand as we rounded the bend. At once the high slope shut out the sound of the children splashing and shouting. We could hear the burble of water and the chirping of birds. I could hear another sound, too—one I hadn't expected. Someone was whistling a tune. And not just any tune, but a Bohemian folk song.

I shaded my eyes with my hand and looked to the tree. A man was reclining in the shade with his feet propped up on one of the roots. It was silly of me to think a place so close to the camp was a secret, but I was disappointed to learn it wasn't.

"It's Mark!" Holena said. She let go of my hand and skipped toward him.

He heard her voice and sat up, the sun lighting his face. He smiled, looking glad to see us.

"Trina! Hello. Come sit in the shade," he said.

Holena was already sitting on the big root of the cottonwood, leaning out over the pool and trailing her fingers on the surface of the water. I stepped over the root, into the narrow wedge of grass, and hesitated. It was too small a space to share with another person, though Mark seemed to be expecting me to sit down there beside him. He saw my hesitation and his smile faltered.

"What's the matter, Trina?" he asked.

"It's just that it's awfully crowded here," I said.

He shook his head. "Not just here. You don't want to talk to me at my house, either, or anywhere else. What have I done?"

The heat of embarrassment filled my cheeks. I wanted to flee, but I could not. I sat down on the root of the tree, trying to decide what to say.

"It's always like this now," he continued. "You hurry to get away from me. You won't even look me in the eye."

I had kept my eyes on Holena, but I could hear the hurt in his voice. I forced my eyes up to meet his.

"You haven't done anything wrong, Mark."

"Then why are you avoiding me?"

"I'm not. It's just—" I thought hard, trying to untangle my feelings. "We used to talk about school, and what we wanted to do afterward. Now that you're working, things have changed."

"I'm still the same," he said.

I studied his face. It was the same—blue eyes with pale lashes, the soft beginnings of whiskers, and a mop of blond hair that wanted to flop across his forehead toward his left eye. Something else was there too, though. A new seriousness, perhaps, or more worries. Things that had aged him faster than me. I wanted him to still be the same, but like everything else in America, what I wanted made little difference.

He reached his hard, coal-stained hand out and took mine. "Trina, I still want to talk about school and our friends there. Just because I had to go to work doesn't mean I wanted to give up everything else."

"I'm sorry," I said, "I just thought—" I was still searching for the right words when I was saved by Holena.

"What's this?" She held up a fishing pole that had been lying in the grass next to Mark.

"I bought that with my paycheck last week," Mark said with a smile.

I jerked my hand out of his. "You're fishing? Here?"

"I thought if I could catch a meal or two it might stretch our income, but I'm not having much luck."

"Maybe there are no fish in this creek," I said.

"You're probably right. There's another stream over that ridge." Mark pointed toward the hill that rose on the other side of the water. "Johnson at the store says there's good fishing there, but I thought I'd try here first. I'm tired, and this is my only day off."

I shaded my eyes and surveyed the slope, my thoughts on the fish in the pool that I did not want him to catch. "It's not too bad of a climb. It might be worth the trouble to have fresh fish for supper, don't you think?"

"If it is worth the trouble, you are welcome to use my pole. I've got a can of worms you can take with you, too." He grinned and held the pole out to me.

"But—" I looked at the pole and the water before turning back to Mark. "But I don't know how—and I'm supposed to be watching my sisters."

"Holena can stay here with me. This is all you have to do," he said, and he explained how to cast the line into the water and how to reel it back in. Uncertainly, I took it and tried casting as he had said, only to whip the hook into the grass practically at my feet. Holena giggled.

"No," Mark said. "Like this."

He got to his feet and stood behind me. Then he wrapped his arms around me, his hands on mine to show me how to hold the pole. He pulled it back gently and cast. Though my hands and arms followed obediently through the motion, I could not concentrate on the lesson. His encircling arms felt strong and safe, and his body was warm and solid. It felt nice. My heart began to hammer unexpectedly. I hoped he couldn't hear it.

"Now you try it," he said, stepping away from me. I forced my thoughts back to the fishing pole again. This time the hook landed in the middle of the pool. I reeled it back in quickly.

"That's it," he said. "Now let me show you how to bait the hook and you're all set. You're not squeamish about worms, I hope." He dangled one in front of me. Then he deftly threaded it onto the hook and held the pole out to me.

"But—" I looked at Holena. I wasn't as eager to get away from Mark as I had been before.

"I will stay with Mark," Holena promised. "I don't mind. And Papa loves fish."

That was true, and fresh fish for supper did sound good. I looked back up at the ridge, then at Mark. My face flushed unexpectedly.

"Okay," I agreed, and set off quickly before I could change my mind.

The ridge was both steeper and higher than it had appeared. When I reached the top, I paused to catch my breath. From this height I could see beyond the mine and the nearby hills to the snow-capped peaks of the Rocky Mountains, cool and white against the sky. Below me on the other side of the ridge ran a green valley with a stream somewhat larger than our own. I looked back the way I had come. I could see the lone cotton-wood. Mark and Holena stood in the sunshine beside it, look-ing up and waving. I waved back and set off down the opposite slope.

Mark had been right about fish in this stream. I caught one almost immediately after casting my line into the water. After catching a fish in one pool, I walked along the water to the next, and I soon learned which places were likely to have fish and which were not. I worked my way upstream for some time, until at last I had twelve trout—one each for me, my sisters, and mother, and two for each of the men. The sun's rays were slanting from the western horizon, and I knew it was time to get home. I gathered the fish into my apron and I tied it into a bundle with the apron strings. Swinging the bundle over my shoulder, I began to walk back toward the ridge. I had been moving upstream all afternoon, and wasn't sure how far I had come. I had planned to climb to the top of the ridge and use the view from there to find my way back home.

The bottom of the valley was choked with willow bushes and shrubs, and I had to fight my way through them to get away from the stream. I burst out into a plowed field and almost into the farmer. A tanned, squarely built man, with thick black hair and a large mustache blinked at me in surprise, as did the two barefoot children beside him.

"Excuse me," I said, taking a quick step back. "I was fishing. I didn't know—" I was afraid I was on his land and he'd take my catch. He only stared at me. His little girl giggled, reminding me of Aneshka.

"*Buenas tardes,*" she said to me, but her papa shushed her.

I recognized the language as Spanish. I had heard it at school, spoken by the children of Mexican miners. At least, the schoolteacher called them Mexican, but I knew some of them had grown up on farms in the area. Farms like the one I had apparently stumbled onto. Now that my surprise was wearing off, I saw that they were planting a field. Each carried a canvas bag of seeds and a sturdy, pointed stick to form the holes for the seeds. I felt a pang of longing—this was exactly the life my father had wanted us to have.

Suddenly I had an idea. I swung my bundle of fish off my shoulder and opened it. "Will you trade?" I asked. "Half my fish for some seeds?"

The man held his hands up and shrugged. "*No hablo inglés, señorita,*" he said.

I took six fish from the apron and held them out. "For seeds?" I repeated, pointing at his canvas bag.

The children and the farmer spoke for a moment in Spanish, then the man smiled at me. He took a handful of seeds from the bag and held it out, pointing between me and the seeds. I nodded and he poured corn kernels into my open hand, saying something to his son. The boy took a handful of beans and added them to the seeds I already held. I accepted them with thanks and poured them carefully into my pocket before gathering the fish and giving them to the man.

"*Muchas gracias,*" he said. He handed the fish to his son, who ran off with them toward the low buildings on the far edge of the field. I retied the apron bundle and hurried away. The load was considerably lighter. There would not even be a whole fish for each of us now, but I was happy with my trade. I planned to plant a garden behind our house and grow some of our food. That way, we could save some of the money that we usually spent at the company store.

The sun had nearly set when I got back to the creek, and everyone had gone home. I found both Mark's family and my own waiting for me at my house.

"Well?" Mark asked when I arrived. "Did you bring us supper?"

I untied my apron so they could see the six fish. With so many expectant people gathered around, the fish seemed smaller than they had before.

"We'll have to share," I said.

"That's not even one apiece!" Aneshka complained.

"Hush, Aneshka," Momma said. "I'll put them in a stew with vegetables and there will be enough for everyone."

"And enough is as good as a feast," Old Jan said, tweaking Aneshka's cheek gently.

"I'd rather have a feast," Aneshka grumbled, but I ignored her.

"I think it will be a fine meal," Mark said, grinning at me.

"I had more," I said, "but I traded some to a farmer for these." I pulled the seeds from my pocket and spread them gently on the porch.

"That's not enough for a feast either," Aneshka said.

"They're not to eat," I told her. "They are for planting a garden behind the house. We can grow fresh vegetables and we won't have to spend our money at the store."

"That's a fine idea, Trina," Papa said, smiling.

"Indeed it is!" said Old Jan. "Fresh vegetables for your table will be very nice to have."

"And, we'll save money," I pointed out again.

"And that means Holena and I can have new dresses for school!" said Aneshka, finally growing excited. "I want yellow calico with blue flowers! What do you want, Holena?"

As my sisters prattled on about new dresses, I glanced at my mother. To my surprise, she was frowning at me, and my heart sank a little.

"What's wrong?" I asked.

She shook her head. "Put those away and come help me get supper now. Everyone is hungry."

I did as she said, confused. I had thought she would be happy and proud that I had made the trade. In the kitchen I chopped vegetables while she cleaned the fish. When they were all bubbling together in the pot, I asked her again what was wrong.

"Trina, I asked you to stay with your sisters. I need to be able to count on your help."

Her words surprised and stung me. Didn't she realize I was trying to help with the fish and the seeds? Couldn't she see the opportunity here? "Mark was watching them," I said.

46

"I thought you'd be pleased. Aren't you glad to have the fish?"

She sighed, wiping her hands on her apron. Her brow drew down and her lips tightened. "I don't want you to get hurt, Trina."

"It was safe, Momma. Really."

She shook her head, and I knew I had mistaken her meaning. "I know it was safe. But a garden, Trina? What do you know about growing a garden?"

"I know I have to—"

"It's another dream that won't work out!" she said. "And now you've got your sisters and your father all excited. And you're already dreaming of the money we'll save and what we'll do with it. But the seeds won't sprout or the crop will be eaten by locusts, and then what?"

"But they might—"

"Then more disappointment! More heartbreak!" she burst out.

I stared at her. How could she be so upset over such a simple plan? She couldn't really believe that we would break our hearts over something so small.

"It's only a garden, Momma," I said quietly.

Momma took a deep breath and returned to her usual resolute expression. "You should have done as you were told and stayed with your sisters. Now set the table."

The matter was closed. She left the kitchen and I obediently set the table, biting back my disappointment.

Momma said nothing more about it for the remainder of the evening, but Papa and Old Jan couldn't stop planning. Old Jan had a shovel I could use to turn the soil, and Papa had a plan for where we should lay out the garden. Aneshka was telling Holena of all the lovely bolts of fabric she'd seen at the store, and the new dresses we would all have. Momma only sat in silence and chewed hard on her food.

"Will you have a garden too?" Holena asked Old Jan. "It was Mark's fishing pole, so half the seeds should be yours."

Old Jan patted her head affectionately. "I had once thought of planting a garden, but I can't till the soil with only one leg. But you've given me an idea. Excuse me for a moment."

He rose from the crowded table and thumped out of the house and up the road. When he returned, he had a bulging paper envelope. He handed it to me with a smile.

Gently I poured the contents out onto the table. A variety of seeds spilled out.

Old Jan leaned over the pile and began sorting them with his finger. "I was saving these when I thought I might plant a garden. I have squash here, and cucumbers. These are tomatoes, and this—" he paused as he picked up a fuzzy gray pod, and his expression softened. "This I brought with me from the old country. My wife always had poppies by the front door."

"Then we will plant them by your door here," I said.

"And yours," he said, smiling. He cracked the pod open with his gnarled fingers and showed me the hundreds of tiny black seeds inside. "There are plenty to go around."

"We're going to have a big garden, aren't we?" Aneshka said.

Momma stood abruptly and began gathering our empty bowls. "And who's going to weed and water and tend this garden? That's what I want to know. Lord knows, we have little enough time for our chores as it is now."

"It won't be a chore, it will be a garden," Holena said.

"Your mother's right—it will be more work," Old Jan said. "I can't till the soil, but I can do other things. I can weed and harvest. I can build trellises for your beans. I'll help out all I can, so it won't be a burden."

"And it will be worth it, Ivana, you will see," Papa said.

Momma only tightened her mouth and set the dishes on the counter.

As I washed the dishes that evening, I thought about the garden and all the plans that had been made at the table as we feasted on fresh fish and plum dumplings. I was excited to get started, proud to be helping my family, and determined to overcome my mother's disapproval. We'd soon have a thriving garden and fresh vegetables, and she'd see that it had been the right thing to do. After all, what harm could possibly come from planting a garden?

Chapter 5

ON MONDAY EVENING, after the washing was done and supper was eaten, I took Old Jan's spade out behind the house and began turning the hard, rocky soil. Old Jan offered advice. Aneshka and Holena picked out the biggest rocks and arranged them in neat borders on the edge of the plot. Momma did not help, but she sat at the back door with her mending and watched our progress. I could see fear in her eyes when she did not know I was looking. It only pushed me to work harder. When she saw our hopes turning into success, she would be pleased. I fell into bed exhausted that night, but happy.

When we had finished planting the patch behind the house, we turned a bit of soil by the front porch steps and planted some of the poppy seeds. The rest we took to Old Jan's house and planted along the porch there, while he instructed us on their placement. He wanted them to be just as his wife had had them in the Old Country. We had just finished planting them when Karel and Mark emerged.

"They won't grow," Karel said. "The seeds are too old. It's been four years since we left Bohemia."

Mark shrugged. "Who knows, it's worth a try."

"A lot of trouble for nothing, if you ask me," Karel said.

"Anything worth having is worth the trouble of getting it, isn't it, Trina," Old Jan said.

I agreed it was, although privately I had to think about my papa and his farm. He had come to America willing to work the coal to get it, but it wasn't enough. There was no promise that hard work got you anywhere—it could just as easily come to nothing. Still, we had to try. So I pretended I agreed with Old Jan.

After the planting was done, we waited. Old Jan came by to pull weeds. On hot days I hauled buckets of water from the creek and he spread them along the rows. Every morning Holena rushed out into the backyard to check for growth, though both Old Jan and I told her it would take time. At last, a week later, she was rewarded with the discovery of thick sprouts in the bean row, pushing their bowed heads up through the soil. Holena came dashing into the kitchen before she had even eaten breakfast. We followed her to the garden, where she showed us her discovery. Aneshka, after some scrutiny, reported the first sign of grassy corn sprouts as well.

I secretly glanced at Momma as my sisters padded barefoot along the rows, squealing with delight at each new discovery. Her face had softened and she was almost smiling, but then she saw me looking her way and her expression tightened again.

"I am glad things are sprouting, Trina, but don't get your hopes up that anything will come of it."

"I know it may not, Momma. But maybe it will. Old Jan says that anything worth having is worth working for."

"So it is," she said. "And we have plenty of work to do today, so enough nonsense. Go start heating the irons and I'll get the clothes from the line."

When the ironing was done that afternoon, Momma took the majority of our laundry earnings from the can on the shelf and sent me to the store for meat, as she did every Tuesday. Since the day Mr. Torentino had sold his plums, I had hated this chore. Mr. Johnson still gave me his usual salesman smile, but his eyes were hard. The previous week I had sent Aneshka in to make our purchases while I waited outside, but Mr. Johnson had tempted her into spending all the change on sweets, and I had gotten a scolding for it. So today I was by myself, with strict instructions to buy only what was on the list.

Mr. Torentino's wagon was just rumbling away from the store. I waited a few minutes before I entered, in case they had had another argument. I didn't want to do anything to offend Mr. Johnson again. Inside, he was stacking canned goods on the shelf behind the counter. I waited in silence for him to finish and notice me. When he did, he glared at me for a moment before pasting on his salesman smile. I knew my week's absence had done nothing to soften him.

Clenching my money nervously, I told him what I wanted. Without comment he set the goods on the counter in front of me. He totaled the amount and I handed him my money.

"Well," he said, looking at the cash in his hand, "you have three cents extra here. That will get you a piece of licorice, three lemon drops, or a stick of horehound." He gestured toward the jars of candy lined up on the counter. "What will it be?"

I swallowed hard and spoke. "I'd like my change, please, sir."

His salesman smile remained on his face, but stiffened. "It's just a few pennies, and I bet you've worked hard all day. You deserve a treat."

"No, thank you, sir. I'd like my change, please," I repeated, holding out my hand.

"What's the matter—you were happy enough to spend your money on Torentino's plums. Isn't my stock good enough for you?"

I did not know what to say to that, so I just waited silently for my change. With a shake of his head, he opened the cash register drawer, dropped my money inside, and took out the pennies he owed me.

My money safely in my pocket, I quickly gathered my purchases. "Thank you," I said, and hurried toward the door.

Mr. Johnson had already turned back to his shelves, but I heard him mutter something about "tightfisted Greeks." I could have kept walking, but I did not. I straightened my shoulders and raised my chin a little.

"Czechy," I said.

"Hmm?" he said, turning from his work. He didn't know I had heard him.

"We are Czechy," I said. "Not Greek."

He waved an impatient hand and went back to his work. "Bohunks, huh? You all look the same to me," he said. "Just like sheep."

My cheeks were flushed as I left the store, but I vowed to keep it to myself at home. My father would be angered by the insult, and my mother would scold me for talking back to Mr. Johnson. And since there was nowhere else for us to buy the things we needed, we couldn't afford to offend him.

When I arrived at our house, Holena was sitting on the front steps, her chin on her knees, staring at the place where we had planted the poppies. I followed her gaze, expecting to see sprouts breaking through the ground, but there was nothing there.

"What are you looking at?" I asked.

"Why haven't the poppies sprouted, Trina?"

"Maybe they just need a little longer," I said.

"Do you think Karel was right?"

"I don't know. We will have to wait and see."

Over the next few days, I went out to the garden in the back each morning to see the progress, but Holena went to look for the poppies. I knew they hadn't sprouted by the look on her face when she sat down at the table for her breakfast.

"I don't know why you're in a bother about them," Aneshka said. "They're only flowers. We can't eat them."

"None of it may come to anything, anyway," Momma reminded us all as she set our usual bowls of porridge on the table.

"But it might," I said. "And then maybe we won't have to spend so much money at the store and we can save a little."

Momma shook her head. "We'll still have to buy all the same things as we do now. Unless you can grow meat or coffee or flour in that garden of yours."

Despite myself, my heart sank. She was right; we couldn't live on the kinds of vegetables growing in my garden. There were just too many things that we needed that weren't in my little garden.

Momma looked at my face, and hers softened a little. "It's a good thing you are doing, Trina, and I am sure our meals will be better if anything comes to fruit. But you have to be realistic."

I nodded and ate, then started my chores, still thinking

about what she had said. Our biggest weekly expense at the store was meat. After wash day and Papa's payday, we had enough money for fresh meat from the store, and we certainly couldn't go without — at least, Papa couldn't. As hard as he worked, he needed something to sustain him. And Momma was right that I couldn't grow meat. I didn't have a cow or a pig, and even if I did, we had no way to feed it or to keep the meat if we butchered it. But I could fish. If I could bring fish home from time to time, even just once a week, I could save us a little money — maybe two or three dollars a week. And that could be one hundred dollars or more in a year!

The thought sent a tingle up my spine. One hundred dollars was an awful lot of money. I thought about it until I was finished with the last of my chores. When my sisters went outside to play, I went along, with one of Papa's old newspapers. I sat down on the porch steps and flipped through it, looking for the pages of advertisements. I knew they were in there, because when we had first arrived in America, Papa had used what little English he had to translate them for us each night — ads for land and farms here in America. I wasn't sure if he still read them or not, but he never read them out loud anymore.

I found the page and flattened it on my lap. A long list of ads in small print offered everything from horses and buggies to the services of laundresses and dress makers. Mixed in were the ads I wanted to read. Most of them were for established farms. My favorites were the ones that had fruit trees. I liked the idea of acres of apples or cherries or plums, so I looked for those first, and I found one right off that sounded perfect. A black border highlighted the ad. Inside the border, large block letters declared LAND! LAND! LAND! and below that ORCHARDS! PLENTY OF WATER! MOUNTAIN VIEWS! I could see it in my mind — at least, until I read the price: $2,500.00! I could never save that kind of money! Still, we didn't need mountain views; we just wanted a farm of our own. I read on, refusing to let my hope collapse, but just as the passing months had worn away at my father's dream, reading these ads wore away at mine, too. Even undeveloped land was selling for two or three hundred dollars, and it would cost much more to turn it into a farm. I couldn't see that we would get out of the coal camp with a penny less than five hundred dollars. Catching fish for one meal a week wouldn't be enough—but if there were other things I could do to save us money, maybe it was a start.

What we needed was a better source of meat—someone who could provide it at a better price than the company store. I remembered the farm where I had traded for seeds, and I had an idea, but I didn't share it with anyone. If my plans didn't work out, it would disappoint my sisters.

The next time I went to the store was on Saturday, after Papa got paid. As usual, there was a bit of change from my purchases, but I didn't return it to the can behind the stove when I got home. I felt guilty and wondered if I was stealing, but I planned to use it to help my family, so I did not see how I could be. After all, when Aneshka had bought candy with the change, she had not been stealing.

That afternoon, I asked Momma's permission to go fishing again, and she agreed. She had enjoyed the fish as much as the rest of us. I walked to Old Jan's house, where he sat on the front porch whittling. I borrowed the fishing pole, promising to bring fish for his supper as well as ours. Then I set off over the ridge.

As before, I caught fish in the stream, and as before I worked my way upstream, but this time I was not surprised to find the farm. This time, I had been looking for it. I left my string of fish and my pole in the bushes and walked to the cluster of buildings, carefully stepping in the space between the rows of young corn in the fields.

The buildings were bigger than they had appeared from across the field and for a moment my courage failed me. The structure was not just a single house, but many. The low adobe buildings formed three sides of a rectangle around an open courtyard. Each flat-roofed building had several doors, all facing into the courtyard, all painted a cheerful, bright blue. The open courtyard was bare dirt and busy with children playing. Their mothers kept a watchful eye from their shaded doorsteps where they worked.

A chorus of barking dogs announced my arrival, and several mongrels ran toward me. I froze until one of the older women came off the porch and called to them. They retreated, wagging their tales, and I let out my breath.

"Hello," I called to her. "Do you speak English?"

She shook her head, then with a quick word in Spanish, she sent a boy running to the cluster of low barns and buildings behind the houses. She smiled at me, and I felt my nerves relax a little. It was a warm smile that formed deep crinkles at the corners of her eyes, as if she had been smiling for most of her life. I smiled back and gave a little curtsy, which only widened her smile.

I took the money from my pocket, and gesturing as I spoke, I said, "I was wondering if I could buy—"

The woman held up a hand and gestured for me to wait, so I closed my hand around the money and stopped speaking. A moment later the boy returned from the barn with three men and several older boys. One of the adult men said something in Spanish to the others, and I recognized him as the man I had met in the fields. I hoped he was telling the others that he recognized me, but I couldn't be sure.

"*Buenas tardes, señorita*. You come here before, no?" another man said, and I quickly nodded. I held the money out to him.

"I—I wanted to buy a chicken, please, sir."

His eyebrows raised and he looked at my money. It was only forty-five cents, less than half what I would have paid at the company store, but I knew Mr. Johnson's prices were high. I held my breath and waited while he translated my request and the men discussed it. Finally, the man nodded.

"Come," he said, and the group walked back toward the barn. I followed with rising excitement. My mother would be so pleased to get a whole chicken for so little—we often could only afford a part of one to put in the pot.

Chickens were everywhere around the barns, scratching and pecking the bare dirt. Several hens had little broods of chicks scurrying around their feet, and young chickens with new pinfeathers in their wings were flapping and chasing each other like school children. The man to whom I had spoken singled out a hen without a brood and snatched her up, deftly catching her legs with one hand and binding them together with a strip of twine with the other. He held the squawking, flapping bird out to me.

I stared. It hadn't occurred to me that the bird would be alive. Of course, I knew it would be alive, but I hadn't thought about carrying it home that way. In my mind I had seen it much like buying a chicken from Mr. Johnson's store, where they hung already dead and plucked over his counters.

The farmer must have seen the uncertain expression on my face. He calmed the bird and turned her for my inspection. "Don't worry, she is strong, a good layer, no? She gives you many eggs."

My mouth fell open and I snapped it shut again. Eggs! I had only been thinking about buying a chicken for the pot, but eggs! If I had hens that could lay eggs, maybe I *could* grow meat! There was enough room behind our house for chickens. But one hen could not lay enough eggs for my family to eat well, or to hatch a brood large enough to fill a henhouse—at least, not soon.

"How much for two or three of those?" I asked, pointing at the young chickens chasing each other in and out around an old cart. "I have a large family; one hen won't give enough eggs for all of us."

"How big is your family?" the man asked.

"There are five of us, plus Old Jan and his two sons."

The man laughed. "Five is not so big," he said, unwinding the twine from the hen's legs and letting her go. He spoke to the other men in the group again, and after a time turned back to me.

"Three pullets," he said, pointing to the young chickens.

"All hens?" I asked.

"*Sí*, pullets," he said.

I nodded and smiled. "Thank you. Thank you very much." I handed him the money and he sent one of the boys into the barn for an old sack made of gray, hand-spun wool. The farmer collected three squawking chickens and put them into the bag, which he handed to me.

"Thank you," I said again. "How long until they lay eggs?"

"A few weeks, *más o menos*," he said.

Carefully holding the squirming bag, I set off back to where I had left my fish and my pole, then over the ridge toward home. I was thinking happily about the fresh eggs we would have when the chicks got old enough to lay. It would not be much at first, but if these were successful, maybe we could hatch more, and

59

have meat. My mouth watered as I imagined roasted chicken for our Sunday dinners.

From the top of the ridge, I looked down into the drab coal camp and my thoughts returned to the present. What would my mother say when I came in with live chickens? And what would she say when she found out I spent the change from the store without her permission? My plan had been to bring a chicken for the pot—there was no foolish dream in that. But my bag filled with squirming chicks was full of dreams. And that was the last thing my mother was going to let me bring into the house! How was I going to explain this? More important, what on earth was my mother going to do when I tried?

Chapter 6

I SAT DOWN on the ridge and looked into my bag. The three little chickens looked up at me with their glossy black eyes and peeped their uncertainty. I stared back the same way. I knew nothing about raising chickens. Maybe I should take them back to the farmer and get my money back rather than try to explain it all to my mother. The farmers would laugh at my foolishness, and I hated that idea. I hated even more the thought that it was foolishness; I wanted my plan to work. I wanted the chickens, and I wanted fresh eggs and meat. Mostly I wanted to prove we didn't have to rely on Mr. Johnson and his awful store.

It was a good plan; I just had to find a way to convince my mother, and that wouldn't be easy. She had protested a garden. I didn't like to think what she would say about chickens. I closed the bag again and got slowly back to my feet. I descended the ridge and entered camp on the west end, so I could pass Old Jan's house before going to my own.

"Ah, here's our fisherman now," Old Jan said as he saw me coming. "Did you have any luck?"

I climbed the porch steps and sat down beside him. "I caught plenty of fish," I said. "And I have something else, too. But I need your advice." I told him of my idea to buy a single chicken for meat and how it had changed, and I showed him the three pullets in the bag.

"That is very serious, Trina, taking money without asking," he said, his tone sober but still gentle. "You shouldn't have done so."

"I was afraid my mother would not let me try."

"Your mother only wants what is best for you," he said.

Frustration welled up inside me again, just as it had the night I brought home the seeds. "How is it best for me—for any of us—to be stuck here, working and working and never getting ahead? If she wanted what is best for me, she'd let me try to make things better. That is all I'm doing—where's the harm in trying?"

Old Jan patted my knee. "You are a brave girl, Trina, and a good girl. How many fish did you catch?"

I held up the string. "Enough for everyone to have a whole one this time. But what about the chickens?"

"Do you think your momma would cook all the fish for us? I will bring potato soup. I have it simmering on the stove already, but your momma's a better cook with fish."

I nodded. "She is always happy to have you."

"Then leave the chickens with me and take the fish to your momma. I'll work something out."

I did as he said and set off for home with the fish. Momma was pleased to get them, and pleased, too, that I had invited Old Jan and his sons to supper.

"It's the neighborly thing to do," she said, "and the least we can do, since they are kind enough to lend you the fishing pole."

I helped Momma prepare supper and filled the tub of wash-water for Papa, as I did every evening. My mind, however, was not on my work. I hoped Momma wouldn't notice. I needed her to be pleased with me, to be in a good mood. I had no idea what Old Jan was planning to do when he arrived. I did not see any way he could bring the pullets to our house without brooking my mother's opposition.

My stomach swirled with butterflies when I saw Old Jan approaching with Papa. They were discussing something in earnest tones, so I slipped back inside the house before they saw me. Old Jan did not appear to have the chickens with him, and I was afraid my expression would reveal that I had a secret.

Papa washed the coal dust and dirt from his face and hands in the tub by the back door as usual before the two of them entered. I watched as Momma greeted Papa, then welcomed Old Jan. Neither gave any hint that anything was out of the ordinary.

"Where are your sons?" Momma asked Old Jan.

"They will be along shortly with the soup," Old Jan said. "I wanted to talk to your husband, so I came along when I saw him passing my house."

Momma looked between the two men, her eyes registering surprise. "Is something wrong?"

Papa glanced at Old Jan, then back at Momma. "There's talk of layoffs at the mine," he said. "Just not as much demand for coal now that summer is here."

Momma's jaw clenched. "Talk? When will we know?"

"They say some people will get their slip with their pay next week," Papa said. "And, they are going to start giving out scrip payments for the summer."

"Scrip?" I asked. I had never heard of such a thing.

"It's not real money," Old Jan explained. "It's like a voucher that you can use to buy things at the store. But you can't buy things anywhere but the company store with it."

"That doesn't worry me. Where else are we going to spend it, anyway? But the layoffs. I don't know what we will do if you're laid off, Tomas," Momma said.

Old Jan put a hand on Papa's shoulder. "Don't worry, Mrs. Prochazkova. I have been here for four years and I have seen this many times. Your husband is a hard worker and a family man. They will keep him on. It will be the lazy ones and the bachelors that will go."

"Let us hope so," Momma said.

"It's a good thing Trina's such a good fisherman," Old Jan said with a wink in my direction. "You won't have to worry about going hungry with her in the family, no matter what."

Momma smiled in my direction, but the creases of worry between her eyes did not go away. "Supper is almost ready," she said. "Sit down and relax while the girls and I finish up in the kitchen."

I understood her worry, and I shared it silently as we finished preparing supper. If Papa lost his job, I didn't know what we would do. I felt a surge of guilt for having spent our money without permission. We would need every last cent we had if there were layoffs at the mine. I was glad that Old Jan hadn't brought the chickens right away—maybe I could still return them and get my money back. My heart fell when I looked out through the open kitchen door and saw Karel and Mark approaching. Mark was carrying a wooden crate, and I had a good idea what was inside it.

He set the crate down outside the back door, putting a rock

on the lid to prevent escape, then came inside just as Momma called everyone to supper. Holena skipped up to Mark and greeted him with a hug.

"Trina caught more fish for us with your pole," she said happily. Her mood, at least, had not been smothered by the news from the mine.

Karel laughed. "So she did. Trina has out-fished you again, Mark."

I shrugged. "I'm sure if you had more time, you'd be the better fisherman," I said to make him feel better. I'd only just started to be able to talk to him again. I didn't need Karel making things more awkward between us.

Papa smiled at me. "Trina has many talents that she's only just discovering," he said, making me wonder if Old Jan had already told him of the hens. Embarrassed, I retrieved the skillet from the stove and put a fried trout on each plate. Luckily, the conversation among the adults turned back to the topic of the mine, and I could breathe more freely. Maybe the chickens would be forgotten.

Karel was especially worried about the possibility of layoffs. He and Mark were bachelors, even though they had an injured father to support. And bachelors were always laid off before men with families.

"If they let one of us go, we could still get by, I suppose," he said. "But I don't know what we'll do if we are both laid off. All the other mines are laying workers off too; there won't be any jobs anywhere."

"I'm good with my hands. I might find some odd jobs," Mark said. "I'm sure they'll take us back once fall comes and the demand for coal goes up again."

"If we can make it through to fall," Karel said.

"We'll help you, Karel, won't we, Papa," Holena said. "We have the garden, and money from washing clothes."

"Of course we will," Papa said, patting Holena's hair. "We are family now, aren't we? That garden will be a big help."

"Well, we will cross that bridge when it comes. No point worrying," Momma said, but I could see she was. If the bachelors in camp were laid off, they wouldn't be paying us to do their laundry anymore, and it would be some time yet before the garden produced any food. Of course we had to help Old Jan's family, but how would we do it? I understood why the lines of worry across Momma's forehead never quite went away anymore.

"What we need," Old Jan said, "is something to see us through the good times and the bad. Something to fall back on."

Papa nodded.

"In the Old Country, I remember we had a cow," Mark said. He glanced in my direction and gave a little grin. "She grazed up on the commons and we had milk, whether we had money or not."

"Can we get a cow, Papa?" Aneshka asked.

"Where would we keep a cow?" Momma said.

"Yes, a cow is much too big, but I have something smaller in mind that might help," Old Jan said.

"If it's small, it's not going to be much help," Aneshka said. "I want a cow."

"Well, I don't know." Old Jan pushed away his empty plate and leaned back in his chair. "Sometimes you have to start with small things to get the big things you really want. Do you know the story of the three brothers who inherited their father's farm?"

"Tell us," Aneshka said, bouncing in her chair and clapping her hands.

66

"Please tell us," Holena added more politely.

"The oldest son took the biggest and best share, and the second son took almost all the rest. For the youngest son all that was left was a good, sturdy rope. Now, a rope, that is not much, is it?"

"No, his brothers should have given him more," Holena said.

"Perhaps. So all he had was one small thing when he set out to make his way in the world. When he came to a forest he made snares from some of that rope, and he caught a squirrel and a hare."

"What did he want those for?" Holena asked.

"Don't interrupt," Aneshka said.

"He put the squirrel and the hare in his basket and continued on until he came to a lake. Beside the lake was a cave and in the cave was a bear, snoring away.

"The boy sat down beside the lake to make a bigger snare to catch the bear, but before he finished, a water sprite that lived in the lake saw him. It was just a small sprite, and very curious, so it rose to the surface and said to the boy, 'What are you doing with that rope?'

"Well, the boy was a clever lad, so he said, 'I plan to tie up the lake so no one can get out.'

"The sprite dropped to the bottom of the lake and told the king of the sprites what he had heard.

"'Go back up and challenge the boy to a race. When he is tired from running, catch him and drag him into the deep water, and we will be rid of him,' said the king.

"So the little sprite rose to the surface again and challenged the boy to a race.

"'I can't right now,' the boy said, still shaping his snare. 'But my younger brother will race you, though he's very small.'

"The sprite accepted the challenge. So the boy let the squirrel out of his bag and the creature zipped away so quickly it was half-way around the lake before the sprite started. Of course, it won. When the sprite told the king what had happened, the king sent him back to try again.

"'I can't. I'm still too busy, but you can race my other brother,' the boy said.

"The sprite agreed, and the boy set the hare loose. Well, what do you know, that hare was even faster than the squirrel had been."

"And the sprite lost again!" Aneshka said with a delighted squeal.

"Yes. So when the sprite returned to the king, it was clear that racing wasn't going to work.

"'Go back up and tell the boy you will wrestle him, and when you have a good grip on him, drag him into the lake and we'll be rid of him for good.'

"So the sprite returned to the surface, and he challenged the boy to a wrestling match.

"'Oh, I am much too busy,' said the boy, 'but my old grand-father is sleeping in that cave, and if you'll wake him up, he might be willing to wrestle with you.'

"'If I win,' said the sprite, 'will you leave our lake alone and not tie it up?'

"'Certainly,' agreed the boy. So the sprite went into the dark cave and saw the sleeping figure.

"'Grandfather, come wrestle with me,' he said, but the figure went on sleeping.

"'Come on, old man,' the little sprite said impatiently, and he slapped the bear hard on the nose.

"Well, that bear came awake with a huge growl and swatted the little sprite so hard he flew backward and landed with a big splash in the middle of the lake. When the king saw that, he knew he had to do something to protect the lake from such a strong, clever, fast family. So he rose to the surface and asked the boy, 'What do you want to leave our lake alone?'

"'Just enough of your gold to fill my hat,' the boy answered.

"'Agreed,' said the king. And while he was at the bottom of the lake gathering the gold, the boy dug a pit in the ground and cut a hole in the top of his hat. So when the king poured his coins into the boy's hat, he kept filling and filling, and the hat did not fill until the boy had nearly all the sprite king's gold.

"And that is how, with nearly nothing, the boy ended up the richest of all the brothers," Old Jan finished.

"We have nearly nothing—maybe we are going to be rich too," Aneshka said, and giggled.

Momma gave her a reproachful look, but Old Jan smiled. "As I said, I have a small thing that may help."

"What is this 'small thing' you have?" Momma asked, her voice skeptical.

"Well," Old Jan said quietly, looking at me, "they are not really mine. But maybe Trina would like to tell this story."

All around the table eyes turned to me. I looked desperately at Old Jan and he gave me an encouraging smile, but nothing more. I was on my own from here; he had done all he planned to do. I had made the choice to take the money and buy the chickens, and I was going to have to tell my parents on my own. I swallowed hard and spoke up.

"I bought chickens," I said simply.

"You what?" Momma said.

"Chickens?" Papa said.

I nodded and hurried to explain everything before I lost my courage. When I finished, there was silence at the table for a long moment. I kept my eyes on my empty plate, not daring to look at my parents.

"Well, where are they?" Papa said at last.

Mark rose from the table and returned a moment later with the crate. He set it on the floor and everyone gathered around as he lifted off the lid.

All of a sudden, Papa began to laugh.

Momma frowned at him. "What is the matter with you?" she said, but he only laughed harder. It was a long moment before the laughter quieted enough for him to speak.

"You remember, Trina, when your sisters made wishes and you would not?"

"I wished for plum dumplings," Aneshka said.

"And I wished for hair ribbons," Holena said.

Papa nodded, still chuckling, "And Trina wouldn't wish, but I did, remember? I said I'd wish for a farm. And here it is—a garden and livestock of our very own. Our little farm here in America. You should have wished, Trina, but since you wouldn't, it looks like I got the third wish instead!"

Chapter 7

I GAPED AT my father in disbelief. Had my wish come true, only to leave us stuck in the mining camp?

"You and your foolish nonsense," Momma snapped at Papa. Then she turned to me. "What were you thinking, Trina? Chickens? Where on earth are we going to keep them?"

"I thought we could keep them behind the house," I said. "They will be old enough to start laying eggs in a few weeks. I just wanted to help us save money to get our farm," I said.

"And just how are we supposed to fence or house them?"

"I hadn't thought of that," I admitted. The truth was, I hadn't really thought of any of it.

"There is always scrap wood in the mine dump," Mark said, surprising everyone. "We could probably dig up enough to make a chicken coop."

"And when will you have time for that?" Momma asked. "You boys work too hard now as it is."

"But we are going to need the extra food if we get laid off

at the mine," Mark pointed out. "I think it's a lucky thing that Trina found that farm and got these chickens." He smiled at me, and I blushed so suddenly I could not hide it. All I could do was smile back, grateful for his support. Then I caught my mother's eye and my smile quickly faded.

"I know I shouldn't have spent the money without permission, Momma. But please let me try. If it doesn't work out, we could still butcher and eat these chickens. I got all three for less than a whole chicken from Mr. Johnson's store."

Momma was watching the little hens scrabble and peck around the crate as Aneshka dropped bits of bread in to them. She sighed. "You do have an eye for a bargain, I suppose, but your head is so full of dreams. You get that from your father."

"Can we keep them then?" Aneshka asked.

Momma looked to Papa for his decision.

"If you can house them and feed them, Trina, you can keep them," Papa said.

I nodded. "They can eat kitchen scraps. And grasshoppers down by the creek."

"But do not do such a thing again without permission," Papa warned.

"I won't. I promise."

"And the first time they start costing us money instead of saving it, they go in the pot," Momma added.

That evening Aneshka and Holena herded the chickens around the small yard, but since we had no house for them, the chickens spent the night in the kitchen in their crate.

The next morning I woke to someone quietly calling my name through the open window. The rest of my family was still asleep, so I slipped outside to see Mark measuring out space and writing down his measurements on a scrap of wood.

"What are you doing?" I asked.

"Good morning, sleepyhead. I'm getting started on your henhouse."

"So early?"

"I only have today off, and I'll have to sleep this afternoon before going back on the night shift tonight, so I thought I'd better get started. It shouldn't take long."

"Really? I wouldn't know where to begin," I admitted.

"Then you're lucky you have me," he said, grinning. He looked like his old self, with his hair flopping over his forehead, and I couldn't help grinning back.

"So I am," I said. "What are we doing first?"

He picked up a stick and scratched out a square on the ground. "This is where we will build it," he said. "And here is what we'll need." He took a scrap of newspaper from his pocket, on which he had written a list of materials.

"Can we really get all this from the mine dump?" It wasn't a long list, but it was more than I imagined we could get for free. As far as I could tell, the stingy mine owners wouldn't let anything go for free if they could charge us for it.

"Let's go find out," Mark said.

"But—won't we get in trouble?"

Mark shook his head. "It's trash. No one will even notice. It all gets buried and forgotten under the mine tailings in a matter of days."

My family was still asleep, so I set off with Mark, up the hill toward the mine.

The slanting rays of the rising sun softened and brightened the drab houses and dirt lanes of the camp, but they could do nothing to alter the ugliness of the mine. As we approached, the hoist and the gaping shaft stood out as starkly as ever, surrounded by tangles of steel cable and grimy coal cars. I could never shake the sense of dread that came over me near the shaft. The thought of descending into the darkness, with all those tons of earth looming over me, made my insides knot. I stepped closer to Mark, glad for the warmth of his presence.

"Over there," he said, pointing. An enormous pile of dirt and crushed rock trailed down the slope toward the creek. The pile was streaked gray, brown, and sulfur yellow from loads brought up from different levels of the mine, and the entire mass seemed to be creeping relentlessly down the slope. On the front edge of the pile, trash and debris had been dumped and was being swallowed up by the advance of the dirt and rock.

We climbed down the slope to inspect the tangled debris. Splintered beams and boards, frayed loops of rusting cable, broken gears, and empty liquor bottles lay scattered on the ground or sticking out of the loose tailings. The whole pile smelled of coal, engine grease, and rot. I couldn't help wrinkling my nose, but Mark was grinning cheerfully.

"It may take us some time, but there's a lot here, if we don't mind getting our hands dirty. And the more we find, the less we have to buy."

"Then let's get started," I said.

Searching through the rubbish was hard work, and my hands were soon scratched and bruised, but with every new discovery of something useful, my spirits soared. It was like a treasure hunt, even if our treasure was really just trash. We soon had a pile of wood in a variety of ragtag sizes and shapes, but all were serviceable. After all, the chickens didn't care if they had a fancy house or not, as long as they had a place to roost.

"We need a fence, too," Mark said as we worked. "That will be the most difficult part."

"I didn't think of that when I got them," I admitted. "Is there any way we could make do without a fence?"

"Well, I suppose if you want them visiting your neighbors and roosting wherever they please," he said. "But if you want them to set in your henhouse, you better keep them there. Besides, there are too many stray dogs in camp to let them wander."

"How do you know so much about chickens?" I asked.

"When we were in Bohemia we had chickens. Collecting the eggs was one of my chores, so I got to know our biddies pretty well."

"You had a cow and chickens in Bohemia? Were you farmers?"

"More or less," he said, prying a board loose from the soil and throwing it onto the pile.

"And you gave that up to come here? To work in a mine?"

"We didn't really give up much. We didn't own the land or the crops. It was more like they owned us. And Papa was already a miner. More than once he left home for the mines all winter when the harvest was poor. So, after my mother died, Papa heard about the better wages here and we came. He believed Karel and I would have a better future."

I knew that land was scarce in Bohemia, and most of it was owned by wealthy families. The peasants who worked the estates were often no better off than beggars, but I couldn't see how working the coal mines here was any better. I said as much, but Mark laughed.

"You weren't farmers in Bohemia, were you."

"What does that have to do with it?"

"Farming's hard, miserable work, Trina. You spend your

days out in the heat all summer and in the cold all winter. And you never get paid. When a crop fails, the farmer goes hungry. When you run out of money here, the store will extend you credit so you can still eat."

"But you'll never get out of here that way. You're always in debt to the company," I protested.

Mark shrugged. "Where is there to go? We've got jobs here, and a house."

"But you don't own anything. It's not yours."

"You bought chickens. And you'll own your chicken coop, and your garden."

"But don't you want more?"

He shrugged again and tossed a board onto our growing pile. "Sure I do. But a farm isn't more. I never want to go back to farming. What about you?"

"My father wants a farm, and I think that would be a fine place for Aneshka and Holena to grow up. I think it would be better for you, too. Your papa doesn't mind farming, I think. He's been happy working in my garden."

Mark laughed. "There's a lot more to having a farm than a little kitchen garden. My papa can't swing a scythe anymore, and I don't ever want to either."

"Better than swinging a pick," I insisted.

He shook his head. "The way I see it, the biggest difference between farming and mining is just in what you're shoveling. And at least in the mine, you're getting paid to shovel it."

Mark was turned away from me, tugging at a timber that was stuck fast, so I scowled at his back. I was annoyed by his opinions, but he was doing me a big favor building my henhouse, so I held my tongue. I began gathering nails that we could reuse.

"Help me with this, will you? Something is holding it down," he said a few minutes later. He was still trying to pull the same timber out of the tailings. Using a bent piece of tin roofing, I scooped away at the dirt that held the end of the beam. Soon we could see why it would not come free. A crossbeam was still nailed to its end at right angles, and the second beam jutted downward into the heap of tailings and trash.

"Get at the corner and pull," Mark said, pointing toward the intersection where the two timbers formed an L. I did as he instructed, and together we heaved and pulled but they still would not come free.

"Maybe we should leave this one," I said.

"No, these are good, sturdy beams. They will be worth the trouble. I wonder what is still holding them." He lifted and pulled on his end again.

"Look," I said, pointing at what I had seen as he pulled. The timber he held was not the only thing that had moved. The dirt and trash around it had lifted and flexed as well. "Do that again," I said. Once again, the ground shifted across a wide area. I stepped into the L of the boards and cleared away the dirt in the area that had moved. Strands of wire appeared in the ground, but I couldn't tell what they were. Once some of the dirt was removed from the wire, I took hold of the wood again.

"Let's try it again now," I said.

Together we heaved and tugged, and suddenly the soil gave way and the wood came free. I staggered back a few steps and sat down hard. Mark looked at me, his eyes glinting with mischief.

"Are you okay?" he asked.

I nodded. "It just caught me by surprise, that's all."

He turned back to the timbers, his shoulders shaking.

"Are you laughing at me?" I demanded, getting to my feet. I tried to sound indignant, but my own laughter was starting to rise as well.

He shook his head, but a little chuckle broke out of him as he did.

"Yes, you are!" I said.

He shook his head again. "I'm not. I'm laughing because—look at what was holding us back."

I looked to where he was pointing. Attached to the L of timbers were strips of wire mesh fencing, the kind the mine used to hold back loose rock, but also the kind used to fence in chickens! I stared, open-mouthed. We had pulled loose about four feet of it, and more had disappeared under the tailings.

"How much do you think there is?" I asked.

"Let's dig it out and see, shall we?" he said.

We set to digging and pulling on the rusty fencing. When at last we had it free, we had enough to enclose a small chicken yard.

"I can't believe it!" I said, looking at it after we had it neatly rolled and added to our pile.

"I can," Mark said, grinning at me.

"You can?"

He nodded. "Because I think you, Trina Prochazkova, are the luckiest person alive. All you have to do is wish for something and it appears."

Chapter 8

MY MOUTH FELL open as what he said washed over me. Lucky things were still happening to me! If he was right, my wish wasn't complete. Hope filled me—the chickens and garden weren't the fulfillment of my wish—finding this wire proved that! And that meant we were still on our way to a real farm. I just had to keep trying and hoping and believing! I smiled at Mark, feeling happier than ever.

He smiled back. "We should get these things back to your house," he said, and I agreed.

By the time we arrived at my house with our first load of supplies, my family was awake. A work crew was soon assembled to bring the remaining boards and timbers to the house and start building. Old Jan and Karel joined us with hammers and saws, ready to start construction. I was eager to help build, but Momma called me inside.

"If you are going to have all these men working for you through their day off, you are going to have to feed them," she said.

"But I want to help them build," I protested. After all, the coop was for my chickens.

Momma shook her head. "You can help by making sure these men are taken care of," she said, and ushered me into the kitchen. We set to work cooking and baking as if it were a holiday. I supposed it was only fair. I did need to show my appreciation. But I still could not resist sneaking to the back door whenever I had a moment, just to take a peek at the progress. At first not much seemed to be happening, but when I stepped outside at noon to announce that dinner was ready, I was amazed to see a little square house there, lacking only part of the roof and a door. It was an odd-looking structure, made as it was from ramshackle bits of wood, the grime of mine tailings still clinging to some of them. To me, though, it was as good as a palace — or at least a palace for chickens.

"What do you think?" Mark said, pushing his hair back off his forehead as we inspected his morning's work.

"I think it's wonderful!" I said. "I am lucky to have such good friends!"

He grinned wider. "Come look." He grasped my hand and pulled me toward the little building. Standing on tiptoe, I could look over the wall through the missing portion of the roof. He stood beside me and pointed.

"You see, I put in five nesting boxes, in case you get more chickens."

"Oh, I plan to!" I said. "I'm going to let some of the eggs hatch so that I will have a whole flock!"

He gave me a quizzical look, then burst out laughing.

"What?" I asked, already feeling the color in my cheeks, though I didn't know why.

"You may have your farm, Trina, but that hasn't made you

80

a farmer just yet. If you plan to hatch chicks, you're going to need a rooster."

I stared at him for a long moment. When I finally realized what he meant, the blood flooded into my cheeks.

Mark tried to straighten his mouth into a serious expression, but the laughter kept bubbling out, despite his efforts.

I turned abruptly back to the house, feeling every inch the fool. "Dinner is ready," I said, a little more shrilly than I had intended. "I have to go put it on the table."

"But you do like my nesting boxes, don't you?" he called after me.

I nodded, too embarrassed to look at him.

"Come inside when you've washed up," I said, and fled into the kitchen.

Momma and I had outdone ourselves cooking, or so the men said as they took big helpings of stew, dumplings, and potatoes.

"Trina should get a cow, too," Karel said, as he spread a knife-full of lard on a thick slice of bread. "A little butter and this meal would be a perfect feast."

"Don't go putting any more ideas in that girl's head," Momma said, but she didn't sound angry. In fact, she sounded a little amused, and that gave me hope. If my chickens supplied us with fresh eggs and saved us money, maybe I could find a way to get a rooster, or at least a few more hens. But since I couldn't take more money, I needed to gain Momma's approval first so I could do it with permission.

My hope rose even higher at the end of the meal when the men finished their coffee to go back to work. Momma smiled in my direction. "You may go out and help them finish, Trina. Aneshka and Holena can wash the dishes."

I went outside with my heart singing. Papa and Old Jan

were fashioning a roof for the henhouse, so I helped Mark dig holes and place the mismatched posts for the short fence. When the posts were in place, we stretched the precious chicken wire across them, and I held it tight while Mark nailed it to the posts. I was intent on my work and did not notice that Papa and Old Jan had finished and left us alone in the back until we had the last bit of wire nailed into place. I stepped back and looked at our work, then exclaimed in surprise.

"What?" Mark asked.

"We haven't made a gate—there's no way to get out," I said. We had stretched the wire in a complete square, connecting it on either side to the chicken house with no openings at all—Mark on the outside and me on the inside.

"But the fence is only waist high," Mark pointed out. "You can step over it."

I might have done so if I were alone, but the thought of hiking my skirts and clambering over in front of Mark made me feel suddenly shy. I gazed at the fence uncertainly.

"Come here," he said. I stepped to him, with only the fence between us. He bent forward, caught me behind the back and legs, and swung me up and over the fence. I gave a little shriek of surprise and clung to him for support, noticing again the hard muscles of his arms and back. He set me down beside him on the right side of the fence, his eyes gleaming with mischief. "Next Sunday we can go get more wood and I will build you a gate," he said.

"Thank you," I said, a little breathless, still thinking about those strong muscles. I took time to brush myself off and straighten my skirts while my heart settled back into its beat. Mark had never had this effect on me when he'd sat next to me in the schoolhouse.

"Let's introduce your chickens to their new home, shall we?" he said.

We retrieved the chickens from where they were pecking and scratching along the roadside. Holena and Aneshka had been watching them and shooing off the occasional stray dog. Mark and I carried the hens, flapping and squawking, to the newly fenced yard. Then we stood and watched as they explored, pecking at the ground, testing the barrier of the fence, and darting in and out of the little house.

"Trina, do you remember this morning, when you asked if I wanted something more?" Mark's voice was unexpectedly nervous, and I turned to look at him. His nervousness made him look like the schoolboy once again, instead of the miner.

"Yes."

"What I want is for you to go with me to the dance at the community hall on Saturday. Would you?"

My heart skipped a beat. The older girls all talked excitedly about the community hall dances they went to with the bachelors in camp, but I had not looked for an invitation to one yet. The idea of it made me giddy.

"I have to ask my parents," I said.

Mark smiled, and I noticed how handsome his smile was. "Go ask, then. I'll wait here," he said.

I nodded and slipped inside, feeling like I was walking in a dream. So many things were going right so quickly it couldn't be real—and yet it was! I found Momma alone in the kitchen, putting away the last stack of plates. Through the open front door, I could see Papa, Jan, and Karel on the porch in conversation. My sisters were playing hopscotch in the dust beyond. I cleared my throat and spoke.

"Momma, Mark—Marek—" I added, remembering my parents'

preference for his Bohemian name. I didn't want to give any reason for her to say no. "Marek has asked me to the community dance on Saturday. May I go with him?"

Momma's face burst into a wide smile. "The community dance? That's a fine idea, Trina. Marek is a good boy—a fine young man, that is."

"I may go, then?"

"Of course you may go. We must find you something nice to wear. You should look your best. I'm glad to see you thinking about practical things and not just dreams. Marek is a good match for you. He's almost family already, and he's a practical boy. And you and Marek are very fond of each other, I think."

"A good match! It's only a community dance," I protested.

Momma smiled. "Don't act so surprised, Trina. You're almost a woman. It's time we started thinking of these things. Marek is handsome, and he already makes a good living. Go tell him you would be glad to go."

She smiled at me again and went out onto the porch to sit with Papa and Old Jan, leaving me in the kitchen, my mind reeling. I liked Mark, but I couldn't see myself marrying him. I hadn't thought of marrying anyone yet, but especially not someone who was content to stay forever working at the coal mine. I couldn't bear being trapped here forever, no matter how kind or handsome a husband I had. I'd made other plans. Of course, it would be years yet before I was ready to marry, but as I stood in the kitchen, I could hear my mother suggesting the idea to Old Jan and Papa on the porch. I did not want to make promises to Mark, or to Momma, that I couldn't keep if we got our farm.

Slowly I returned to the backyard. Mark was waiting. He pushed his hair away from his face and smiled when he saw me coming. I felt a pang in my heart, but it couldn't be helped.

"Well?" he asked.

I bit my lip, my eyes on the ground. "I'm sorry, Mark. I'm not ready," I said softly.

He frowned. "You'll be fourteen soon. Will your parents let you go then?"

"Maybe," I said, trying to decide whether it was wrong to let him think my mother had said no. Before I could decide, Karel came around the house to remind Mark that they had a night shift at the mine and should go home for a few hours' rest. I watched them go, already regretting my answer.

Holena suddenly came running around the corner of the house, bursting with so much excitement that I couldn't make out what she was telling me. She tugged at my sleeve. I took one last glance toward Mark and let her pull me away. She stopped by the front porch and pointed excitedly.

"See, Trina, see? The poppies! They've sprouted at last!"

There where she pointed, gray-green sprouts were curling up out of the ground.

"Well, I'll be," Old Jan said quietly from his seat above us on the porch. "And to think I had nearly given up on them! Tereza's poppies!" The faint tremor in his voice made us all look up at him. The corners of his eyes glistened with tears. Holena climbed the steps to him and took his gnarled hand in hers.

"Don't cry, Jan," she said gently. "Be happy. They will be beautiful when they bloom."

Old Jan smiled and patted her soft cheek. "You are a wise child, Holena. I was caught up in thoughts of what was, but you . . . You are right to hope for the future. After all, that is why we came to America, isn't it? To grow our hopes for the future. You are a wise child, indeed."

And with that, I knew I had done the right thing too.

Chapter 9

IT DID NOT take long for everyone in the coal camp to hear about my chickens, and at least half of them came by to catch a glimpse for themselves. The children came eagerly to the backyard to stare over the fence while their mothers walked slowly by on the road, trying to slyly glance past the house to the chicken yard. I could tell how far the news had spread each day by the changing nationalities of my visitors. We all had our own neighborhoods and we didn't mix much. The coal company preferred it that way—if we didn't mix, we couldn't organize against them. My chickens, however, managed what the union leaders could not. In no time Polish, Greek, Italian, Mexican, and Bohemian children were all mixed together, talking and laughing. By the end of the week, even Mr. Johnson knew of my chickens, as I discovered on my next trip to the store.

"Ah, it's the not-Greek girl," he said. I gave him a polite smile and listed the things I needed. He set each item dutifully on the counter in front of me.

"No eggs for you today?" he asked, smirking as if he knew a secret.

I could not help but stiffen, but I only said, "No, thank you."

"What about chicken feed?" he asked.

I hesitated. Was he merely trying to confirm the rumor? Something sinister in his manner made me afraid to tell him anything, though I could think of no reason not to. There was no law against keeping chickens, as far as I knew.

"No, thank you, sir," I said again and held out my money to him, wanting to get away from him more than ever. He did not take my money but continued to look at me with the same cold smirk. My outstretched hand began to tremble, but I said nothing. What was there to say?

Finally he took my money and made change. I hurried out of the store, relieved to get away.

"Never mind him," someone said as I stepped out onto the porch. I nearly jumped out of my skin—I'd had no idea anyone had been watching or listening. I turned to see one of the other Bohemian girls in the camp, sitting in one of the chairs on the porch. Her name was Martina, and she was three or four years older than me. She'd been in school with me when I had first arrived, but soon after she left school to marry. She had no children to come watch my chickens, but still I had seen her walking by our house, glancing curiously toward the backyard. I nodded a greeting in her direction. She rose and began to walk with me.

"My Charlie is on the same crew as your papa," she said as we began down the steps together. "Don't worry about Mr. Johnson. He's just afraid of the competition, that's all."

"Competition?" The idea surprised me—how could my three chickens be competition for Mr. Johnson?

"He's afraid you'll be selling eggs," she said.

"Oh."

"Will you be?" There was an eagerness behind her question that made me think she would be a ready customer if I had eggs to sell.

"I haven't really thought about it," I admitted. "I only have three hens, and they won't start laying for at least two more weeks."

Martina's face fell a little. "I see. But if you did have any to sell, I wouldn't require many. It's only my Charlie and me, and he'd sure be delighted to taste a really fresh egg now and then. You will let me know, won't you?"

I nodded. "I will let you know."

We had been walking as we talked and had come to her house. I thought she would say good-bye and go inside, but she hesitated.

"You have a garden too? And cucumbers?" she asked.

"Yes."

"Mr. Johnson never has cucumbers fresh enough to make a crisp pickle," she said. "Do you think —"

My mother called me from up the street. I could see her on the porch of our house, shielding her eyes from the sun, trying to see who I was talking to.

"Coming, Momma!" I called to her, then turned back to Martina. "You would buy cucumbers, too?" I asked.

She nodded eagerly.

"I'll let you know when they are ripe," I said. When I got home, Momma asked who I'd been talking to. I told her what Martina wanted.

"I said we probably wouldn't have anything to sell," I said. "But if we did have anything extra, from the garden or the chickens, she would like to know."

Momma gave a little snort and went back to work in the kitchen. "You've got everyone in town caught up in this nonsense. You'd be much better off to let Marek court you, and to forget your grand plans."

I did not reply, only put away the tins of food I'd brought and returned the change to the money can. Then I went out to the backyard and looked at my garden. The squash and cucumber vines were sprawling out from their hills, their wide, shady leaves sheltering the blossoms that would soon turn to fruit. The beans were climbing the simple trellises Old Jan had made from sticks and twine, and the corn was almost knee high.

What if there was enough here to sell? We were still going to have to purchase the necessities at the store. The garden would only produce a few extra things that would make my family happier. But Martina had given me something to think about. If these fresh vegetables would be a luxury to my family, they would be to others, as well. And people would pay money for a luxury, even if they could only get a little of it! All this time I had only been thinking of *saving* money—but maybe with my garden, I could be *making* money! And it must be possible, otherwise Mr. Johnson would not be so suspicious. It made me laugh to think that Mr. Johnson's suspicion had led to this discovery, but it gave me an odd feeling, too. It was yet another lucky coincidence—another unexpected occurrence that opened an opportunity. How could I account for so many lucky coincidences?

Holena and Aneshka came skipping out of the house, having finished their chores for the day as well. They each carried an empty plum can.

"We are going down by the creek to catch grasshoppers for the chickens," Aneshka said. "Do you want to come?"

I nodded and found a can for myself, and we set off for the creek. It probably would have been more efficient to bring the chickens to the creek to catch their own meal, but my sisters enjoyed chasing grasshoppers and trying to trap them in tin cans. As for me, I had been so busy with the garden, the chickens, and my regular chores, I had spent little time at the creek lately. So when my sisters tired of catching bugs, I sent them home, and I wandered alone around the bend to where the high bank silenced the mine. I needed the silence and the solitude to think.

I settled myself in the space between the tree's roots and waited, wondering if I would see the fish again, wondering if it really was a magic fish. I knew it couldn't be, but how else could I explain what was happening? I heard a noise behind me and turned to see Holena. She was watching me, her eyes uncertain. I smiled at her and patted the tree root beside me. She sat down on it, still looking at me with questioning eyes.

"What is it?" I asked.

"I like this place," she said. "It feels special."

"I think so too," I said.

Her face brightened. "You do?"

I nodded.

She chewed her lip, looking at the pool. I waited and soon her question spilled out. "You didn't see a magic fish in the washwater like Aneshka said, did you?"

"No, I didn't," I said.

"You saw it here, didn't you?"

I was so surprised by the question, I could only gape at her.

"I saw it too, the day I was here with Mark."

"You did? How do you know it was a magic fish?"

"I knew it was because you didn't want Mark to catch it. Why else did you make him stop fishing here?"

I couldn't help but smile. She had seen through everything.

Holena sighed and hugged her knees. "I wish you had made a wish, Trina," she said.

"Why is that?"

"Aneshka and I used our wishes on little things, just like you said. You would have wished for something smarter."

"Do you regret your wish, then?" I asked. People in the stories always did.

Holena shook her head. "But you would have wished for something wonderful and you'd be happy."

We sat in silence for a long moment before she spoke again. "If we see it now, Trina, will you make a wish? Please?"

I hesitated. I hadn't told anyone about my wish. It had seemed like an embarrassing secret all these weeks, but Holena was different. I took a deep breath. "I already have."

She looked at me, her eyes round with surprise. "You have?"

I nodded. "After your wishes came true, I came here and saw the fish, so I made a wish."

"What did you wish for?" Holena asked.

"I wished for a farm here in America, where we could all be together and happy."

"That was Papa's wish too! And that's why you got your farm!"

"That may be why we got the garden and chickens," I said slowly, "but I don't think that's the farm. Things are still happening. Lucky things. And we've never been lucky before. Not in America, anyway."

"You mean we're going to get a *real* farm? And Papa won't have to work in the mine anymore?"

It sounded so big when she said it—I couldn't promise such a thing to sweet Holena. I couldn't bear to disappoint her, despite my own hope.

"I don't know, Holena. But I do know things are getting better for us. And I have a new idea, to help make a little extra money, to help even more." I told her we might sell extra eggs or produce. "Maybe I'll make enough money to buy a rooster, and then our flock can grow. With more chickens, we could sell more eggs, too. What do you think?"

Her eyes gleamed happily. "I think your wish is coming true, Trina!"

"Don't tell anyone, please?"

"Not even Aneshka?"

"For now, not even Aneshka," I said. I stood and brushed the dirt off my skirt. "We should get back home."

I offered her my hand. As she took it, she glanced back at the pool. "I'm glad you believe in the wishes."

I followed her gaze. I had come here alone to decide what I believed, but I hadn't decided. At least, I thought I hadn't. Now, as I thought about it, I couldn't explain away our luck any other way. Slowly, I nodded.

"Yes," I said, "I suppose I do believe."

We turned and started toward home. Behind me in the water, I heard a soft plop and, looking back, saw ripples. Holena, it seemed, was not the only one who had heard me, and I had a feeling that I had made a commitment to more than just myself.

Chapter 10

I TENDED MY backyard empire with extra care after that, watching eagerly for our first harvest. I fished, too, and as I'd hoped, the free fish one day a week saved a few dollars at the store. Unfortunately, the layoffs at the mine had sent many of the bachelors away. As they left, they took their laundry—and their laundry money—with them, so the money can on the shelf stayed as empty as ever. I didn't worry, though. Opportunities had come along ever since I had made my wish. All I had to do was watch for them and snatch them up when they appeared. And although I had discouraged Holena from hoping for too much, I was once again reading the advertisements for land and daydreaming of shady orchards and fields of ripening wheat to the horizon.

Right on schedule, my hens began laying eggs, enough for us each to have one with our breakfast porridge several times a week. Even Momma agreed they were a treat.

The next opportunity came one morning in mid-June as I

worked in my garden. I was searching among the broad squash leaves for the first of the bright yellow vegetables when I saw a pair of unfamiliar shoes in front of me on the edge of the vegetable patch. I looked up to see Martina holding her pocketbook before her.

"Good morning," I said, and straightened to face her. I couldn't help a curious glance at her pocketbook as I waited for her to speak.

She shifted uncomfortably and gave me a shy smile. "It's my Charlie's birthday today."

"That's nice."

"And I want to bake him a cake. But I have no eggs. I was wondering if I could buy two from you."

I knew we had eggs in the house that we were saving up to make a meal's worth, but I suspected Momma wouldn't let me sell those. But I hadn't checked my henhouse yet today. My young hens didn't lay every day anyway, so two fewer eggs could be explained away easily enough.

"Let me see what I can do." I crossed to the chicken yard and entered through the fine new gate that Mark had made me. As luck would have it—especially the kind of luck I'd been having—there were three eggs in the nesting boxes. I removed them carefully and gave two to Martina. She gave me a nickel. I thanked her and slipped the nickel into my pocket, intending to put it in the can when Momma wasn't looking so I wouldn't have to explain what I had done. But as I continued to work in the garden, I started thinking again about a rooster. If I was going to get one, this nickel could be the first step. Then once I had a rooster, we could have more chickens, and more eggs, and even meat from time to time. And, more important, there would be more to sell—we'd be saving *and* making money.

This was the next opportunity I'd been waiting for. The money didn't have to go into the can.

Later that same day, another neighbor showed up in the yard. "I hear Mrs. Pearsonova bought eggs from you," she said. I smiled and nodded. Martina had married an American, but in the Bohemian district, the older women couldn't resist adding the "-ova" ending to the name of a married woman, whether her married name was Bohemian or not.

"I sold her two," I said, "but my hens don't lay many yet."

"What else do you have? Do you have cucumbers?" she asked, sounding as if she were inquiring across Mr. Johnson's counter.

"I do," I said. "They are small yet, though."

She strode into my garden and bent over my plants. To my surprise, she plucked a tiny cucumber off the vine without even asking permission. She put three cents into my hand, thanked me, and marched away. I stared after her, unable to say a word.

Once again, rumor spread quickly among our neighbors. Within the week, I had more requests than I could fill. Those I could, however, brought in a few cents here, a few there, until my apron pocket jingled when I walked. By the end of the week I had enough to buy a rooster. That I could not do without my mother's permission, so I waited until the chores were done and my mother sat down for a few minutes before starting supper. Then I showed her the money and told her where it had come from.

"Forty-eight cents this week, Momma, and that's with our garden barely starting to produce. When everything is growing and if we had more chickens—"

Momma sighed heavily and held up her hand to stop me. "What is it you want, Trina?"

"I want to buy a rooster. Then we could get more chickens, more eggs. We need a rooster if we want enough for eggs every day and some to sell as well."

"The eggs are nice to have, but it worries me that you always want more, Trina."

"Please, Momma? A rooster will make things even better."

She sighed again, but there was an unexpected gleam of humor in her eyes. "Roosters are trouble, Trina. Haven't you heard the story of Kuratko the Terrible?"

I looked at her in surprise. I had not heard my mother tell a story since I was a little girl in Bohemia. "Who was Kuratko the Terrible?" I asked.

"He was a rooster, of course," she said, and began the story. "There was once an old woman who wanted a baby, but she had never been able to have one. So she got a chick from a neighbor's chicken, and she babied it and cared for it like a real child.

"'Don't do that,' her husband warned her, but she wouldn't listen. She named that silly little rooster Kuratko, and it grew bigger and more spoiled every day. It ate and ate, and grew and grew until it was bigger than the dog."

"A rooster bigger than a dog?" I smiled at the ridiculous thought.

"Yes. And as it grew it got greedier and greedier until it had eaten up nearly everything in the house.

"'Put it out!' said the husband, but that silly old woman refused, saying, 'It's my baby!'

"But when that rooster had eaten up all the food and the old woman had nothing left to feed it, Kuratko gobbled up the old woman, all in one peck. Then it ate the old man and the dog, too."

"That's not a very happy ending," I observed.

"That isn't the ending. After eating the old man and the dog, the rooster was still hungry, so it went out in the yard, where it swallowed up the pig and the cat. But the cat used its sharp claw to cut the rooster's craw as it was swallowed, and when Kuratko went to crow at sunrise the next morning, his craw split open and he fell over dead. And the cat jumped out, followed by the pig, the dog, the man, and the old woman, who promised never to be so silly again. And that is the story of Kuratko the Terrible."

I laughed. "I don't think I will let my rooster grow that big."

"But you've let your dreams," Momma said. "And just like the old woman's, they may swallow you up if you aren't careful."

"But the garden hasn't, and neither have the chickens. You said yourself they are a help."

Momma nodded. "So they are. Very well, Trina, get your rooster. But don't look to me for help if it gobbles you up."

I climbed the ridge that afternoon, feeling light and happy. Momma's opposition had been the only thing wrong with my plans for the future, and now even that was beginning to give way. And when she saw how much money we could make — as well as save, once we had eggs to sell — it would disappear entirely!

I acquired a rooster easily enough, a cocky little red fellow who had most likely been headed for the pot at the other farm. He strutted around as king of his own kingdom in my little chicken yard. Momma christened him Kuratko, and Papa and Old Jan, who related the story to my sisters, agreed the name fit his character. And this time, we didn't have to wait for rumors of his arrival to spread. He announced it gleefully at the crack of dawn the very first morning, and every morning thereafter.

Chapter 11

WITH KURATKO making his presence known, my house once again drew visitors, the children bringing gifts of worms and grasshoppers so they could watch him strut and crow. I even saw Mr. Johnson pass by once, craning his neck toward my backyard. I stayed out of sight, but afterward when I thought about it, I felt a small satisfaction that he was worried enough to come take a look for himself.

For the next two weeks, everything went back to normal, but with more anticipation than usual, for we had one hen brooding on eggs. Mark said it would take about three weeks before they would hatch. Counting down the days in my head, I wished it would all go a bit faster. I was so eager for the new arrivals to my flock that it was nearly all I thought about, even as I washed and ironed clothes, kneaded bread dough, or endured Mr. Johnson's glares and insults at the store.

July arrived. There were only two or three days left in my reckoning, and I had started checking regularly to see if the eggs had hatched. I was in the garden with my sisters, thinking as always about my new chicks and planning for how I would feed them, when the air was split by a long, loud screech of metal on metal that raked along my spine like fingernails on slate.

Momma appeared in the back doorway. "What on earth?"

Our eyes locked in the horror of recognition as a muffled boom shook the earth. The mine!

I dropped my hoe and began running, my mother and sisters beside me. We weren't the only ones. Within minutes the streets were filled with other wives, mothers, daughters, and sisters, all running for the mine, all wearing the same expressions of dread.

A choking cloud of dust and smoke was roiling out of the open shaft and enveloping the gathering crowd. It smelled of coal and dirt, burning rubber, and hot metal. We joined a crowd of women gathering near the great framework of the hoist. The thick cables that hauled the mesh cage of the lift into and out of the shaft had snapped, and raw-edged tangles of wire jammed the huge gears of the hoist. Ropes of cable dangled from the framework, sweeping in slowing arcs over the shaft. Beside the shaft, which should have been obscured by the lift but now gaped open, was a small booth where the lift operator manned the levers to raise and lower the lift. It was considered to be a better job than blasting through rock in the deep tunnels below, and the man who held the job was considered lucky. Today that luck had run out. The body of the hoist operator lay crumpled over his levers, his neck twisted back into an impossible position, his body gouged and scored where the broken cables had whipped him as they ripped loose. Four or five other men were sprawled on the ground nearby, gashed and bloodied by the cables, one of them screaming in pain.

My hand went to my mouth to hold back the rising fear and nausea. Crowds were gathering around the bodies, including women crying out their husbands' names. As the man's screams sank to moans, I wrenched my eyes away. Death, I thought, should not be a public spectacle.

My mother had drawn my sisters' faces into her skirts so they couldn't see the carnage. I wished I was small enough for someone to do the same for me. Momma's face was gray and her lips were pressed so tightly together that they were turning blue. I stepped to her and put my arm around her waist, though I'm not sure who I was trying to comfort. She caught my hand in hers and squeezed, her own fear turning her grip into a vise.

"He wasn't on it. He wasn't on it," she said, as if trying to reassure me, but I knew it was really a prayer.

I looked again at the broken hoist cables and let the same prayer run through my mind. The lift, a mesh cage that lowered men into the mine and brought them back to the surface when their shifts ended, must have dropped when the cables snapped. How far had it dropped, and who had been on it? Or beneath it? I remembered the muffled boom somewhere far underground, and knew that more bodies would be coming out of the mine.

Indifferent to the scene, the mine's automatic whistle blew, reminding all of us that the shift had been changing. All the men were either entering or leaving the mine at this hour. Anyone could have been on or near the lift. Anyone. Papa, or Karel, or Mark.

I looked desperately through the men still on the surface. They were mostly clean — men on the night shift, reporting for duty and not yet into the mine. Already their wives and families were finding them, hugging and crying with relief, but there was no such relief for me. None of the faces I loved could be found.

Old Jan hobbled up beside us.

"Where are Karel and Mark?" I blurted out, hoping against hope they were late to work today and still at home.

He shook his head, then tipped it toward the mine. Around us, a grim silence was spreading through the crowd, though I could hear women whispering "trapped" or "no other way out." I could hear men's names, too, names of husbands, brothers, and fathers, spoken like prayers.

I said nothing. My lips were tightening down just like my mother's, and my own determination was all channeling into that one, fervent hope. Papa wasn't on it. None of them were on it!

An alarm bell was clanging now, and mine officials were arriving from their fine houses and offices at the bottom of the hill. They kept well away from the open shaft and the settling dust that might soil their fine black jackets and waistcoats. Workers were gathering around the open shaft, looking down it, and men were climbing into the mangled gear housings of the hoist to examine the damage. Without the hoist, they wouldn't be bringing anyone out of the mine. The crowd of women continued to grow.

We stood for some time, watching and waiting. Finally an official came and pushed us back to a safe distance. He said they were doing all they could, that we would be taken care of, and that we should go home. I did my best to translate his words into Czech for my mother, just as other daughters were doing in Welsh, Polish, Greek, and Spanish. Despite so many tongues, we all wore a universal expression of fear. Questions were thrown back at the man in many languages, but he had no answers. We refused to go home, so we were left once again to our silent vigil.

"Trina," Momma said, her words stiff and tight in her throat, "take your sisters home and feed them. Then get them to bed. There is no need for them to be here."

Although I wanted to stay, I did not protest. I understood her meaning. This was no place for children. They deserved to keep whatever bit of innocence life here still left them. I wanted to be useful in whatever small way I could, so I gently pulled their hands loose from my mother's skirts and began walking toward home.

The town seemed deserted—the houses mostly empty and unlit. I could smell burned food and coffee from more than one house we passed—many wives had been preparing supper and left it, forgotten on their stoves. Whether we knew the families or not, we went inside and removed the scorched pots from the stove tops. I was glad to do something to fight off the helplessness I felt.

Our own supper had been on the warmer when the accident had happened and so was fit to eat, but we were not fit to eat it. I filled three bowls with stew and put them on the table, but we only picked at it, and in the end it went back into the pot. Without our usual bickering, we washed our bowls and put them away. Afterward we sat briefly on the porch in the cool air, but the unnatural silence of the camp weighed too heavily upon us.

"Perhaps we should get ready for bed," I said.

"When will Papa be home, Trina?" Holena asked.

"I don't know."

"Will he be here when we wake up?"

"I don't know, Holena," I said, putting my arm around her

and pulling her to me. It was all the comfort I could offer, and yet it was so little.

Aneshka burrowed her hand into mine. "Say he will," she begged in a small voice, her usual sassiness gone. I did not know what to say.

"Come on, let's get ready for bed. Fretting won't do any good," I said.

I helped my sisters into their nightgowns and together we said our prayers with extra fervor. We lay down on top of the covers, for the summer evening was hot. I stared at the ceiling as the room grew dim, afraid to close my eyes and see again the bloody body of the hoist operator, or the dying man on the ground. Neither of my sisters were sleeping either. I turned and looked at Aneshka. She was curled into a tight ball, her eyes squeezed shut. Holena pressed her small body up against me.

"Will you tell us a story?" she asked.

I thought for a moment, but I couldn't make my mind focus, so I told her the first story that I could think of. "Once upon a time, there was a poor fisherman and his wife," I began. Holena closed her eyes as I told the story, and by the time I finished, she was breathing in soft, steady breaths. As for Aneshka, she hadn't moved at all, but when I came to the end, she whispered something. I tilted my head closer to hear.

"I would wish for Papa to be all right," she said.

"Me too," I answered softly.

Tears squeezed from between her closed eyelids and slid down her cheeks. Then suddenly she was convulsing with sobs.

I rubbed her back and told her to be brave, but she only sobbed harder until she at last cried herself into a shuddering sleep.

When both girls were peaceful, I rose silently from the bed

and dressed again. I took the pot of stew, the bowls from the kitchen, and blankets from my mother's bed, and I returned to the mine.

Bright gaslights illuminated the area around the open shaft, and a crowd of men was gathered around the hoist, but I could not tell what they were doing. I could not keep my eyes from trailing back to the hoist controls, so I was relieved that the mangled body of the operator had been removed.

On the edge of the bright light the crowd of women still waited. Among them, I found Momma and Old Jan.

"You must sit down, Momma," I said. "You must save your strength." It was the sort of thing I had heard people say in a crisis, though I didn't know what she had to save her strength for. I didn't want to think about that.

I coaxed the two of them away from the crowd a bit and they sat. For each, I filled a bowl of stew, but they had no more appetite than my sisters or me.

"Is there any news?" I asked Old Jan. He shook his head. "The hoist is ruined and the lift cage is gone. They won't be getting anyone out without it. They're trying to get men out of the top levels with ropes and pulleys, but most of the men are in the deeper levels. The top played out years ago."

"But they have to get them out!" I said.

"They've telegraphed the head office to get a new lift down here, but it will take some time. The gears in the hoist are stripped, too. It will take three or four days to get the parts here and installed, I think."

"Four days!" I said.

Old Jan squeezed my hand. "Now listen, your papa is a strong man and a hard worker; he'll be all right. He wasn't one to leave his shift before the whistle blew. He wasn't one to

104

crowd by the lift to get out at the first chance, either. He's probably got some food and water left in his lunch bucket. I imagine he's already bunked down for the night and is sound asleep."

I smiled weakly at Old Jan. I appreciated his effort, but no matter how much I wanted to believe, I knew this was just another one of his stories—he couldn't know for sure.

"And Karel and Mark," I said. "Their dinner buckets were full, so they will be fine too, right?"

"That's a good girl. That is how we must think," Old Jan said, but I saw the pain of uncertainty in his eyes. I looked at Momma. She gave a little warning shake of her head that I knew meant I shouldn't ask, and I pieced together the rest. The lift must have been taking men into the shaft when the cable broke. That meant Papa would not have been on it, but Karel or Mark might have been. And no one on it could have survived. I fought back my tears, but they were coming all the same.

"There, there," Old Jan said. "We know nothing for certain yet. We have to keep hoping. Keep believing."

I nodded and wiped my eyes, but not even I could stretch hope that far. This was a far cry from wishing for a few chickens.

Old Jan gave a thankful smile and wrapped one of the blankets I had brought around my mother's shoulders. She clasped it there with one hand, but she said nothing. We sat with her in silence for a long time. Finally, Old Jan patted my hand.

"Go back and get some sleep, Trina. Your sisters may need you. Nothing more is going to happen here tonight."

"Then we should all go home," I said.

"I'm not leaving," Momma said, her tone fierce.

"I'll stay here with her, Trina, until she is ready to go home."

I didn't want to leave Momma there, but I finally returned alone to our dark house. It felt empty, even as I lay between my two sisters and listened to their steady breathing. The absence of my parents seemed to fill the house.

I did not sleep much that night. I woke before dawn, at the time Papa usually set off for work. I lay half asleep and waited for the automatic whistle at the mine. It blew, jerking me awake to an empty house, no cooking smells coming from the kitchen. I remembered then, and fear overwhelmed me again, just like it had the first time. I turned to see my parents' bed still empty and unused.

I rose quietly and went to the kitchen. It felt strange to be doing normal chores—lighting the stove, making coffee, measuring out oats—in a world that was no longer normal. And yet, what else could I do?

When my sisters were dressed and fed, I left them to do the morning chores and I took my pan of oatmeal and the coffee pot to Momma and Old Jan at the mine. All was quiet there. No one was working near the shaft or the hoist. The mine officials had declared that nothing more could be done until a new lift was installed, and the workers who were not trapped in the mine had all been sent home. The only people there now were the small clusters of women who had settled into camps on the margins of the scene. In the full daylight I could see just how many there were. The accident, happening as it did when the new shift was entering and the old had not all come out, had trapped more than a hundred men in the mine.

"If nothing is happening here, why not come home?" I said when Old Jan had explained everything to me.

"We will wait here for our husbands," Momma said. "We will not go home and let them forget the urgency of the situation."

I looked around and saw the grim determination on the face of not only my mother, but of the other women scattered across the hillside. It was an expression all too common to miners' wives. I could feel it settling onto my own features as well. "Then let me stay today, Momma. I want to help."

Momma smiled at me, one small flash, before her face turned hard again. "You are a big help, Trina, but I need you most to take care of your sisters."

I would rather have stayed, but this was not the time to argue with my mother. Once the meager breakfast had been eaten, I returned home.

For two long days, the routine was the same. If Momma and Old Jan slept at all, they did so beside the mine. Holena and Aneshka wanted to help as well, so we started each day with our chores. Then we gathered all the food we could from our garden, our henhouse, and our kitchen. We baked and cooked meals enough to feed not just Momma and Old Jan, but other women, too, who were holding their vigil at the mine. They opened their larders to us so we could prepare pots of food and coffee for ten or fifteen of the women from the Bohemian part of town. Under other circumstances such gatherings would have felt festive, but nothing could dispel the oppressive quiet.

The afternoon of the third day, my sisters and I were in the kitchen shaping dumplings when we heard the whistle of a train approaching camp. With the mine shut down, the train that transported the coal had been silent too. I paused and listened to be sure of what I had heard. It blew again and now I could also hear the chug of the engine. My heart pounded with urgent excitement. This would be the new lift! At last! I dropped the dough and, not even taking time to clean the flour from my hands, I ran to the mine. I was not the only one. Aneshka and Holena came with me, and the streets were once again filling with people—not just women, but men, too, pulling up suspenders or putting on work gloves as they went.

At the mine, men and boys were assembled into a work crew before the train came to a stop. They got to work at once, unloading the new cables and gears for the hoist, and the parts for a new lift. A mine official came to the hillside where the women were camped and told them to go home, but they refused. In the end, the officials set up a rope barrier that we were required to stay behind.

The grim silence of the past two days was now replaced by urgent action, as every able-bodied man in camp went to work getting the hoist operating and the mine open. Wives and daughters, including me, took turns carrying water and coffee to the work crews so the usual water boys could be put to other tasks. Lights were again set up, and work continued through the night. No one quit when their shift was over. Every man there knew that it could have been him trapped below—that it could be him next time.

The new lift was in place by sunrise, and a cheer went up when the lever was pulled and the hoist gears jolted into action, pulling the cables tight. Still, the ordeal was far from over. The shaft had been damaged or blocked in places by the erratic course of the falling lift, so the descent of the new lift into the mine was gradual. At each level men got off the lift to clear a section of the shaft below before it could descend farther.

It was past noon before they raised the twisted wreckage of the original lift to the surface, and with it, the first of the dead. Like the lift, those who had been on it were crushed beyond recognition. They were laid out by the train track, where ashen-faced women filed by, looking for a familiar patched boot or shirtsleeve to know for certain. The lucky ones came away having recognized nothing; the unlucky collapsed in despair.

Momma ordered me to stay at the rope with my sisters while she and Old Jan joined the line. I was glad to be spared a closer view of the dead, but I could not help watching as Old Jan and Momma moved slowly past them. I did not breathe until I saw Old Jan shake his head and turn away. My hopes that Karel and Mark had not been on the lift rose, and I told myself again that they were all right. They had to be. They were with Papa now, cheering at the sight of the new lift arriving to bring them home!

My anticipation was not to be satisfied so quickly, though. As the afternoon passed and the day grew hotter, we remained in the crowd, watching. Men had been working on three levels in the mine, and it was being cleared of both the living and the dead from the top down. As the day progressed, the line of bodies by the train track grew, and the crowd of waiting women dwindled. Some slipped under the rope and ran, screaming with joy to embrace a man as he emerged, blinking and squinting into the daylight. Others crouched, weeping, beside the tracks, their shawls or aprons over their heads. Those of us still behind the rope waited in tense silence.

By dusk, only a handful of women remained behind the rope, but we were still among them. The lift rose to the surface once again, and the gates opened to pour out more men. One of them carried a body toward the train track. I saw Martina— who had baked a cake for her Charlie just a few short weeks ago—gasp and go white. She seemed to shrink as she watched. Then, with a soundless sob, she pulled her shawl over her head and walked slowly toward the tracks. The knot of fear tightened around my heart, squeezing out my breath. Charlie had been on Papa's crew.

I turned my eyes back to the lift, now descending smoothly

into the shaft. The gears of the hoist stopped turning, indicating the lift had stopped somewhere far below. We waited in silence. A wagon clattered up the street and stopped by the train, driven by Mr. Johnson. Inside it were stacked coffins, their pine boards still fresh and smelling of sap. Mr. Johnson jumped down from his seat and approached the mourning wives and mothers, his sales ledger in his hand. His face was composed in a respectful expression, but it looked too practiced to be sincere. I turned away feeling sick, unsure I could bear one thing more.

Just then, the hoist clanked into action and the cables began to move. The handful of us still behind the rope drew in a collective breath and held it as the lift came into view and stopped, the cage filled with more grimy men. More women slipped under the rope as the men staggered out. The last to come out were Papa and Karel, carrying between them a limp and bloodied body.

Mark.

Chapter 12

MOMMA, ANESHKA, and Holena were under the rope in an instant, but Old Jan stood frozen, staring at the still form of his youngest son. The same shock and fear rooted me beside him. I took his hand, and together we tried to go forward, but it was like trudging through deep water.

Momma and my sisters were already with the men, Momma taking the tragic burden from Papa while my sisters clung to his legs. At once Papa collapsed to his knees, holding the little girls to him.

Momma turned, and I knew she was looking for me.

"Quickly, Trina, go to Jan's and prepare hot water and bandages. Quickly!"

The desperation in her voice broke me from my trance. Water and bandages? Surely it was too late for that. Then I saw Papa on his knees and all the fear came back—he must be hurt too! I let go of Old Jan's hand. I turned and ran, as my Momma had told me to. I wanted to run forever—run from the pain and from my regret that I had never told Mark how I felt. But I had a job to do, and the living still needed me. Old Jan's house was not far.

Once inside, I lit the stove and began heating water. Then I found clean rags and tore them into strips. I had a mound of them ready when Momma and Karel came through the door with Mark between them, Papa and Old Jan hobbling behind. I saw now that Karel wore no shirt or suspenders. He had fastened his own shirt as a bandage across his brother's chest and secured it there with his suspenders to stanch the bleeding. The makeshift bandage was now brown and stiff with dried blood.

They laid Mark on his bed before collapsing themselves into chairs. I ventured a glance into Mark's face, and to my amazement I saw him wince with pain as they settled him onto the mattress.

"He's alive!" I gasped.

Momma gave me a surprised look. "Of course he's alive — why did you think we needed bandages?"

"I thought— Oh, Papa!" I cried, and like a child threw myself into his arms, sobbing with relief.

Papa held me, patting my hair. "There's my good girl," he said. "Now get me a drink of water — I'm parched!"

I dried my eyes and hurried to fill and refill cups of water for Karel and Papa as they drank deeply. Old Jan, meantime, was feeling his younger son's forehead and cutting the suspender straps to remove the bandage.

"We were the last group off the lift before the cable broke," Karel explained. "We were still signing out tools with the foreman when the lift came crashing down. A piece of flying metal caught him across the chest. Something hit his leg, too. He's lost a lot of blood, Papa."

I went to the bedroom doorway and watched while old Jan peeled back the bloody bandage. Mark groaned and clenched the sheets as the stiff bandage pulled the scab from the wound. New blood bubbled up through the ragged gash that ran for eight inches across his chest.

Papa staggered to his feet. "I'll fetch the doctor," he said.

"Nonsense, Tomas," Old Jan said. "You're hardly fit to be standing yourself, and the doctor has worse than this to attend to." Old Jan turned back to his son and probed the edges of the gash with his fingers before speaking again. "You are lucky, Marek. If it had caught you two inches lower, it would have torn your stomach and we'd have lost you. This is only skin and muscle. Trina, bring me the water and those rags."

Together we bathed Mark's wounds. Then I did what I could to soothe away the sweat from his brow while Old Jan stitched the edges of the gash shut with a length of thread and a sewing needle that he had heated in a candle flame. I might have emptied my stomach at the sight of the needle pulling through Mark's skin had I eaten anything that day. As it was, I swallowed my nausea and tried to find comforting words for Mark until he passed out from the pain.

When the wound was sewn up, we smeared it with a salve my mother provided and wrapped it with the clean rag bandages. Then Old Jan inspected Mark's leg, which was swollen and blue at the ankle. Another deep gash cut to the bone across the front of his leg, just above his boot. Mark jerked back to consciousness as his father removed the boot, torn beyond repair by whatever had cut his leg.

"Lucky again," Old Jan said with a look of relief. "If it hadn't been for your sturdy boot, you might have lost this foot. As it is, it's just a deep cut, not even a broken bone."

I stayed beside Mark until he slept, then I went to the kitchen, where our families were eating supper. I could barely keep my eyes open long enough to finish my meal. My sisters, mother, and I cleared the dishes while my father staggered off to home. When the dishes were all washed, Momma, Aneshka, and Holena followed. I looked in on Mark once again. I thought a bit of color had returned to his face, but I couldn't be sure.

"He'll be all right," Old Jan said.

I jumped in surprise. I hadn't realized he was standing at my shoulder.

"Are you sure?"

"I've seen men survive worse, and he's as strong as a horse. The only danger now is infection, but we'll take good care of him. Now go on home and get some rest yourself."

Reassured by his calm, I agreed. It was well past dark as I walked the short distance from Old Jan's house to my own. With each step my weariness grew heavier until I was stumbling across the threshold. I stepped into the bedroom and breathed in the fullness of my family, all of them here and asleep. With a simple, silent prayer of thanks, I settled myself beside my sisters and slipped at once into a dreamless peace.

I slept until the sun was high in the eastern sky and the air was becoming warm and stale. My sisters were still asleep, so I slipped quietly out of bed and padded barefoot into the kitchen. Momma was sitting at the table, drinking a cup of coffee and darning stockings.

"Where is Papa?" I asked, after glancing around and seeing no sign of him.

"He's gone to work," Momma said.

"At the mine?"

"Of course at the mine."

"But—" I stared, paralyzed with fear. How could he go back down that lift after all that had happened? "But he can't!"

"And what are we going to live on if he doesn't?" Momma said, but the lines of worry were deeply furrowed on her forehead. She was afraid but, as usual, the practical needs were foremost in her mind. "He has already lost three days' pay this week."

"But he was trapped! The mine surely owes him something for all he's been through!"

"We have much to be thankful for; we must remember that," Momma said, not looking up from her work. "Many families were not as fortunate as us."

I remembered again Martina's Charlie, and I knew she was right. Still, all I could think about was how we had to get out of here so that Papa would never go through such a thing again. I vowed to myself that I would work extra hard in my garden so that we could buy our farm.

"Thank you, Trina," Momma said.

I looked at her in surprise. I had no idea what she was thanking me for.

"You worked hard these past few days to look after everyone. I don't know how I would have gotten through it without you. I am proud of you."

I hurried to dress after that, eager to work in my garden. I wanted to do the things that would earn the money to get us away from the mine.

I swept the kitchen and the porch, and as I did I remembered for the first time in days that I had a brooding hen. I put away the broom and took up my basket with rising excitement, hoping to see a nest full of cheeping chicks in the henhouse. It wasn't until I stepped out the back door and saw the gate swinging crookedly on torn hinges that I realized I hadn't heard Kuratko crow that morning. I looked around, hopeful that the chickens were simply loose in the yard and garden, but they were not. There was no sign of life in the yard at all—but there were signs of death everywhere. Feathers littered the ground, and a smear of blood ran across the chicken coop wall near the door. I hurried through the open gate, searching the ground. The tracks of large dogs were everywhere in the yard among the chaos of feathers. The limp body of one of my hens lay in the corner of the yard, tossed against the fence and forgotten. Everyone in town had been at the mine; no one had been in the neighborhood to hear stray dogs in the chickens.

I remembered the brooding hen and hurried to the hen-house, hoping against hope. It was no use. The brood had hatched, but without their mother's care the bald hatchlings had all died in their nest.

I backed out of the henhouse, anger and grief stinging my eyes. Then I saw my garden. The battle of dogs and chickens had ranged beyond the broken gate. Row after row of vegetables were trampled flat. The bean trellis had been torn down and had uprooted most of the stalks when it toppled. The remains of bold little Kuratko were tangled in its strands of twine.

I looked for one long moment of despair, then collapsed on the back step in tears. Every grief and fear of the past week tore from my throat in racking sobs. My mother found me there sometime later, still weeping uncontrollably.

"Trina, what on earth . . . ?" Then she stopped and looked around at the carnage. "Oh, Trina. I'm so sorry," she said, her voice mixing sympathy with resignation. I knew that tone too well. She had to be thinking she had told me so.

"No, you're not!" I blurted out before I could stop myself. "You never wanted me to succeed!"

"What we want and what life gives us are seldom the same thing, Trina."

A new burst of sobs kept me from answering. She stood silently beside me for a long moment before she said, "Hush now, Trina. We have work to do."

I wanted to stop crying, but I couldn't. It was all too much.

"Hush now," Momma said again. "How can you carry on like this for a few chickens? Men died in that mine and all you can think about are your silly chickens?"

"No, Momma! Don't you see, the chickens were to be our way out! So Papa would never have to go back into that mine."

"It was a dream, Trina. You're crying for the loss of something you never had to start with."

"And you don't believe in dreams," I said bitterly. "You don't believe in anything but staying stuck here."

Momma sighed heavily and sat down on the stoop beside me. "Trina, dreams aren't real. You can't eat them; you can't keep your papa safe with them. And believe me, you'll never feed your children with them. We only have what life has given us, and dreams . . ." She paused, fumbling for the words. "Dreams get you hurt, just like this one's hurt you. Just like your papa's dream put him in that horrible mine."

"So you'd have us never try to make our lives better," I said. "To have something more."

"Believing I could have something more made me what I am today," she said. "I could have been a tailor's wife, living in a comfortable cottage in Bohemia, but instead I married the man who filled my head with dreams. And look where it got me!"

I looked at her in surprise. For the briefest moment, I saw her not as the resilient mother I had always known, but as a young, vulnerable dreamer herself. Her usual hard expression quickly returned when she saw me looking.

"But—you love Papa, don't you?" I asked.

"Of course. I love all of you. But these dreams! Dreams only crush the things you love!"

She turned her face away from me, and for the first time I understood. I ached from the loss of a few chickens and a garden. What pain must she feel from the weight of years of disappointments? No wonder she had warned me against this dream. I put my hand on her shoulder. She straightened, strong again.

"We have other things to keep us busy now, Trina. Put this behind you and look to all you still have. Papa still has a job, we still have our family and friends, and you have a handsome young man who wants to court you. That should be enough for anyone. To want more than what you need is a vanity."

I wiped my eyes and nodded.

"Now, see if there is anything you can salvage in your garden."

I took a basket to the vegetable patch and began searching through the trampled and wilted leaves. A few squash clung to the torn vines, and I picked those. The corn was all ruined, without a single ear having ever formed, and only about one-fourth of the bean plants could be saved. The cucumbers at the very edge of the garden were the only crop that had been spared. The few surviving beanstalks might produce enough for a meal now and then, but my hopes of selling anything more were gone.

The disappointment was a steady ache in my chest that wouldn't go away, though I tried not to think of it. And I could see now that a few eggs and vegetables would never have earned us enough money to get out of here. The dream had clouded my judgment. I had wanted far more than I could ever have. I told myself it was best that it should come apart now while it was still only a small thing. I thought again of Martina and others who had lost someone in the mine, and I felt ashamed.

I was putting the trellis back in place along the few bean plants when I noticed a bootprint in the soil. I had seen the tracks of the dogs everywhere, but this surprised me. Had someone been in my garden while we were at the mine? I couldn't imagine that anyone had taken any vegetables. Maybe someone had seen the dogs and tried to chase them off. Surely no one would steal anything at such a time—everyone in town was connected to the disaster; no one would be thinking of robbing a garden.

I looked again at the bootprint. A pawprint partially obscured it—it was from before the dogs had done their mischief. It must have been Old Jan's, I decided, from before the accident. I put the question out of my head and finished collecting vegetables.

When I finished, I had more than enough for a meal. I set aside a few, but most of them wouldn't keep. They were bruised and had been withering on the ground for too long. I looked again at the two chicken carcasses. They hadn't been chewed by the dogs, and were still fresh enough to use, and that gave me an idea. I wanted to make up for my foolishness, so with Momma's help, I plucked and cleaned the chickens and put them into a big kettle of soup with the trampled vegetables from the garden. When it was done, I put some into two pans and set out.

I went first to Martina's house. Charlie was laid out in the bedroom and a small group was gathered around him, sobbing or fidgeting uncomfortably with the hats they had removed

119

upon entering. Martina sat at the kitchen table, staring into a cup of tea, her face like marble.

I knocked at the open door and held up the soup pot. "For you," I said.

She raised her eyes to mine. They glinted with a look of panic. I entered and set the pan of soup on the table beside her.

"What am I going to do?" she whispered. "The mine says I can only stay through the end of the month now that there's no worker living here. Where am I going to go?"

Rage rose in me again at the mine owners, but I bit it back. "What about your papa?" I said. Her family had been at the mine before she'd married.

She shook her head. "They've moved to the mine at Cokedale. They don't know about any of this yet. But there are seven kids in that house. I couldn't burden them by going back."

"You'll think of something," I said.

A loud sob rose from the other room and Martina choked back one of her own. Her face was so white I thought she might faint. "They've been here all day," she whispered. I looked past her to the woman keening at the bedside and the silent men that surrounded her like a queen's attendants.

"Who are they?"

"Charlie's mother and brothers. They arrived from Pueblo on the train this morning. She hates me. She didn't want Charlie to marry a foreigner. She won't let me near him."

Martina clung to my hand now, as if I were the only solid thing in her world. I had only intended to pay my respects and be gone, but I couldn't leave her like this.

"Walk with me," I said. "You need some fresh air."

"And leave Charlie?" She glanced guiltily toward the back room.

Leave his mother, I thought, but instead I only said, "You have to think of your own health, too." I coaxed her to the front door and through it. She stepped out into the sunlight and blinked, like a dazed creature pulled from its burrow.

We walked slowly up the road, past my house and toward Old Jan's, where I intended to leave my second pot of soup. The fresh air did bring a little color to her pale face. When we reached Old Jan's, I paused.

"I have another errand here, Martina. Do you mind?"

She shook her head, so we walked to the front door. The door was open in the hot afternoon, but Old Jan was not sitting on the porch. I called in a greeting and he called back from the bedroom, inviting us in. I stepped inside, but Martina only hovered in the kitchen.

Mark was propped up in bed, though he was leaning far back to ease his chest. His face wore an expression of pain.

"How are you feeling?" I asked him, scrutinizing his face for any sign of fever. I was relieved to see none, but frightened by how pale he looked.

"Sore," he admitted with a twitch of a grin. His voice was weak, but at least he had tried to smile.

"He's resting easy. That's the best thing for him now," Old Jan said.

"I brought you some soup," I said. "I thought it might help."

As they thanked me, Karel came in through the back door, carrying two buckets of water. I supposed that, like Papa, he was expected to return to work for his regular shift. He started to say something, then he caught sight of Martina, standing uncertainly near the kitchen door. A look of tender sadness came over his face and he set down his buckets.

"I am sorry about Charlie," he said to her. "He was a good

121

man and a hard worker. He was near us there, waiting to get on the lift, to get home to you." He shook his head regretfully.

I looked at Martina. Tears were welling from her eyes. Karel took a handkerchief from his pocket and carried it to her. They were speaking in hushed tones when I turned back to Mark.

"They are evicting her," I said, trying to control the outrage in my voice. "And they're docking your pay for the time you were trapped in the mine. How could they!"

"They can do as they please," Mark said.

"But it's wrong!"

Mark sighed, and I immediately regretted my anger. He didn't have the strength for it. I laid my hand softly on his.

"You should sleep," I told him. "It will help you get your strength back."

"I'd rather have a bowl of your soup," he said, this time managing a small smile at me.

I filled a bowl and, sitting beside him, spooned soup carefully into his mouth.

"It is delicious," he said. "Are the vegetables from your garden?"

I nodded. "It is all there will be, though." I told him what had happened to my chickens and the garden, struggling to hold back my grief. It was silly to cry over such a small thing, and I could not explain that my tears were for something so much larger.

"There, there," Old Jan said, patting my hand. "It's a blow to be sure, but we survived without it, and we will again. You can plant again next summer."

He was right, of course, and so was my mother. Survival was the most we could expect in this world. I looked at Mark and knew that survival itself was a blessing.

Karel reappeared in the kitchen to collect the dinner bucket his father had prepared for him. "I'm off to work. Enjoy lying about while I'm laboring away," he said to Mark with a grin.

"I should get back to Martina," I said when Karel had gone. "And you should rest."

"Thank you, Trina," Mark said. He clasped my hand in thanks, but he did not let go when I tried to leave, so I turned back to him. "Trina, I'll be laid up here for a short while, but I'll heal fast. I'll be back on my feet before the next dance." He squeezed my hand and looked into my eyes. "Will you go with me?"

Before, when I had refused him, I had thought I'd had a future—that I'd be leaving the coal camp soon. Now, I saw otherwise. I saw the foolishness in believing in anything other than what was real right now. And in the four days the men had been trapped in the mine, I had also learned how fragile my real world could be. I hadn't appreciated what I had, and I had almost lost it. I'd almost lost Mark.

I looked into his pale, sick face, waiting eagerly for my answer. I could not know what the future held for either of us. All I could do was make the most of each moment that I had, whatever or wherever it was. And where it was—where it would always be—was here. But at least it could be with Mark.

"I would be honored," I said.

Chapter 13

THE NEXT WEEK did not start with dancing. It started with funerals. In all, twenty-seven men had died and countless more were injured in the disaster at the mine, and no family in our community was untouched. The mine closed on Tuesday, and everyone in town crowded into one service or another. There were so many services held in so many different languages that they took place wherever space could be made. Afterward, the wagons full of coffins converged in the hilltop cemetery to the south of the mine. The whole community watched as one after another was lowered into the long row of open graves. Final prayers were said before the first shovelfuls of dirt were thrown onto the pine boxes. Then we united, no matter what our religion or language, in grief for our shared loss.

Mark insisted on going to the funerals, though we all begged him to stay home in bed. He could not walk on his injured foot, and the stitches across his chest made leaning on crutches unbearable. Papa and Karel carried him much of the way, though they were still pale and wrung out by the ordeal. It took all their strength to get Mark to the hilltop cemetery, and all Mark's strength to stand through the prayers and scriptures read there.

It was past noon when the mourners dispersed from the hill. The mine officials shooed us all away from the graves, telling us to go home and mourn in private. Rumors had spread that union organizers would be at the funerals, so wakes and public gatherings had been forbidden.

Papa and Karel started back down the hill with Mark, struggling to keep their footing on the loose, gravely slope. Fortunately, other men came to their aid, healthy men who had not been trapped underground. Two bachelors took over and carried Mark down the hill and all the way back to his house. Old Jan was beside himself with gratitude for the men and, since they had no families to spend the afternoon with them, he invited them to stay for dinner.

Amid the commotion, it took several minutes for us to realize that Karel had stayed behind to assist Martina from the cemetery. Still snubbed by her mother- and brothers-in-law, she had stood alone at the funeral. She had collapsed, wailing with grief as the first shovelful of dirt was thrown on Charlie's coffin, and Karel had gone to her aid. Now, as they approached down the road, she moved like a sleepwalker, relying on Karel's strong but gentle arm to guide her. As they arrived at the house, Old Jan took one look at her and declared that she would not go home alone either.

Momma looked around at everyone—Mark, propped in a chair, his face tight with pain; the lonely bachelors; the desolate Martina. She squared her shoulders.

"Yes, Jan, you are right. We must all have a meal together. We must keep up our strength and support each other through these times."

"I'm not hungry," Martina protested weakly.

"Come now. The living must live," Momma said.

Old Jan nodded and gently guided Martina to a chair. "Life goes on, my dear. Even at times like these."

"Trina, go to the store and get us enough meat for a decent stew. We've got potatoes and a few vegetables left from the garden," Momma said.

"The superintendent forbade gatherings," Karel reminded us.

Momma made an impatient, dismissive gesture. "This is no gathering. It is family, and a few people who need family. They can't deny us that. Besides, we've no interest in the union. Trina, run along. We must get started."

I did as she said. Old Jan came along too, insisting that the bachelors had helped his son, so he intended to pay. Mr. Johnson's store was open, but he had no customers, so Mr. Johnson was sitting outside on the porch. I stopped and stared when I saw him. He was leaning back in his chair, a bottle of soda pop in one hand while his other hand scratched a big yellow dog behind the ear. A second dog, equally large, lay at his feet, its tongue lolling out of its mouth in the summer heat. I stood staring until he looked up and saw me. His eyes tracked my gaze to his dogs before returning to my face. Then his lips curled into a slow smile.

"Do you like dogs?" he asked with mock innocence. "These are a special breed. They're *bird* dogs." His smile widened even more as anger flooded my face with color. "I believe you have pets too, don't you? Tell me, how are your chickens these days?"

I couldn't answer. I was seeing in my mind all that had really happened. It made sense now. Stray dogs couldn't have broken through the gate or done so much damage by themselves, and hungry mongrels wouldn't have left carcasses uneaten. And there had been that bootprint in the garden. I clamped my mouth shut, unwilling to respond to his taunt. I smiled back, though my insides were boiling, and walked into his store as if nothing was wrong, refusing to let him get the better of me. Mr. Johnson followed. I could feel him still smirking behind me.

Inside the store, Old Jan got busy selecting meat and a few other items. I wasn't sure just what. My head was pounding with anger, and I could barely see.

"Looks like you're having a little party," Johnson observed as Old Jan counted out his money.

"Only a family supper," Old Jan said.

Mr. Johnson shot me a suspicious look. "Didn't know she was part of your family."

I said nothing. I hoped Mr. Johnson would soon forget this encounter. I did not want his hatred of me to harm Old Jan and his sons, especially now that I knew what Mr. Johnson was capable of.

At home I helped my mother prepare a hearty meal and tried to forget the encounter myself. When dinner was ready, we carried it to Old Jan's house, where we ate on the porch, as it was too hot inside. The men had dragged a mattress outside for Mark, and I sat beside him and helped him eat. He had little appetite, but could at least eat some of the gravy from the stew, and a few bites of the chewy meat.

As the afternoon wore on, his color grew worse. His sweaty face looked like a wax doll, with a high flush of pink in his cheeks. I left his side again only when I had to wash the dishes. When I returned, I was more alarmed than ever. He was leaning against the wall, his eyes closed and his lips slightly parted. Flies were crawling on his face and shirt. For a moment I thought he was dead, and I gasped. My gasp awakened him, as well as drawing the attention of the others. He stirred and brushed at the flies on his face, grimacing with pain as he did so.

"I think it's time you were back in bed, Marek," Old Jan said.

"And time we went home and gave you some peace and quiet," Momma added.

Taking her meaning, the two bachelors thanked my mother and Old Jan and set out for their own home. Karel offered his arm to Martina, who stood to leave as well.

"Perhaps Trina might stay long enough to help me get Marek settled," Old Jan suggested.

Mark protested, insisting that he didn't need help. By the time we got his mattress back on his bed and moved him, however, his jaw was clenched with pain. He leaned heavily on me and hopped the short distance to his bed. Once there, he collapsed, spent. I tucked a pillow under his head.

"Holena told me today that you made a wish for a farm," he said, managing a brief, teasing smile. "No wonder you've had so much good luck. It's magic!"

I scowled. She had promised to keep it a secret. "I don't feel very lucky."

"But you are," he insisted. "You got your little farm — chickens, garden, chicken coop."

"That wasn't a farm. And anyway, it's all gone now."

He sighed as I gently tucked his bare feet under the sheets. "Maybe that's my good luck."

"What do you mean by that?" I asked.

"With your chickens and garden, you were too busy for me. Now we are going to the dance."

I did not reply to that, only busied myself arranging the sheets comfortably around his feet, then helped him out of his shirt. His skin felt warm, and I looked again with concern at his face. Sweat stood out on his brow, but it had been a warm day, and he had exerted himself. I hoped desperately there was nothing more to it.

"We are going to dance all night," he murmured, shutting his eyes and settling back comfortably once his shirt was off him. I looked at the bandages on his chest. There were a few dark spots of blood, but not enough to give alarm.

I smoothed his damp hair back off his forehead. "Rest," I whispered, but needlessly—he was already asleep.

The next day Papa was back at work once again. Old Jan arrived at our house midmorning.

"How is Mark this morning?" I asked. My concern had only grown in the night, but Old Jan did not look worried.

"He is still sleeping," he said. "He was worn out from yesterday, so I did not wake him for breakfast. Sleep is the best thing for him. I came to see if there is something I might do for the garden."

I did not want to think about the garden or see the ruined chicken yard, so I stayed inside to help my mother with the mending while Old Jan and my sisters worked outside. Still, I was fidgety and my mind was not on my work. The third time I had to remove a big tangle from my thread, Momma asked me what was the matter.

"If you want to go out to your garden, go on," she said. "Heaven knows you're not very useful here as you are."

I dropped my hands to my lap and sighed. "I'm worried about Mark. He felt warm last night when I helped him to bed."

Momma's needle stopped in midair.

"A fever?"

"I—I don't know. It was a warm day. Maybe he was just worn out, like Old Jan said."

"There's broth for our lunch on the stove," Momma said. "Perhaps you should take some and look in on him."

"Old Jan said he's resting."

"But you won't be easy till you're sure he's all right, and I won't either, now. Go on. If all's well with him, you can come right back."

I already felt better just to be checking on him myself. I poured some of the broth into a small pan and set off at once up the hill to Mark's house.

Inside, the house was still and quiet. I set the pan of broth on the stove and tiptoed through to the bedroom. The curtain was closed, so the room was dim. Karel was snoring in one corner. In the other corner, Mark lay still on his back in Old Jan's bed, his face turned toward the wall. I stood in the doorway and watched him, his chest rising and falling with each breath. At first, I felt a rush of relief at how peacefully he slept, but as I stood watching, I realized something was wrong. His breaths were not the slow, deep breaths of a restful sleep. They were too quick and shallow.

I crossed the few steps to his bedside and leaned over him, trying to see his face. His hair was plastered to his neck with sweat. Dread filled me. I reached out and put a hand on his forehead. Even before I touched him, I could feel the heat of fever.

He stirred at my touch and turned his head. The flush in his cheeks and, his hair, curling with sweat, made him look so young. His eyes fluttered open and swept past my face before closing again. He mumbled something about dancing.

I bit my lip hard to hold back the sob of fear that lurched up from my gut. I didn't know what to do. Should I wake him? Feed him? Let him sleep? I did nothing—only stood staring at his burning face, thinking how young he was. Thinking he was too young to die.

Chapter 14

I DON'T KNOW how long I stood there before my mother called my name from the front porch.

"Trina? When you didn't come back, I—" She stopped talking when she stepped through the bedroom door and saw me there.

"He's burning up with fever!" My voice cracked with desperation.

She whisked past me and pushed the curtain aside, flooding the room with light. Karel groaned and turned over, his face to the wall. Momma bent over Mark and felt his forehead.

"Get cool water and a cloth to bathe his face," she said, her voice calm but serious. I hurried to do as she said—of course it was what you did for fever. I felt foolish for not thinking of it myself. When I returned from the kitchen with the water, Momma had peeled back the damp sheet and was cutting away the bandages on Mark's chest. I began to bathe his face with the cool damp cloth, but stopped dead when my mother removed the bandages and I saw the gash in his chest. The wound was still mostly closed, but the skin around the scab was red and puffy. Near his shoulder, the stitches had torn loose, and the gash had split open. My mother pressed her fingers along it, and thick, bloody pus oozed out, giving off a foul smell.

Momma sucked in air through clenched teeth. Her expression was as grim and pinched as it had been during those nights and days of waiting at the mine.

"Momma—"

"Go fetch Old Jan," she said.

I ran, tears blinding me along the way.

"It's Mark," I told him when I reached the garden plot. "He's— Fever."

Old Jan dropped the hoe he had been using and grabbed his crutches. Together we headed up the road as fast as the old man could go. Back inside his house we met up with Momma in the kitchen, where she was heating water at the stove. Old Jan looked at her inquiringly.

"Infection," my mother said through tight lips. Old Jan paled and clomped past her into the bedroom.

I stood tentatively in the doorway, watching as he bent over his son, feeling his forehead and examining the gash on his chest. My mother nudged my arm, her hands full with a washbasin of warm water and clean rags.

"We must open the wound again to clean out the infection. It will be very painful for Mark. Perhaps you should go home."

I straightened my shoulders. "I want to help," I said. "Maybe I could be a comfort to him."

Momma nodded. "Then bring those towels," she said, indicating a stack on the kitchen table. "And that new block of lye soap."

While I hurried to get those things, Momma woke Karel

and sent him to our house to sleep. She knew there would be no sleeping with us tending to Mark.

In the bedroom, Old Jan was holding his son's hand and calling his name. Mark woke and looked at his father, his eyes glassy.

"Time to go to work already?" he said, and tried to sit up. Old Jan pushed him back down and gently shushed him.

"No work for you today, son. You have to rest, get your strength back."

Mark sighed, and I could see he remembered now, all that had happened and why he wasn't working. A hard shiver racked though him.

"Your wound's infected, Mark; we're going to have to clean it out," Momma said in her matter-of-fact way. "It's going to hurt, I'm afraid, but it can't be helped."

Mark's eyes traveled from my mother to his father to me. He reached for my hand.

Lancing and cleaning the infected gash was horrible, and the worst of it was Mark's pain. Where the wound had torn open, cleaning it was easiest. Along the rest of the gash Momma cut away all the stitches Mark had suffered through a few days before, and lanced the tender scab that had formed. Then she squeezed the stinking puss and blood from the wound, wiping it away with towels before using rags and the harsh soap to wash it again.

At first Mark gritted his teeth and squeezed my hand to resist making a sound, but before long he gave in to the misery, crying out as my mother cut and squeezed and wiped. I held his hand, though my own was soon bruised and aching from his grip, and mopped his burning face with the cool rag I'd brought in earlier.

When my mother at last finished, she laid a clean towel gently over his chest and examined his ankle. The cut there looked angry and red as well, though not oozing pus like the wound on his chest. She left it alone, though she looked worried.

"Stay with him until he's resting again, Trina," she said. She motioned Old Jan toward the kitchen with her.

I stayed where I was, holding Mark's hand. Gradually his grip loosened and his jaw unclenched.

"It's bad, isn't it?" he said after a time.

I cupped his hand between my own. "Just rest now," I said.

"Am I going to die?"

I swallowed hard. "Shh. Just rest," I said.

"Will you stay with me, Trina?"

"I'll stay as long as you like."

He closed his eyes and sighed. "Forever?"

"As long as you like," I repeated. "Now get some sleep, if you can."

"I'd like forever," he murmured.

I said nothing, just held his hand and watched him drift toward sleep. My mother and Old Jan were talking in low tones in the kitchen. I strained to hear them over Mark's shallow, panting breath.

"I don't know where the money will come from," Old Jan was saying.

"Wait until tomorrow and we will see, but if he doesn't improve quickly, we will have to find the money," my mother said. "Trina made a little selling eggs. It may not all be gone."

They were speaking of the doctor. I knew my mother would not suggest it if it wasn't serious. I looked again at Mark's face and blinked back my tears. They were welcome to all the money I had left.

I stayed at Old Jan's house all the rest of that day, mopping Mark's brow with a cool cloth to try to ease the fever. In the evening my mother returned with a kettle of soup and tended Mark while Old Jan and I ate. I took my bowl to the porch, eager for some fresh air after the long hours in the still, stale air of the bedroom. When I finished my supper, I asked my mother if I might stay the night.

"I can tend to Mark if he needs anything, and that way Old Jan can get some rest too."

Momma nodded. "I think that is a very good idea, Trina. If you need anything, we are just down the hill, and you can come get me."

She went home and returned with blankets to make a bed for me on the kitchen floor. I slept poorly that night in that strange room. Mark moaned and mumbled as he sank deeper into the delirium of fever. He thrashed and tangled himself in his sheets. The next morning when he jerked awake, he did not know us.

The doctor wouldn't take the scrip the mine was issuing, so we had to scrape together every last bit of cash we had to get him to come. He restitched the wound, using a bit of whiskey to numb the skin as he did so, and he left a small bottle of opium syrup to help Mark rest. As for the infection and the fever, we would just have to wait and see. I stayed on, taking turns sitting with Mark so that Old Jan could rest himself, but the old man would not go far from his son's side.

On the fourth day the fever subsided gradually. I wasn't sure, at first, but by midday, Mark was resting peacefully for an hour at a time without the aid of the syrup. Toward evening, he opened his eyes and looked at me as I mopped his brow, and he was sensible of who I was. I smiled with relief and called

Old Jan to the bedside, but by the time he arrived, Mark had slipped back into sleep.

Old Jan and I stood together and watched him sleeping peacefully.

"He's been improving all day," I said. "I'm sure the fever is down."

Old Jan said nothing at first, only stood leaning on his crutches, looking down at his son. At last he gave a deep sigh. "He is so young," he said. "Too young to be throwing his life away in that mine."

A knot tangled up inside me and all I could do was nod.

"Do you know, in the Old Country, my wife and I had five children."

"Five?" I didn't know. While Old Jan had told us many stories, this had never been among them.

He nodded, sighing again. "Five. Karel and Marek were my youngest. The first three are all dead now, just like my beloved Tereza."

"What happened to them?"

"It was long ago, child; it doesn't matter now. I came to America for these last two — so they might have a better future. And they would have, too, if I hadn't lost my leg."

I tried to push down the lump in my throat, but it was stuck fast. Old Jan brushed a gnarled hand across the top of my head, smoothing the hair that had pulled loose from my braids.

"If he recovers, Trina—"

"He will, Jan! I'm sure he's better tonight!" I knew not to interrupt my elders, but I could not bear the thought that Mark might die.

"He is better," Jan agreed. "And I have you to thank for that, Trina. You have taken good care of him."

I shrugged, embarrassed, but pleased, too.

"I think you are more fond of my Marek than you have admitted," he continued.

"I am fond of him," I said. "I'm fond of all of you."

"But with Marek, I think there is something more. When he recovers, Trina, go to the dance with him. He likes you very much, and it would make us all happy, don't you think?"

I wasn't sure who he meant when he said "all," but I knew it would make Momma happy, as well as Old Jan and Mark. I supposed it would make me happy too. I saw that more now than I had before. Now that I had come so close to losing him.

I nodded. "I've told him I will, if he's well enough," I said.

Old Jan smiled at me and patted my cheek. "You are a good girl, Trina. You take such good care of my boy. You will keep taking care of him, won't you?"

"Of course! He isn't better yet. Of course I will tend him, as long as he needs me."

"He will need you for a long time, my dear. A long, long time. You know what your mother wants, and I think Marek wants it too. You and Marek are a good match. With you, I think my dreams for him could grow again. I think he could build a good life here in America."

I listened to him while I watched Mark sleep, his cheeks still flushed but his breathing deeper and quieter than it had been in days. I was suddenly aware of the ache at my heart. It had been there for days, but I realized that now it was different. Watching over Mark, fearing for him, being by his side every day, I realized how fond of him I had grown.

My plans to get the farm had been crushed, and with them, my hope. But I hadn't lost Mark. Before, I had felt like I had to choose, but that choice had been taken from me. All that was left was Mark, and as I looked at him, my heart swelled within me. Slowly, I nodded.

"I will take care of him, Jan. For as long as he needs me. I promise," I said.

Old Jan smiled and hugged me. Before the day was out, my mother knew of my promise and couldn't wait to tell my father of the match. The whole family was excited and spoke of nothing else that evening. Everyone except Aneshka. She glared at me, stomped her feet everywhere she went, and wouldn't speak a word to me. I simply ignored her and tried to enjoy the happiness the rest of my family shared.

Mark's fever broke at last the next day, and the wounds at his chest and foot began to heal in earnest. His strength had been sorely taxed, though, and he did not get out of bed for some time. I returned to my own house at night and to help with chores, but whenever I had free time, I was at Mark's bedside. Momma, delighted with my promise, released me from my chores as often as she could spare me, so that I could help Old Jan and Mark.

When I was with Mark, I could almost forget the empty feeling inside me from my lost dreams. I cooked and cleaned for them, thinking that this is what it would be like to someday marry Mark. I was glad to have work that kept me from my wrecked dreams in the backyard at home.

Unfortunately, the more time I spent with Mark, the angrier Aneshka seemed to be about it all. Whenever we made beds or washed dishes or scrubbed laundry together, she was surly and uncooperative. I tried to ignore her, thinking it would pass. But after several weeks, I lost my temper one afternoon, when she threw an armload of shirts into the washkettle, nearly splashing the scalding water over the edge and onto me.

"What is the matter with you?" I shouted, feeling almost as close to the boiling point as the washwater.

"What do you care what's the matter!" she shouted back. "You don't care about us anymore. You just care about Mark!"

"Mark's been very sick! He needed me," I protested.

"But he doesn't need you anymore. I think it's that you *like* Mark," she said, making the word *like* into a taunt. Then she puckered up her lips and made kissing sounds.

My cheeks flamed with anger and embarrassment. "Stop it, Aneshka!"

"Well, you're always with him! It's not fair!"

"What's not fair?" my mother said, arriving with a bundle of laundry from Old Jan's house.

Aneshka crossed her arms and glared at me. "It's not fair that Trina's always with Mark when she's supposed to be getting us a farm."

Momma gave an exasperated little sigh and began vigorously stirring the shirts in the tub. "Don't be silly, Aneshka. Trina can't get us a farm. Whatever put such an idea into your head?"

Aneshka only glared harder. "Trina knows what I'm talking about," she said.

"I don't," I said stoutly. At least I didn't know how she had pried the secret of my wish out of Holena. "Besides, Mark has nothing to do with it."

Aneshka scowled and stomped her foot. "It's not fair!" she said again.

"Stop that, Aneshka," Momma said. "We have work to do."

Aneshka did as she was told, but she was surly for the rest of the afternoon. I was too. I could not explain the truth to her. The wish had not failed because I was with Mark. The truth was, I was with Mark because the wish had failed.

Chapter 15

SOON MARK was up, doing his own chores and walking to help rebuild his strength. He went striding by our house, up and down the road, farther and farther each day. Though his strength was coming back, his gait was still awkward. He could not seem to flex his foot upward properly, causing it to drag when he walked, and it did not improve with practice.

Old Jan wanted to consult the doctor about it, but Mark refused. They were out of money and a month behind on their rent as it was. The mine had extended them credit; however, rumors were spreading of another round of layoffs. Karel was one of the few bachelors left at the mine, and the family feared he would lose his job as well, and Mark would have no job to go to even when he recovered. Everyone in town was struggling and praying their jobs would last. Martina, who could not bear to return to her parents' home, had resolved to sell Charlie's clothing and whatever of her own possessions she could spare. She hoped to pay off her debts to the mining company and have enough left over for train fare to Denver, or perhaps Kansas City. There she hoped to find a factory job. I did not dare ask what she might do if there were no jobs to be had. The thought of being alone in a big city was too terrible for me to imagine.

When Karel and Mark heard of Martina's plan, they went to her house, though they themselves were in debt. Mark came back up the road a short time later with Charlie's old boots. They were worn, but he needed something to replace the boot that had been ruined in the accident, he said. He could not go back into the mine without boots.

"Where is Karel?" I asked.

Mark sat down on the porch step. "It's Saturday, his night off, so he's taking his time coming home. He stayed to visit with Martina."

I thought nothing more of Karel's absence that evening, or the next day when Old Jan and Mark came to our house to share our Sunday dinner. We were just about to sit down to eat when Karel and Martina came walking up the road toward us. They stopped and stood before the porch, Karel looking up uncertainly at his father while Martina's eyes stayed shyly on the dirt before her.

Karel took a deep breath and cleared his throat. "We've gotten married, Papa."

We all stared, our mouths hanging open stupidly. When there was no response, Karel continued.

"The priest was here, and he won't be back for two weeks. This is best for everyone. I'm not a bachelor now, so the mine will keep me on. And Charlie would have wanted Martina taken care of. I'll do that."

Momma was the first to recover her composure. She stood

141

and beckoned to them. "Come in, come in. You are family here now."

Karel took Martina's hand and led her up onto the porch. Momma clasped her and gave her a kiss on either cheek in congratulations. Old Jan leaped up to do the same, and the rest of us followed. I did not know what to think as I kissed her blushing cheek. It had been barely two weeks since she had wailed at Charlie's funeral. Perhaps it should have been shocking, but all I felt was relief that she would not be alone and penniless in a distant town.

"Dinner is almost ready," Momma said. "It will serve for a wedding feast, I think."

We all went into a flurry of activity at that. Papa and Karel carried the table and chairs out into the yard. I spread Momma's fine linen tablecloth on the table. In the kitchen Momma mixed up batter and used the last can of plums to make dumplings. She had been saving it for a special occasion, she said, and this was it.

We did not have time for many wedding traditions, since the marriage had already occurred, but Mark did tie two spoons together with a ribbon. As we sat down to eat, Mark brought a bowl of potato soup out for the newlyweds to share. We all watched as they struggled to eat it with their joined spoons. It was supposed to bring good luck, but mostly it was good fun. We laughed as they spilled, and yet I thought they did very well for two people joined on a moment's notice as a practical necessity. There was a careful, tender courtesy between them that seemed very comforting. It occurred to me as I watched them that there was a certain wisdom to my mother's views — that accepting what life gave you and being grateful for it could bring a comfortable life.

Mark was seated across the table from me, and I couldn't resist a glance at him. He was looking at me, too, and when our eyes met he smiled. I smiled back.

After dinner was complete, Momma and Aneshka took the broom and mop and marched off to Martina's house to prepare it for the new couple. Holena and I stayed behind to wash the dishes and though it was her wedding feast, Martina insisted on helping.

"I'll not have Karel thinking I'm a lazy wife," she said.

We began working in silence, but soon she spoke. "Do you think poorly of me for marrying now, with Charlie barely in the grave?" She kept her eyes on her work, but I could see tears welling in her eyes. "I loved Charlie, and I wouldn't do anything to dishonor his memory. But I was afraid, Trina. And Karel is a good man. He was Charlie's friend."

I stopped her flow of words with a hand on her arm. "You haven't done anything wrong," I reassured her. "Charlie would not have wanted you alone in the city. And Karel *is* a good man; he'll be good to you."

"He was Charlie's friend," she said again. "He was afraid of being laid off. With his father and brother unable to work, he had to keep his job somehow. And I had nowhere to go. Maybe that's not a good reason to marry, but I swear I'll take good care of him, Trina."

I nodded. "We are glad to have you in the family," I said. Not that Karel and Mark were my family yet, but we spent so much time together it felt like it.

I heard a noise from the doorway and turned to see Mark.

"Your groom awaits you, Mrs. Kocekova." He gave a stiff little bow and swept his arm toward the porch.

Martina startled a little at the sound of her new title, but then she smiled and went outside. Everyone was gathered there and applauded her. Aneshka gave her a little bouquet of flowers, mostly dandelions and grass, and the family paraded the couple to Martina's house. Karel swept Martina up and carried her through the doorway, and the rest of us returned home. We all settled comfortably into the shade on the porch.

"Do you think they will be happy?" Mark asked, to no one in particular.

Aneshka gave a little snort. "How can they be when they are so poor? Martina shouldn't have sold her things."

"Aneshka," Momma said sharply.

"They will have a hard time of it in that respect, I'm afraid," Old Jan said. "They are at her house for now, but she can only keep it through the end of the month. I'm afraid until Marek is back to work, they will have to crowd in with us, and that is not pleasant for newlyweds."

"It can't be helped," Momma said. "Some things in life we simply must accept, and the sooner we do that, the better off we are."

I had worked hard to believe that view of things in recent weeks. Still, it didn't seem the same as being happy.

"What do you think, Trina?" Mark asked. "Do you think they will be happy together?"

I thought again about the gentle courtesy I had seen that day between Martina and Karel. I sighed. I wasn't sure I knew what happiness was anymore.

"I think they are kind to each other, and that is a good start," I said.

"A very good start, indeed," Old Jan said. "Kindness and respect are more important than all the riches in the world."

Aneshka, sensing that Old Jan had a story to prove his

point, scooted closer to him. Holena watched him eagerly as well. He smiled at them obligingly.

"Let's see. There once was a shepherd who was cheated by his rich neighbor. For his work, the shepherd was to receive a fine heifer, but when the work was done, the neighbor refused. So the shepherd and the neighbor went before the burgomaster, a young man, new to his position. The burgomaster did not know who was in the right, so he decided the case by saying, 'Each of you go home. Return tomorrow with the answer to this riddle: Of all things in the world, tell me, what is the swiftest? What is the sweetest? And what is the richest? Whichever of you answers best shall have the heifer.'

"So the two men went home with their questions. The rich neighbor consulted his wife, who was as greedy as he was. The poor shepherd had only his clever, gentle daughter at home, but he told her the riddle too.

"In the morning, the two men returned to the burgomaster, who put his question to them again. 'What is the swiftest thing in the world? What is the sweetest? And what is the richest?'

"The rich neighbor gave his wife's answer. 'It is simple, sir. The swiftest thing is my fine gray mare, for no one passes me on the road. The sweetest is the honey from my hives, for they are the best in the world. The richest is my sack of gold ducats, for I have been saving them away for years.'

"'Hmm,' said the burgomaster. Then he turned to the humble shepherd and asked him. And thanks to his clever daughter, the shepherd answered, 'I believe the swiftest thing in the world is a kind thought, for a kind thought comforts a loved one in no time at all. The sweetest thing is another's love, for it can soothe any suffering. The richest thing is the earth itself, from which honest labor brings forth all other riches.'

"At once the burgomaster saw the shepherd had answered most wisely, and so he gave the man the heifer and sent the rich neighbor home to quarrel with his wife. But to the shepherd he said, 'I must know who gave you this answer.'

"'My clever daughter, Manka, told me these things,' the shepherd replied.

"Now, the burgomaster had been thinking of taking a wife for some time, and at once he was intrigued by such a clever girl. So he gave the shepherd six eggs to take to Manka and said, 'Tell your clever daughter that if she will hatch these eggs into chicks and bring them to me tomorrow, I will marry her.'"

"That's not fair," Aneshka interrupted. "You can't hatch eggs overnight."

"They would need their momma to hatch," Holena said. I knew she was thinking of my chicks, dead in their nest. I wished Old Jan had picked a different story.

Old Jan smiled at my sisters and nodded. "The shepherd thought the same thing, and he was sorry, for he thought the burgomaster would make a fine son-in-law. But he took the eggs to his daughter and told her of the man's request.

"Manka only laughed. The next morning she gave her father a handful of grain and said, 'Take this to the burgomaster and tell him that if he will grow a field of wheat for me and bring it to me tomorrow, I will know he is my equal and I will consent to be his wife.'

"When the burgomaster received this reply, he mounted his horse at once and rode to the shepherd's home, where on one knee, he asked the clever girl to marry him. She consented and they were wed. That night, after the wedding feast, he said to her, 'You have proved to me that you will be a kind and honest wife, and so we will be happy. But you must never use your cleverness against me or I will turn you out of my home.'

"They lived together for some time in happiness, for they lived by the principles of kindness and fairness that Manka had shown in her answers. But as the burgomaster grew older he grew lazy and eager for gain in his duties. One day, a dispute was brought to him from the marketplace. A farmer's mare had given birth to a foal, but a loud noise had scared the foal under a merchant's wagon, so the merchant claimed the foal was his. Now, the burgomaster knew the farmer was a poor man, while the merchant was wealthy and powerful, capable of giving many gifts and favors. So without much thought, the burgomaster gave the foal to the merchant, and the poor farmer went home with nothing for his trouble. When Manka saw the sad farmer leaving, she asked what was wrong and he told her. Manka at once told the farmer what to do.

"The next morning, the burgomaster stepped out his front door to see a fishnet strung across the road. The farmer was sitting nearby, watching it eagerly.

"'What are you doing?' the burgomaster asked.

"'Why, I am fishing,' replied the farmer."

"Fishing in the road?" Aneshka said with a shriek of laughter.

"That is exactly what the burgomaster said. And the farmer replied, 'Why, yes, for if a wagon can foal in this town, I would suppose that fish could be caught in its streets.'

"At once the burgomaster saw the wrong judgment he had made. But he also saw Manka's hand in the farmer's clever act, and so he went back inside and said to her, 'I warned you never to use your cleverness against me. Now you must leave my house, as I said. But I am not hard-hearted. Take with you whatever you like best from our home, and return to your father.'

147

"'Very well,' Manka said. 'But please, husband, let us sup together one last time before I go.'

"The burgomaster agreed to this, so that evening Manka served him a fine, heavy supper and many tankards of good, strong beer, and before long, the burgomaster was snoring in his chair at the table. When he was asleep, Manka did as she had been told. She took her favorite thing and returned to her father's house.

"The next morning the burgomaster woke, confused, for he was in a shepherd's hut on the edge of the forest. He looked around, and there was Manka, preparing breakfast at the humble hearth.

"'Where am I?' the burgomaster asked. 'And how did I get here?'

"'You are in my father's house,' Manka said, 'for you said I could take with me my favorite thing in the house, and that, dear husband, is you.'

"When the burgomaster saw that she had once again out-witted him, he might have been angry, but he was not. For he saw what she said was true—she was his favorite thing too. He had married her for her cleverness, but he found that as they had given each other the kind thoughts, sweet love, and honest labor over the years, she had become his greatest treasure. And so he returned the foal to its rightful owner, apologized to his wife, and took her home, promising to never behave so badly again. And from that day on, when a particularly difficult case came before him, he always consulted his clever wife before he made his judgment. And with kindness and respect, they lived out their days in happiness."

Aneshka clapped her hands in delight at the end of the story. I think she liked best that Manka had outsmarted her husband.

But Holena seemed to better understand Old Jan's meaning.

"I think Karel and Martina will be kind to each other too. I think they will be happy, even if they don't have much," she said.

"I do too," Mark said. "I think if you care about someone, you don't need much else to make you happy. What do you think, Trina?"

I had a hard time answering. As Old Jan had told the story, Mark's hand had found mine and closed around it. Now all I could think about was the feel of that hand and the happiness that eased the ache in my heart at its touch.

"It's the last Saturday of July this week. That means the community dance," Mark said. "I think dancing with you is the last thing I need to completely heal me, Trina."

I looked up to see Momma smiling and Aneshka glaring at me. I ignored them both and turned to Mark with a smile of my own. "I'll be ready at six," I said.

Chapter 16

MARK'S UNEVEN gait did not improve much over the coming week, but he was determined to keep walking and gaining his strength. The day of the dance he stopped by our house in the morning and danced me around our porch in front of Momma and my sisters, just to prove he was well enough to go.

That afternoon, Momma helped me prepare. I bathed, and she brushed out my hair. I would wear it in a bun rather than my usual girlish braids. From her own trunk, she found her best dress, the one she had married in. She had not worn it since we left the Old Country. Now she offered it to me.

It felt good to put on a dress that reached to the floor, like an elegant lady. I was not yet a lady, though, as the loose bodice proved. My mother only smiled at the way the shapely dress fit my mostly shapeless frame.

"Soon, Trina. Don't worry," she said, and she pinned the bodice under the arms where a few tucks would create a serviceable fit. She made the alterations without cutting the fabric. There was no point in making the dress fit a girl's body now, when mine was on the verge of becoming a woman, she said.

My mother hummed happily as she worked, and it made me happy to see her so cheerful. It didn't even bother me when Aneshka came into the kitchen, scowled at us, and then stomped off to the backyard with an angry snort. She stayed in the back all afternoon, though I couldn't imagine why. The ruined chicken yard and garden had been such painful reminders of our failed dreams that I spent as little time as possible behind the house. How Aneshka could spend hours at a time with those reminders was beyond me.

By suppertime, I was ready for the dance, wearing my mother's fine dress and with my hair pinned neatly at the nape of my neck. My father smiled with pride when he saw me.

"My little Trina is becoming a woman," he said, kissing me on the forehead. "And a beautiful woman, at that. Marek is a lucky fellow."

My family sat down to supper, but I hardly ate a bite. I was afraid of spoiling my dress and I was feeling nervous. Even though I'd seen Mark every day since the accident, going to a dance with him was different.

Mark was in high spirits when he arrived to escort me to the dance. He, too, was clean and polished, in a suit that probably belonged to his father. His hair was trimmed and slicked down smoothly. He smiled hugely when he saw me, which made me blush. He complimented me politely and greeted my parents even more politely.

"You are looking well, Marek," Papa said. "Why, to look at you now, no one would know you've been sick."

"I am much better, thanks to your daughter. I am going back to work on Monday!" he announced.

He had meant this as good news, but the knot of fear I'd carried since the accident twisted tighter inside me. He wasn't yet well enough for the long hours of hard labor. He showed no sign of pain that evening as we danced or visited with the other young couples, though. In fact, he was so merry that I buried my misgivings. By the end of the evening I, too, was merry, and I was sorry when the fiddlers announced the last song.

Afterward, as Mark and I walked up the road toward home we could hear other couples whispering and giggling in the darkness. Mark's hand found mine and they clasped together. Our pace slowed, neither of us eager to end the evening. It was very romantic, at least until Mark broke the silence between us.

"Will we be getting more chickens?" he asked.

I was surprised by the question. My chickens were the last thing I'd been thinking about—or wanted to think about. "No. We haven't got the money, and besides, it all came to nothing last time."

"That's not to say that it would come to nothing again, though, is it?"

I frowned, thinking that Mr. Johnson would not let me succeed, but I didn't say it. Mark had enough to worry about. "I was just thinking," he said, "that the chickens would be a good idea for us now. With me having been out of work, it would be good if we had some means of food that costs no money at the store."

"Maybe we should get chickens for you and your papa," I said. "If you can bear to be a farmer."

"The chicken house and fence is in your yard, but perhaps we could share the cost of the chickens. My papa can come and help you care for them. I don't mind that much farming for a good meal now and then."

"What about the dogs?"

"We have to be more careful, that's all. That happened because no one was home. But if my papa came to look after them, that couldn't happen."

"I don't know. It didn't work last time."

"You aren't going to give up that easily, are you? It's just a minor setback," he said a little impatiently.

"Minor? I lost everything."

We were in front of my house now, and we had stopped walking. In the darkness Mark pulled me to him and wrapped his arms around my waist. "Not everything," he breathed into my hair. "You didn't lose me."

I leaned my head against his chest, my chin just above the still-tender scar that had nearly killed him. I felt lucky to be wrapped in his arms, and I felt safe, too.

He bent forward and kissed me lightly on the forehead. I wanted to stay there like that, but he spoke again. "I think we can make the chickens work, and the garden. In a few more years we'll be the envy of the camp."

I pressed my cheek in tighter against his chest, listening to his heartbeat. I tried not to think about the future when we would still be here, doing the same things, forever. He squeezed me to him in his strong arms for a long moment before finally bidding me good night and releasing me. I climbed the steps to my house and went inside alone. In the darkness, I changed into my nightdress and lay down on the bed. Aneshka rolled over immediately to face me.

"Did you set a date to marry him?" she whispered.

"Of course not! He's barely sixteen. That won't be for years yet."

Aneshka slipped her hand into mine, much as she had the first horrible night after the mine accident. "Please, Trina. You can't give up on your wish—you just can't. I know I was selfish with my wish, but I'll work extra hard for yours to make up for it, if you will just try too."

I sighed. "Aneshka, I didn't give up on the wish. Everything was ruined, remember? Besides, wishes aren't real. It was just a game."

"But you said you saw the fish," whispered Holena from my other side. I hadn't even known she was awake. "You said you believed!"

"That was before, when there was something to believe in."

"Before you gave up," Aneshka insisted.

"What else am I supposed to do?" I said, my whisper sharp as annoyance rose in me. "There's nothing left!"

"Yes, there is," Holena whispered.

Suddenly Aneshka was out of bed and pulling me up as well. "There is," she said. "Come on, I'll show you."

"Aneshka, go to sleep," I said, but now Holena was up too, so I got out of bed myself before they woke our parents. Quietly we slipped out the front door and around the house to the back.

"See?" Aneshka said, pointing.

Across the garden, which should have been only bare earth or weeds, I could see a dark mass of leaves in the moonlight. Not the neat, orderly rows I had originally planted, but a sprawling expanse of luxurious growth. I stepped closer, to the very edge of the garden, but it was too dark to see properly.

"What is it?" I asked.

"It's your cucumbers," Aneshka said.

"We've been tending them for you," Holena said.

"Because you won't," Aneshka added.

I stared in disbelief. The tiny corner of cucumber plants that had been spared by Mr. Johnson seemed to have magically expanded to fill the desolation of the destroyed garden.

The ugly emptiness of the ruined rows had been replaced by a carpet of wide leaves and curling tendrils of vine. I bent over the plants and raked through the leaves with my fingers. I could feel several hard fruits sheltered beneath them.

"I don't believe it," I said. "How could they have grown so much in such a short time?" I thought about it. "I suppose we have had some good rains."

"It's not the rain; it's the *wish*," Holena said, as if my suggestion was the silliest thing she'd ever heard.

I straightened. "It's not the wish. No matter how many cucumbers we get, they aren't going to get us a farm."

"You could sell them."

"We'd have to have acres of cucumbers to earn enough money for a farm," I said, still looking at the patch before me. "But maybe we have enough to make pickles. Papa likes pickles with his meat. We'll have another look in the morning."

I took both of my sisters by the hand and walked them back the way we'd come and into the house. I got them into bed, then slipped in beside them. Someone stirred across the room.

"Trina, is that you?" came my mother's sleepy voice.

"Yes, Momma."

"How was the dance? Did you have a nice time?"

"Yes."

"You are happy, then?"

"Yes, Momma," I said softly. "Yes, I'm very happy." It was true. I had had a wonderful evening with Mark, but there was more to it than that. My discovery of the unexpected cucumber plants seemed to have delighted me like nothing had in weeks.

"Good. Good night, then," Momma said. The bedsprings squeaked as she settled back into her bed.

I lay still, listening to the soft breathing of my family and looking up at the ceiling. Why had those plants made such a difference? I had told my sisters it wouldn't, and I had believed that when I said it. So why was I feeling so happy? I couldn't explain it, but I knew if I asked Holena, she would easily do so. She would say it was the wish, and she would be content in her innocent trust.

I closed my eyes, refusing to slip back into the foolishness. *It's not the wish*, I told myself. *Wishes and dreams are for fools.* But though I repeated it several times before falling asleep, I dreamed once again that night of fields of ripening wheat.

Chapter 17

THE NEXT MORNING was Sunday, so we had no chores. I got up early before church, and taking my basket with me, I went out to the garden to inspect it in the daylight, half expecting the sprawling cucumber vines to have been a dream. They were not, and by the time my mother called me in, I brought with me a full basket.

Momma looked at the basket in surprise. "Where on earth did you get those?"

"The garden, and there are more on the vine," I said. I couldn't keep from grinning. "Do you think it's enough to make pickles?"

"Enough?" Momma said with a laugh. "I think we'll have enough pickles for the year."

We went to church that morning, but all I was thinking about through the hot, airless service was getting home to the cucumbers.

After church I walked back up the hill toward home with

Mark and his father, going slowly so that Old Jan could keep up on his crutches. I told them of the cucumber vines as we walked.

"You see," Mark said, "I told you it was only a minor setback. Your farm is back on its feet already."

"A cucumber patch is hardly a farm!" I pointed out.

"But you can turn it into one," he said. "As you get more chickens or other seeds, we can expand into our backyard, too. Maybe we could get a goat—or maybe even a cow, like Aneshka wanted. We'll be the richest folks in the coal camp."

"But we'll still be in the coal camp," I said.

"For now," Old Jan said. "But you have your whole lives ahead of you to build your dreams. You've got to have dreams."

I did not contradict him, but I knew better. It was better not to have dreams, and I wasn't going to be pulled into them again by a few cucumbers. Besides, I couldn't see how being the richest family in the coal camp was much to believe in anyway.

Back at the house, Mark and Old Jan talked with Papa while Momma and I prepared Sunday dinner. Karel and Martina arrived with a pot of soup and dumplings. We dined outside, as if we were all one big family. Afterward the women gathered in the kitchen to talk of pickles while the men moved Martina's sparse possessions to Old Jan's house.

"The first thing we must do is make a brine," Momma said. "We can do that today and get started in the washtub. In Bohemia, I had a pickle crock, but we will have to get a new one here, or jars. Here in America they use jars. See?" She flipped through the paper and showed me the advertisement for Mason jars at the mercantile in Trinidad. Momma did not know enough English to read the paper, but she was learning a little about America from the pictures in the ads and stories.

"With jars they can be shared more easily," Martina said, a little nervously. "I would pay half on the jars and provide sugar and spices, in exchange for some of the pickles."

"That's a fine idea," Momma said.

We were a cheerful party that afternoon. The first stage of making the pickles only required a brine of hot water, salt, and a chunk of alum, all of which we had without a trip to the store. We could get sugar and jars later; the store was closed on Sunday. I enjoyed starting the pickles, but I dreaded the prospect of a trip to the store for jars. If Mr. Johnson really had been the one to destroy my garden and kill my chickens—and I was sure he was—what would he do when he found out that something had survived and that we were making pickles? Would we come home from a day of doing laundry to find our jars of pickles all smashed in the backyard?

I tried to convince Momma that Martina should buy the jars. But the next day was Monday, laundry day, and Martina was washing Old Jan's and Mark's clothes as well as Karel's these days. Momma admonished me and sent me off to the store. I couldn't explain why I didn't want to go, because I had not told Momma of Mr. Johnson's hatred for me. So I had no choice but to go obediently, though my dread grew with every step. To make matters worse, a wagon was hitched in front of the store. As I drew nearer, I saw that it was Mr. Torentino's supply wagon, the same one that had brought the plums. I had liked Mr. Torentino, and everyone had been happy to get his plums. But I didn't need another reminder of why Mr. Johnson had a grudge against me. My steps faltered and I considered coming back later.

"Trina!" The call came from the shaded porch, and I looked up to see Mark sitting there. "Come join me."

Though his invitation was warm, his expression and the sag of his shoulders gave off heavy melancholy. I climbed the steps and sat down beside him. "I thought you were going back to work today," I said.

He nodded. "So did I, but when I reported for my shift last night, they said they couldn't use me. They don't have much work, and what they have they aren't giving to a fellow with a bad foot."

"Your foot's getting better," I said, trying to sound hopeful for his sake.

He looked down at it and shook his head. "I don't think so. I don't think it will ever be right again."

I didn't know what to say. I understood his desire to work and his fears about the future, but I felt relieved that he wouldn't be returning to the mine just yet. I sat beside him in a heavy silence for a long moment, searching for the right words.

The door swung open, and Mr. Torentino stomped across the porch to his wagon. I remembered then why I was there. Eager to end the awkward silence between us, I excused myself and hurried into the store, momentarily forgetting my fear of Mr. Johnson.

"I need jars," I blurted out when he acknowledged me.

"Jars?"

"Pickle jars," I swallowed, my fear coming back to me. "For making pickles."

Several women in the store raised their eyes to me, curious.

"You're making pickles, are you? I suppose you'll be needing cucumbers, too, then," Mr. Johnson said.

"No, thank you, sir."

His eyes narrowed, and I felt a stab of satisfaction. He thought he had destroyed me, and now he was wondering. *Let him wonder*, I thought. *Better yet, let him know he hasn't beaten me entirely.*

I raised my chin and my voice, so everyone in the store could hear. "They're from my garden."

"Are they now," he said, and there was a dangerous quiet in his voice that caused my defiance to wither as quickly as it had risen. "Well, I don't see any jars here, do you?"

I glanced around. "Can I order them, then?"

"Certainly." He pulled a dog-eared Sears and Roebuck catalog from under the counter. "It will cost extra, of course. Postage is expensive way out here, and someone has to haul it up from Trinidad." He was flipping through the catalog as he spoke, until he came to a page filled with pictures of jars of various sizes and shapes. I could see the price beside the picture of pickle jars—eighty-five cents a dozen.

"That will be four dollars," Mr. Johnson said. "Paid in advance."

"But—it says right there eighty-five cents," I said, pointing at the picture.

He shrugged and slapped the catalog shut. "Shipping is expensive."

"That's not a fair price!"

"Take it or leave it," he said with a nasty smile.

I didn't want to do either. If I didn't buy jars, we couldn't preserve the cucumbers we had already begun pickling. If I did place the order, I was agreeing to a price that we both knew was highway robbery. He had gotten the best of me once before, and I couldn't let him do it again.

Then I remembered the picture in the newspaper that Momma had seen. If she had seen jars in the paper, that meant someone in Trinidad had them for sale. And that gave me an idea.

161

"Never mind," I said to Mr. Johnson, "excuse me," and I hurried out of the store.

Mark was still on the porch, and out of the corner of my eye I saw his mouth open to speak, but I hurried past and down the steps. Mr. Torentino's wagon was disappearing down the road in a cloud of dust and I had to hurry to catch it. I gathered my skirts into my hands and I ran. I had to shout several times before he heard me over the creak and clatter of his wagon. He pulled up on the reins and looked down at me, breathing too hard to speak.

"Yes, missy? What is it?" he said in his musical Italian accent.

"Do you have a store in Trinidad?" I asked.

"Yes, ma'am. Torentino and Sons, on Main Street."

"I need pickle jars, but Mr. Johnson doesn't carry them. Could I get them from your store?"

"Sure. We have plenty. With so many farms around, there's ready demand at this time of year. Come in the next time you're in Trinidad."

"But we don't go to Trinidad," I said. It was too far, and with Papa off work only one day a week and always needing to rest on that day, we hadn't left the camp since we'd arrived. I took a deep breath before venturing further on my idea. "If I paid you for them now, would you bring them with you on your next trip back up here?"

Mr. Torentino stroked his mustache as he considered it. "I don't usually make deliveries outside of town, but since I bring the supply wagon up here every Monday anyway, I don't see why not. Do you have the money?"

"How much are they?" I asked, praying he wouldn't add too much for delivering them so far from his store.

"Eighty-five cents a dozen," he said.

"That's so much cheaper than what Mr. Johnson's asking. Could you bring two dozen?"

Torentino glanced back toward Johnson's store. "I imagine everything seems cheap to you after dealing with Johnson," he said. "All right. Two dozen, next Monday at this same time."

"Thank you, sir!" I counted out the money and handed it up to him, then stepped back so he could be on his way again. I remembered Mark then, and how he'd probably been about to say something to me when I had run past him and after Torentino. I walked back to the store to apologize and explain, but when I got there, Mark had gone.

I walked home again, hoping I had done the right thing. What if Mr. Torentino forgot, or what if he had taken my money with no real intention of bringing me the jars? I realized he hadn't given me any receipt or anything to prove the deal. In my heart, though, I had a good feeling about the man. He had granted Aneshka's wish—not that he had known anything about the wish itself—and he'd been polite and kind.

Since I wasn't sure whether or not I'd done the right thing, I only told my mother that I had had to order the jars. Things had been so much better between us since I had stopped dreaming of a farm and agreed to a match with Mark. I didn't want to tell her that I was scheming again. Besides, I didn't want to worry her by telling her of Mr. Johnson's grudge against me.

I was finishing the ironing the next afternoon when I heard Old Jan call a greeting to my mother from the street. I stepped outside behind Momma, hoping Mark would be with him, but he was not. Old Jan was standing in the road, grinning from ear to ear, and I saw why right off. He had no crutches. His leg stump was neatly cradled in a wooden leg.

"My heavens," Momma said.

He grinned and waved at us with both hands.

"What do you think? My hands are free now—no more crutches for me!"

"It's wonderful! Where did you get it?" I asked. I couldn't imagine how they had come up with the money for it now, with all their other troubles.

"My Marek made it for me," he said, "from a post he found in the mine dump."

I looked again at the leg, and I could see now that it was homemade, but made well, shaped and smoothed with care. The cup at the top that cradled Old Jan's leg stump was padded with rags, and the strap that secured the wooden leg to the real one was an old leather belt.

"He's always been clever at making things," Old Jan said.

"Where is he?" I asked.

Old Jan sighed heavily. "Down at the creek, I think. I suppose you've heard they wouldn't take him back at the mine. Frankly, I don't think he is ready either, but it's certain now that we'll have to rely on Karel until the fall. That means we can't start catching up on the doctor bills or the rent, and that Karel and his bride will have to suffer the company of me and Marek for a while still. Marek blames himself, though I told him it couldn't be helped. If you'd go find him, Trina, I'm sure you could cheer him up."

Momma gave me permission to go even before I asked, so I set off for the creek, taking with me the buckets for Papa's washwater. I knew where Mark would be—exactly the place I would be if I were upset.

As I expected, Mark was sitting under the tree by the pool. He was throwing pebbles into the water. I called his name and he glanced up, then returned to glumly tossing pebbles without so much as a greeting. Though he didn't invite me to join him, I stepped under the tree and sat down on its raised root. He shifted, keeping his back to me.

"Mark, what is the matter?" I asked.

He shrugged and said nothing. I waited. I knew he would speak when he was ready.

"I could have been something, you know. If things had been different. If Papa hadn't gotten hurt, I could have gone to high school. If I hadn't gotten hurt, I'd have a job."

"You'll have a job again," I said. "You just need time to heal."

"But it's not good enough, is it? I'll never walk right. I don't blame you. I can see why you don't want a lame husband."

"What are you talking about? I never said—"

"When you found out I couldn't work yesterday, you couldn't wait to get away from me. You ran off into the store, and then when you'd finished with Mr. Johnson you left without even looking at me."

"No, Mark! I ran after the supply wagon to buy jars," I said.

"Jars?"

Quickly I explained to him what had happened at the store. "He's bringing them, and for much less than Mr. Johnson wanted to charge me."

"It's still true, though, isn't it. I'm not worth much to anyone anymore—a cripple who can't get a job."

"You're hardly a cripple!" I insisted. "You'll get a job again, and in the meantime you can do other things. Look at the leg you made for your father. It's beautiful! How can you say you're of no use?"

He shrugged, but I could see he was proud of the leg and pleased by the compliment, so I went on.

"The mine isn't the only job in the world. There must be other things you could do."

"If you're trying to talk me into farming, forget it."

"It wouldn't have to be farming. There are all kinds of jobs in town."

"Not for me. We owe the mine owners here, two months' back rent on the house, and all that credit at the store. We'd have to pay it back if we left here, and we don't have the money."

"But you'll never have the money if you stay here," I said. It was so unfair the way the mine trapped us all with debt. "Karel is still working in the mine. He could take care of things here and you could look for work in town. Surely you could find work there where your foot wouldn't matter."

Mark looked at me, his eyes reflecting both hope and fear. "You want me to go? To leave here?"

"I want to get out of here, don't you? And if they don't hire you back soon, the debt is only going to grow. There must be something you could do in town, but you won't know if you never try."

His face had been brightening as we talked, the hope slowly overpowering the fear. "I wish you could come with me, Trina."

I nodded, wishing I could too, but we both knew that was impossible. Mark reached over and took my hand.

"You will wait for me, won't you? Promise me you will," he said.

"I promise," I said, my heart swelling until I could barely speak. Suddenly I regretted encouraging him. Life would be so dreary here with him gone, and what if he never came back? What were the chances he would still even want me after he'd been away, meeting the pretty, sophisticated girls in town?

"I promise to come back, Trina," he said, as if he had read my fear. Perhaps he had. "The mines always need more men by

September or October. That's just two months away. And by then I'll be stronger; surely they will hire me. When I'm back and our debts are paid, I promise we will get on with all our other plans, Trina."

"If you get out of here, Mark—" I began, but he suddenly clutched me in a tight hug and repeated his words.

"I'll come back, Trina. I promise. And I'll think about you every minute that I'm gone."

I wrapped my arms around him and shut my eyes. I wanted my whole world to be him for a moment—his warmth, his smell, and the strong muscles of his chest against my cheek. I breathed in the mingled scents of shaving soap, sweat, and coal dust, with the faintest perfume of Old Jan's pipe tobacco. For just a moment, I wanted to let the warmth and strength of his embrace push away any thoughts of the future. I didn't want to think about the dreams or plans or problems before us. *Dreams only hurt us*, I reminded myself, and I held him tighter while I still could.

Too soon Mark released me from the embrace and I opened my eyes. He was fishing around in his pocket. He drew out a piece of copper wire and began twisting it around itself into a single braid. Then he curled it into a ring, knotting the ends together to finish it. Smiling, he slipped the band onto my finger.

"This is so you will remember my promise, okay?"

I nodded, my heart thumping as I looked at the simple wire ring on my finger.

I had nothing to offer in return, so I bent to the edge of the pool where pebbles glinted colorfully from under the water, and I picked a pretty red-and-yellow-speckled stone, smooth and wet and glistening.

"So you will remember too," I said, placing it in his hand and curling his fingers around it.

He grinned, a little mischievously, then quickly leaned forward and stole a kiss, right on my lips. He pulled back and looked at me, and when I gave no objection he leaned in again. This time, I kissed him back — at least, until we were interrupted by the whistle from the mine.

"Oh — Papa's washwater!" I said, remembering the buckets I had abandoned just upstream.

"I'll help you," he said.

He stepped over the tree root awkwardly, holding the trunk for support as he swung his bad foot over. Despite his own difficulty, he turned and held his hand out to assist me once he was on the other side. I had stepped over the root many times without help, but it was a gentlemanly gesture, so I took his hand. But as I stepped over to his side, I saw his gaze was falling somewhere behind me.

"Look," he said, pointing toward the pool. Even before I turned, I knew what I would see. The fish was there, waving softly in the current in the center of the pool.

"I've seen that fish before, but I can never catch it," Mark said. "I guess it can see us, too."

And it had seen me accept Mark's ring and give him my promise. "Holena says it's a lucky fish," I said. "Like in your papa's stories."

"Maybe it is," Mark said, encircling my waist with his arm and pulling me toward him. "Maybe we can make a wish for our future, and it will all come true."

I shook my head and pulled him away from the pool. Wishes and dreams were for fools; that was what I had learned. That was the moral of all the stories, including my own. I felt the twist of copper wire around my finger. Whatever my future would be, I refused to make a magic fish a part of it again.

Chapter 18

ANESHKA WENT into a fit when she saw the copper band on my finger, then refused to talk to me for the rest of the evening. I didn't care. Mark had decided to look for work in town, so it was my last evening with him for a while. I was just as glad to have Aneshka leaving us alone. Her silence didn't last, however. In the morning, I woke to her glaring at me.

"What about the pickles, Trina?" she said accusingly.

"What about them?"

"You're planning to marry Mark, but you promised to finish the pickles with us."

"I'm promised to Mark is all. Momma and Old Jan have agreed on the match, so it's none of your business."

"What about the wish?" she demanded.

I groaned and flopped onto my back, shielding my eyes with my arm. "Why did you tell her, Holena? It was supposed to be a secret."

"She was sad," Holena whispered from my other side. "I thought if she knew, she wouldn't be so sad."

"Well, it was my wish, so it's mine to do with as I please, isn't it? Maybe Mark is going to get a job on a farm and take me there," I said.

"But the farm was supposed to be for all of us," Aneshka said.

I got out of bed, angry now. We were all disappointed; it didn't help to have Aneshka always bringing it up and accusing me with it. "Well, it didn't work out that way, did it? What am I supposed to do about it?"

"You're supposed to make it work out!" Aneshka screamed, throwing her pillow at me.

"What is going on?" Momma said, looking in from the kitchen. "Aneshka, pick that up."

"It's not fair!" Aneshka said, tears now welling from her eyes. "Trina's going to leave us here and go somewhere nice with Mark, and she promised she wouldn't. She promised—"

"Hush, Aneshka!" Momma's words were firm, but she sat down on the edge of the bed and wrapped her arms around the girl, who was fighting back angry sobs. "Trina's growing up, that's all. Things change when you grow up. Marek will probably get another job at the mine in no time, and we will all be here together, just like before."

Momma had meant her words as comfort, but they were not. I wished that I was still young enough to be able to pour out my disappointment as Aneshka did, in sobs and rages and thrown pillows. Instead, I said good-bye to Mark an hour later and, as the week progressed, I had only chores to distract me from my loneliness and my broken dreams.

✳ ✳ ✳

Aneshka was still sulking on Monday when Mr. Torentino was to return with my jars, so I asked Martina to help me retrieve them. I couldn't carry them all myself, and I didn't want to listen to any more of Aneshka's scolding. We skirted around the store so we could meet Mr. Torentino where I did not think Mr. Johnson could see us, then we sat down to wait.

"Why did you arrange this, rather than just buying the jars from Mr. Johnson?" Martina asked as we watched for the wagon.

"You remember how Mr. Johnson doesn't like me much," I said, and told her the story.

"You mean, you're getting the jars for eighty-five cents a dozen? The same price he charges in town?"

"I think so."

"Do you think he'd sell me boots at his town rates, too?" Martina asked. "Karel's boots have worn through, and we gave Charlie's boots to Mark."

"You could ask," I said.

The wagon came into view, climbing the dirt road to the mine, kicking up a cloud of dust into the dry summer air. Our wait wasn't over, however, because Mr. Torentino wanted to conduct his business at the store first. We watched from a short distance away as Mr. Torentino carried crates into the store, then carried some of the same crates back out. When he returned to us, he was angry.

"That man," he said, glancing over his shoulder toward the store, "is a robber baron!"

I did not know what that meant, but I could tell Mr. Torentino shared my view of the storekeeper, so I agreed with a nod. "Did you bring the jars?"

"I've got them right here." He climbed over the seat and into the bed of the wagon. He handed the crates down to me one at a time, and I thanked him. Martina nudged me with her elbow.

"Mr. Torentino, Martina is newly married and her husband needs new boots, but she can't afford them at Mr. Johnson's store. Could she buy them from you, like I did the jars?"

Mr. Torentino's eyebrows raised. "Well, I hadn't thought to do this more than once, but I do sell boots." He told Martina what he had, and she was soon paying him and thanking him.

"Karel will be so pleased!" she said as we walked back toward home. "I am going to surprise him with the boots when they come!" Her face glowed with the idea, and I felt a pang of envy. I was missing Mark.

Finally the next Saturday afternoon I saw him returning up the street toward our house. Though his shoulders still sagged, his gait was stronger and more even than it had been when he had left almost two weeks before. I rushed to him and threw my arms around him, right in the middle of the street. He hugged me back and told me he was happy to see me, but there was no enthusiasm in the greeting. I pulled back and looked him in the eye.

"What's the matter?" I asked.

He sighed heavily. "I couldn't find work. Too many other coal miners are looking for jobs too. No one wants a cripple like me."

"You're not a cripple, Mark! You're walking much better than when you left."

"I should be, after all the useless miles I've walked looking for work. I'm sorry, Trina. I didn't want to disappoint you."

"The mine will be hiring again come fall, and you'll be better by then," I said, trying to sound hopeful. Trying not to let my disappointment show.

"But what about our plans? Our dreams?" He brushed his fingers tenderly along my cheek.

His plans had never been my dreams, but I couldn't tell him that. I shrugged. "My momma says dreams just make you unhappy, that to be happy, you have to appreciate the things you have. When I thought I had lost you, I saw she was right."

"She's not right!" came an angry shout from behind me. It was Aneshka. I hadn't known she had followed me out into the street to greet Mark. Now her hands were firmly planted on her hips and she was glaring at us both. "You can't give up on the farm, Trina! It's not fair!"

I was fuming mad at her for eavesdropping, but Mark tousled her hair.

"You're right, Aneshka. We won't give up," Mark said. "We'll get those chickens back, and the garden, too. Maybe even buy some goats. We have time yet."

"That's not a farm, and Trina knows it!" Aneshka said.

"Stop it, Aneshka," I said. "Mark only just got home. Stop being so selfish."

Aneshka thrust out her bottom lip in a pout, but I ignored her and turned to Mark.

"Go greet your papa and bring him back to our house. Karel and Martina, as well," I said, squeezing Mark with the arm I still had wrapped around his waist. "We will have a welcome-home feast for you!"

Momma and I prepared supper, and everyone was there, but we weren't very cheerful. Our money was already stretched thin, and Mark still without work was bad news for us all.

"I'll keep asking every day at the mine," Mark said. "Sooner or later they will have something for me."

Old Jan looked at his son and shook his head. "It's no wonder you couldn't find work in town. Look at those trousers—you've got patches on your patches, and your elbow's coming through your shirt. You're too poor to get a job."

I could see Old Jan's point. How could Mark convince folks in town that he was a hard worker when he looked like a ragged beggar? That thought stayed with me that night, along with the general sense of desperation that had run through the whole evening. There had to be something we could do.

"Is it true that Mark didn't get a job because of his trousers?" Holena asked from beside me in the bed.

I hesitated. "I don't know. Maybe partly."

"That nice man could get him new trousers, I bet," she said.

Aneshka reached across me and gave her a little push. "We don't want Mark to get a job, remember?" she hissed. "We want Trina to get us a farm like she's supposed to."

"I wish I'd never told you about her wish," Holena murmured. Silently I agreed.

Momma hushed us from her bed across the room and our conversation ended, but I thought about what Holena had said. Mr. Torentino had been willing to bring jars and boots; why not new pants for Mark? Then again, Mark didn't have the money for them, not even at Mr. Torentino's prices. But what if Old Jan was right? What if Mark could get a job—a better job, in town, if he had new clothes and looked a little neater? I could patch the elbows of his shirt so the patches would barely show.

By the next morning I had hit upon an idea. I walked to church with Mark and explained it to him. We could catch fish after church and sell them to our neighbors. I was sure there were plenty of folks around camp who would buy fresh fish from us. We could make enough money to buy him new trousers and he could try again to find work in town.

He shook his head. "It wasn't my pants, Trina. It was my limp, my lack of education, and my foreign accent."

"But you need money. We could still sell fish, even if you don't want new trousers. Can we at least try?" I asked.

Mark smiled. "Why not? We can take a picnic. And if we can't sell the fish, we can always eat them."

The plan worked better than I had expected, though it angered Aneshka. She glared at me the whole time I was packing the picnic, and I could still feel her eyes boring into my back as I set out with Mark to go fishing. It was a pleasant afternoon, and the fish were biting. Soon we had two long strings of trout. It was late afternoon when we returned to the coal camp, and all through town, parents were relaxing on their porches while their children played in the streets.

"How do we sell them?" I asked Mark.

He grinned at me. "That's easy enough." He cleared his throat and called out, "Fish! Fresh fish! Caught today, nice and fresh!"

I had to laugh. He sounded exactly like the hawkers in the village square on market day back in Bohemia. In no time at all we had a crowd of women around us. We hadn't discussed a price, but it didn't matter. The women seemed to know what was fair and were eagerly pressing their payment into Mark's hand to ensure that they got the fish before others beat them to it. In no time the fish were all gone, and Mark had three dollars and seventy-five cents, nearly as much as he got for a day of work in the mine. It was almost entirely in scrip, only good at the company store, but his family owed so much there, they could certainly use it.

"We should have thought of this sooner," Mark said as he counted his money. "If I can make this much money fishing each day, we just might get by until the mine's hiring again."

"Maybe you shouldn't go back to the mine. Maybe you should become a fisherman," I suggested.

He shook his head. "I don't think there are enough fish in that creek to keep this up. But maybe I could keep it up for a few months. It's good to have something like this to fall back on."

I couldn't help thinking sadly about my chickens and garden. They had been my hope for a bit extra to fall back on. I pushed away the sadness and tried to feel joy for Mark's success. Maybe eventually he'd get paid in real money instead of scrip, and I could still talk him into buying new trousers and looking for work again. I would at least ask Mr. Torentino if he'd be willing to do me one more favor.

The next afternoon, Martina was busy, so I was alone as I waited for Mr. Torentino. Once again, I met him a short distance from the store, where Mr. Johnson wouldn't see me. Once again, I saw Mr. Torentino's disgruntled expression as he left the store and came in my direction. He smiled, however, when he saw me at the side of the road and pulled the horses to a stop.

"Where is your friend?" he asked.

"She couldn't come, but I can take the boots to her," I said. He nodded and handed me a sturdy new pair of work boots.

"I was also wondering what it might cost to get us a pair of trousers. For a friend."

Mr. Torentino considered me for a long moment. "This seems to be turning into a habit, doesn't it?"

"I didn't mean for it to. But—" An idea was sparking to life in my mind, and as it formed, I let it come tumbling out. "But would it be a problem if it did?"

"Depends on who you're asking," he said with a glance up toward the store. Of course I knew what he meant. I had already experienced firsthand what Mr. Johnson did to competitors.

"But would there be anything wrong with it? I mean, it isn't illegal or anything, right?"

He smiled. "It's a free country, as they say. No, it's not illegal. What are you thinking of, anyway?"

I swallowed and told him, even though I knew the risk. "I was thinking that there are a lot of other people in camp who need things and can't afford them at Mr. Johnson's store. If I brought a list each week of what was wanted, would you bring the goods?"

"Johnson won't like that," he said, stroking his mustache, but he sounded more amused than concerned.

"It wouldn't really be competing with Mr. Johnson. If they don't buy them from you, they'll just be doing without. They can't afford to buy them from the store."

"I don't know that he'd see it that way."

"Mr. Johnson is cheating us," I said in a sudden flare of anger. "He's cheating you, too—I see how angry you are when you come out of there each week."

Mr. Torentino nodded. "That's true—some weeks I barely break even, hauling up so much that he sends back without paying for it. But what's in this for you?"

"Well, I was thinking I could add a little to the price for my services: taking orders, picking up the goods from you, and delivering them to people. It would still be cheaper than buying things at Mr. Johnson's store."

"A sound plan. If you added ten percent on everything, that would add up for you."

I nodded. "That's what I was thinking."

Mr. Torentino's bushy mustache twitched as his mouth curled into a grin. "How old are you?"

I bit my lip. Perhaps I should lie about my age, as Mark had done to get a job in the mine. But I didn't like the idea of lying when Mr. Torentino had been so good to me, so I told the truth. "Nearly fourteen, sir," I said, hoping that he wouldn't back out when he heard how young I was.

"And this was your idea?"

"Yes, sir."

"You have a good head for business. I never really considered taking on a girl as a business partner before."

I drew in a breath. I hadn't thought of it in those terms. Business partner! It sounded exciting when he put it that way.

"I'd want the money in advance," Mr. Torentino said. "I don't want to be hauling things up here for folks that have changed their minds. I already do too much of that. And it has to be cash. I can't use that worthless scrip."

"I could get the money in advance if I knew your prices."

Mr. Torentino took a pencil and a little booklet out of his pocket. "It will have to stay to the things folks aren't buying from the robber baron," he said with a nod in the direction of the store. "What goods would that be?"

"Dry goods, mostly. Buckets, washtubs, pots and pans. And school's starting soon, so plenty of mothers will be needing dress material," I said, painfully aware of my own bare legs showing below my skirt hem.

As I listed these things and more, Mr. Torentino scribbled down prices. When I finished, he handed the booklet to me.

"There are your prices. You can write down your orders in that and give it to me with the money next week."

I nodded excitedly. "Thank you!"

"Good luck, partner," Mr. Torentino called as he climbed up to his seat and started his horses with a slap of the reins.

I felt triumphant as I climbed the hill back to town. I didn't know what would come of my scheme. Maybe I could make a few dollars, maybe replace our chickens, or maybe— I stopped myself. I wasn't going to dream—I had promised myself. I wasn't going to be disappointed again.

The next day I set out to visit the neighbors I knew best. I explained that they could order things through me, that the goods would arrive a week after I put in the order and the prices would be reasonable. Everyone was interested, though many had no cash. A few people placed orders with me, however. Most families had hoarded away a little cash for emergencies, and they were willing to use it to get a bargain. Gradually over the week, my list grew. By the following Monday, I had a list of twenty items. I met Mr. Torentino and gave him my list and eighteen dollars, keeping one dollar and eighty cents for myself on my first order.

Mr. Torentino looked over the list, and I could see he was impressed. "This is a good start," he said. "Bring someone with you next week, so you can carry it all."

He tipped his hat and drove away, and I walked home jingling my money in my pocket. I hadn't told my plan to anyone in my family—I didn't want to disappoint them again—but Aneshka caught me putting my money in the can on the kitchen shelf.

"Where did you get that?" she demanded.

"Um—it's the change from going to the store this afternoon," I said. But I had hesitated too long in coming up with an explanation, and she knew it. She glared at me, demanding the truth. Holena stood in the doorway behind her.

"Let's go out to the garden," I said. I picked up a basket and we walked out to the sprawling patch of cucumbers. I bent and started picking.

"Well?" Aneshka said, her hands on her hips.

I explained the plan to her. "But you can't tell anyone!" I said as I finished.

"But we have to tell people," she protested. "How else will they know to buy from you?"

She had a point. "Mostly don't tell Momma or Mr. Johnson."

"Momma's going to notice the extra money in the can," Holena said.

"We won't put it in the can," Aneshka said. She ran into the house and returned carrying an old cigar box that she kept under our bed. It was where she kept her treasures, but she had dumped those things out and the box was empty. "We will keep it in here, and when we have enough to buy a farm, we will surprise Momma and Papa with it."

"Aneshka." I wanted to stop her before she got her hopes up again, but it was already too late for that. Hope was shining out from both girls' eyes. "This won't get us a farm. I won't be making that much money."

Aneshka wasn't listening; she was already headed back into the house to get the money from the can. I looked at Holena, hoping she would understand. She only grasped me in a hug.

"Thank you, Trina," she said.

"For what?"

"For believing in your wish again so it can finally come true."

I held her to me, filled with fear for her. What a huge responsibility my wish had become.

Chapter 19

MY NEW PLAN was the worst-kept secret in the world, thanks to Aneshka. She made sure everyone had a chance to order from me, and I think that she nagged a few of them into doing so. Nearly every day, someone would come looking for me, and I would take my little booklet and my pencil from my pocket to record his or her order. Momma could not be kept in the dark under such circumstances, but I was vague on the details of the arrangement. After all, I wasn't that sure of the plan myself. I made a few dollars the first few weeks, but since we had agreed to sell only dry goods, I doubted business would continue. After all, how often did a family need a new bucket? Besides, since I could only take cash, and the mine had been paying mainly in scrip all summer, it couldn't hold out much longer.

I tried to explain this to Aneshka so she wouldn't be disappointed, but she only accused me of giving up, so I left her alone. She and Holena would accompany me to pick up the goods and deliver them, and I let Aneshka take charge of the money, since she had designated her treasure box as our bank. She and Holena had even cut pictures of farms and advertisements for land out of Papa's newspapers and pasted them onto the box. I paid little attention. I helped them add up the total each week and determine our portion, and I kept the money that had to go to Mr. Torentino, but I left the rest to my sisters. The temptation to dream of a farm crept into my head occasionally. To resist it, I spent as much time with Mark as I could. He was at the mine asking for work every day, and occasionally they did have odd jobs for him. When they did not, he fished.

As he predicted, his catch steadily dwindled, but even so, he was doing better business than I was, since he was willing to take payment in scrip. His family was gradually paying off some of their debt and he was once again talking of all the things we would do in the future. I listened and tried to smile at his dreams, even though none of them were big enough to get us out of the coal camp. I knew he was being practical. I knew, too, that I should be—his modest plans would not hurt anyone, and yet I couldn't get rid of a growing dissatisfaction. I loved Mark as much as ever, but a hollow feeling inside me would not go away when I thought of our future together in the coal camp.

The new school term was quickly approaching, and the question of dresses plagued my mother. One Tuesday afternoon, after Momma and I had finished the ironing, Momma took down the money can and dumped its contents out on the kitchen table. She counted through it and shook her head.

"I don't know how we'll manage school dresses, with Holena starting this year."

"Mr. Torentino can sell us the cloth for less than the company store," Aneshka said.

"That may be," Momma said, "but even so . . ." She went to the small pantry cupboard and took out the stack of flour sacks she'd been saving. They were a thin cotton, but printed with pretty flower patterns. Momma sorted out those that were enough alike to go together.

"We can make Aneshka a new dress from these, and Holena can have Aneshka's school dress, with a little mending. But Trina's bursting out of that dress everywhere, and we don't have enough flour sacks for that," Momma said. "We will just have to buy fabric on credit, I suppose. I don't know what else to do."

I looked meaningfully at Aneshka, but she refused to meet my eyes, so I spoke up. "We have some money, Momma. From working for Mr. Torentino. It's in Aneshka's box."

"But that's for our farm!" Aneshka protested.

Momma raised her eyebrows and looked at me. "For a farm?"

I shook my head. "It wasn't my idea," I said.

"Yes it was! It was your wish!" Aneshka said.

"We need the money now," I insisted.

"Why, just so you can get a new dress?" Aneshka scowled at me.

"Show me this money," Momma broke in.

Aneshka could not disobey Momma, so she retrieved the box. She set it on the table and Momma opened it. I gasped at the same time Momma did when we saw the contents. I knew the money had been accumulating, but seeing it all together startled me.

Momma counted it, laying it out on the table in neat rows.

"Fourteen dollars!" she said when she finished. She looked from the money to me and back to the money with an expression of bewilderment. "How on earth did you get so much money?"

"I told you, we've been delivering goods for Mr. Torentino. From his store in Trinidad."

She frowned. "Yes, that's what you told me, but delivery girls don't make this much money. What is really going on, Trina?"

I told her the details of the business, omitting any mention of Mr. Johnson's anger that had inspired it. I had been careful to avoid him since we had started the deliveries, but word of my business had spread around camp. I was pretty sure Mr. Johnson had heard, or at least suspected. I had never told my parents of his role in destroying my previous plans, or even that he harbored a grudge against me. I saw no point in bringing that up now. Especially since I expected my mother to be angry enough with us as it was. Nervously I tried to read her mood as I explained, but her expression remained closed. She kept staring at the pile of money.

"How long have you been doing this?" she asked at last.

"Four weeks," I said.

"Four weeks," she repeated thoughtfully. "You have saved fourteen dollars in only four weeks?"

"It's been going up every week, too," Aneshka said proudly. "This week we made almost six dollars, and Trina's already taken two orders for next week."

"I had no idea," Momma said. "Who orders from you?"

"Mostly our neighbors," I said quickly. "And sometimes people find me after church."

"If we went across the tracks, we could make a lot more," Aneshka said.

I shot her a warning glance. Momma had a strict rule that my sisters and I were never to cross the tracks that ran through the middle of the coal town. The houses on the other side were exactly like our own, but we didn't mix with the Welsh and Scottish families who lived there. Even at school we avoided those children. Rumor had it, the Scots collaborated with the mine officials. They would betray union organizers or trouble-makers to the bosses. And Papa said a Welshman was at fault in the accident that had crushed Old Jan's leg, as they so often were. Even if they could be trusted, we had a hard time under-standing their English, and they ours, so it seemed best for everyone if we didn't mix.

"You mean you have made all this from only this side of town?" Momma asked.

"Mostly. It's enough for dresses, isn't it?" I said, trying to return the conversation to the safety of our original topic.

"Yes, it's certainly enough for that," Momma said, but the tone in her voice was one I didn't recognize. She turned to Aneshka with a smile. "Run along and play," she said. "We will work on dresses later. You too, Holena."

It was all too clear that, though my sisters were being dis-missed, I was not. Aneshka noticed too, and she gave me one more hard glare before taking Holena's hand and leaving the kitchen.

"Does Marek know of these plans?" Momma asked when we were alone.

"Momma, I didn't tell Aneshka to save for a farm. I haven't said anything about it—it's her idea."

"But the orders, the deal with Mr. Torentino, that was all your doing."

"Mark knows of all that. In fact, he gave me the idea," I said. "But I wasn't really doing it for the farm. I've learned my lesson about those kinds of dreams."

Momma wasn't looking at me. Her eyes were on Aneshka's box and the advertisements my sisters had pasted there. Momma couldn't read the English text, but she could certainly read the prices. When she spoke, it wasn't directed at me so much as thinking out loud.

"Fourteen dollars in just four weeks, and just on this side of town, when the mine isn't even at full production—" She paused and seemed to be adding in her head. "If we can save this much now, by the end of the year . . ."

I stared at her, my mouth open. "Do you mean—Momma, do you think by the end of the year we would have enough for something big?"

"Everyone here needs more than they can name, but we're all scrimping to get by. Come fall, when work picks up again, people will be buying more. Everyone in town is counting the days till the mine is in full production and giving out cash payments again to get what we are doing without for now. And the bachelors will be back, and they are looser with their money than families are. In another month or two your business will boom, I think."

"Enough to buy a farm?"

Momma's eyes snapped up to my face, as if the mention of a farm had startled her awake. Her expression hardened.

"You have to tell Marek of this. You know he has no interest in being a farmer. You shouldn't be thinking of a farm, either. You should be setting a share of these earnings aside to set up a household when you marry. Whatever plans you are making, you should be making them with him."

"But—" I felt a knot tightening in my gut again, the same knot that had been there ever since the accident at the mine. I swallowed hard.

"But what? What's the matter, Trina? You should be happy to share this with Marek. He has so many good, solid ideas you can start working on together. Go on and tell him now, why don't you."

I nodded and stepped outside into the street. I couldn't tell her what I was thinking—that I had only promised myself to Mark because I thought a farm was impossible. I hated myself now for even thinking it. I loved Mark. But I had seen my mother's expression as she looked at those ads and calculated. I had seen hope. And if even Momma thought we might be able to get out of the coal camp, how could I turn my back on that? How could I bear spending money to build something here with Mark when it could have been enough for my family to get our farm?

At Mark's house, Old Jan was stumping around the kitchen, helping Martina wash and put away dishes. He smiled at me, offering a cup of coffee from the pot simmering on the back of the stove.

"Is Mark here?" I asked.

"He's out walking. He's determined to have that foot strong by the time the mine's hiring again." He set the cup of coffee on the table before me, but I stood chewing my lip, trying to decide if I should go after him.

Old Jan raised his eyebrows. "You look like you have heavy matters on your shoulders, child."

I nodded. "I have a lot to think about."

"Can I help?"

I sighed and sat down at the table. How could I explain it to him? "Have you ever wanted something so much that even after you know you can't have it, you still can't stop thinking about it?"

He smiled and nodded. "Once hope has a hold on you, it doesn't want to let go. I think that's for the best, don't you? Where would any of us be if hope abandoned us?"

"Hope did abandon me," I said, remembering the terrible weeks after the accident when I had lost so much.

"Did it?" he asked. "Or did you abandon it?"

"I don't know what you mean."

He smiled. "Do you know the story of the boy betrothed to the frog?"

"I'm a little too old for such stories," I pointed out. My problems were real-world matters now; I didn't need more fairy tales in my head. "I'm almost a woman."

"So you are," Jan said. "But no one's ever too old for the lessons. We are always still young enough to learn."

Martina poured herself a cup of coffee, and one for Jan, and sat down beside us. "And I'm not too old to want to listen, if it means sitting down for a few minutes," she said. So Old Jan began his story.

"There once was a man with one small farm and three sons, and he did not know which of them should get his farm. So he sent his sons into the world to find a bride.

"'Whoever returns with the finest betrothal ring, he shall have the farm,' the father decreed.

"So the three sons set out, each in a different direction. The two older brothers traveled the road, and it was left to the youngest to clamber through the forest. The boy traveled a full day without meeting another person, and he was about to give up entirely when an ugly toad jumped onto a log in front of him and spoke.

"'What are you doing so deep in the forest, boy?' the toad asked.

"'I am seeking a bride who will make me the betrothal gift of a ring,' the boy answered.

"'I have a daughter who will gladly marry you, and she has a fine betrothal ring for you,' the toad said.

"The boy was too kind to reject the ugly creature, so he followed her to her home, a rough cave, and the toad called in to her daughter to come out. The creature that emerged from the cave was the ugliest thing the boy had ever seen. Splay legged, bulgy eyed, and covered in crusty warts."

I couldn't resist a little shiver, and Old Jan smiled.

"But the ugly creature had with her a small chest and told the boy, 'If you will accept a betrothal gift from me, you may choose it yourself from these.'

"She opened the chest to reveal the most costly and beautiful rings the boy had ever seen! Not wishing to be greedy, the boy took the least valuable, but the toad mother protested and insisted he take the finest ring in the box—a perfect diamond the size of a robin's egg.

"Well, of course the boy had high hopes of getting the farm, as you once did, Trina. When the boy returned home with his gift, his brothers were already there, so his father called them all to show the rings they had received. The first brother had a small copper ring, worth only a few pennies. The second had a ring of poor silver, worth only a bit more. But when the father saw the fine ring the youngest son brought, he was sure the boy had stolen it. So he beat the boy and told him he must return it to its owner. Then he set a new challenge to his sons: They must each find a girl who would give them a fine embroidered handkerchief. The brother who brought back the finest would inherit the farm.

"Once again, the youngest son set out through the woods,

this time in a different direction, but once again, he encountered the toad. Though he tried to get around it, he was soon on his way to meet her daughter, who produced the finest silk handkerchief he had ever seen.

"Once again, the boy returned home hopeful, and once again, though he had the finest gift, he received a punishment instead of the farm."

"So the moral is, no matter how you try, you cannot succeed?" I asked bitterly.

"So it might seem," Old Jan said. "But let me finish, because the father sent the three boys out a third time. 'Produce the girls who have given you these gifts and whoever has the loveliest bride shall inherit the farm,' he said.

"Now the youngest son was truly wretched. For while his bride had fine gifts for him, he could not bear to bring the ugly toad before his father. So he chose once again to go in a different direction, hoping against hope to avoid the toads. But much to his dismay, the mother toad found him and begged him to come to her house. So the boy went, and told them what his father had decreed. Still the boy hoped to save himself, and to spare their feelings. So he said, 'I am too tired to return tonight. Let me sleep the night here, and tomorrow we will venture to my father's house,' for he planned to sneak away in the night.

"He lay down to sleep on the stone floor of the cave, and surprisingly enough, fell into a deep, dreamless sleep. It was full light when he woke the next day, and he looked around amazed, for he was no longer in a cave, but in a stately palace. He left his room and wandered to the great hall, where a graceful queen awaited him.

"'You have broken the enchantment!' she told him. 'I am the queen of this land, laid under a curse by a jealous sorcerer.

We were doomed to be toads until a good man would promise to marry my daughter and stay the night to seal the pact. And now, behold your bride.'

"The most beautiful princess ever seen—who, of course, had been the ugliest toad—stepped forward from the shadows and took the boy's hand, and they were married right then and there. And though the boy did return to his father with the most beautiful bride, he did not need his father's farm. For he was now prince of a fine kingdom, where he ruled happily for many a long year."

"It is a fine story," I said. "And what is the lesson?"

"Well, the lesson is whatever you take from it. But it seems to me that the boy was much like you. He thought his efforts had failed again and again, but he didn't give up. And because things once started had a course of their own, good came of it all in the end, even when the end wasn't the one he'd expected. He set out in a different direction each day, but the important thing is that he kept setting out."

"The problem is, I set out in a different direction, and now I don't know which direction is the right one," I said.

"No one can tell you which is right for you, child," Old Jan said, patting me on the back kindly. "But maybe you'll have the luck of the boy in the story and discover that all directions lead to success. Sometimes things have a way of working themselves out."

I nodded and sighed. "I hope you are right."

He looked past me out the open kitchen door and smiled. "Here is my Marek. I'll leave the two of you to talk, shall I?" He picked up a bucket and set off toward the creek.

I greeted Mark on the porch so we could talk and wouldn't be in Martina's way in the cramped kitchen. He smiled when

191

he saw me, and the smile warmed me deep inside. It felt good to be near him, and to know I could make him happy just by being here.

"I'm glad to see you, Trina. I've got good news!"

"Tell me," I said, happy enough not to have to say what I had come for.

"On my walk today I passed by the mine office and the superintendent was there. He noticed how much better I was walking, and he said he thought they could hire me back on, come fall."

"That is good news," I said.

He nodded, still grinning. "And they'll be hiring again soon. Once I'm back to work, Martina and Karel can move back to their own place. And once we've paid off some of our debt, maybe Papa and I can move to a better house, plant a garden, buy some new chickens. What do you think?"

I hugged him and told him it was a good plan, and then I let him talk about all his plans and hopes. I couldn't bear to tell him I had money now to start building that dream. And I certainly didn't want to undermine his happiness by bringing up the possibility of getting a farm.

When I left his house a short time later, my feet took me to the quiet pool by the creek seemingly on their own. I settled myself in the shade under the tree to think. I thought back over recent months and my new business plan. Old Jan was right. Hope for a farm had never really died in my heart. It had always been there, compelling me to set out once again. I had tried to deny it—had denied it to Holena and Aneshka—but it had lingered all the same. My heart was still looking for the other path. But I loved Mark, too, and I didn't want to break my promise to him. And so many things could still stand between us and the farm. I was scared to hope—but scared not to.

"You tell me what to do," I said to the pool, but I saw no sign of the fish. I was apparently on my own for the hard decisions. I thought again about the box under Aneshka's bed and my mother's reaction to our savings. Of everything that had happened, that seemed the most magical of all. It seemed I had made a wish that would come to fruition whether I was still trying or not—it was going to keep jumping out in front of me like that toad in the story. The question was, was that a blessing or a curse? A chance, or another disappointment? And what was I going to tell Mark? It was mid-September. If the schoolmaster wasn't coming until October, we had two weeks yet before school started, and probably about two weeks before the mine would be hiring again.

"All right," I said to the pool. "All right, I will give this two more weeks. I will try selling on the other side of the tracks. If it doesn't work out, I'm done with you and your wish."

A leaf fluttered down to the surface of the pool and I watched, strangely expectant, as it spun slowly across the surface. I saw no sign of the fish.

It didn't matter, I decided, as I climbed the slope and walked home. I had made a decision, whether the fish had heard my bargain or not. Two weeks. I couldn't wait forever for a dream—not when I seemed to have promised that same forever to Mark, and I was going to have to choose.

Chapter 20

THE NEXT DAY, I asked my mother if I could go across the tracks and take orders in the Welsh and Scottish districts. Momma consented, as long as my sisters and I went together and stayed together. She needn't have worried. After having been warned to stay on our own side for so long, it felt strange and daring to step across the tracks and walk down the streets that had for so long been forbidden.

In truth, this part of town looked no different from ours, with ragged children and tired women on the streets and doorsteps. But the refrains of Welsh and Scottish and the flashes of red hair among the children made it all feel foreign.

My sisters and I were too shy to knock on doors. We only approached women in the street or called out to those on their porches. We had little luck. Several old women who were mending together on one porch just stared at us and spoke secretively to each other in Welsh. Another shooed us away, mistaking us for beggars. My heart sank. My mother had reawakened my hope for nothing.

We were about to give up when we saw several young women in the street ahead of us. They were a cheerful group, laughing over their gossip, so we decided to give it one more try.

"Are you in need of anything I could order for you, ladies? I can get things delivered for much lower prices than the store," I said politely.

The tallest, and apparently oldest, of the women looked suspiciously at me. "Can you?"

"Oh, she's that Polish lass we've heard about," said a second, younger woman. Her curly hair was escaping from her loose bun and playing in ringlets around her face.

"Czechy, actually," I said, taking my order book from my pocket. "Is there anything you need?"

"Are your prices really that good? How much for, say, a bag of flour?"

"I only sell dry goods, I'm afraid."

"A yard of dress fabric, then?"

"Three cents a yard," I answered.

"That is much better than the store," the first woman said, considering.

"How many yards do you need, then? And I will need payment in advance."

"Actually, I was thinking of the Llewellyns. They need all the help they can get right now," said the curly-haired one.

"Oh, aye, Glenys," agreed the older woman. "His old parents— eleven children, including a wee babe, and she's laid up with the gout. And there's something wrong with that poor baby. Oh, aye, they need all the help they can get. Go see them, lass, last house down that way."

"Here, I'll show you," said curly-haired Glenys. She led the way down the street to the very last house. It was a decrepit structure, the yard cluttered with old cans and slats from a broken-down picket fence. Two little boys were shouting and chasing a skinny yellow dog through the yard. The steps creaked threateningly as our new guide climbed onto the porch and knocked on the door. A small, pale, blue-eyed child opened it. Though she was about Aneshka's age, I could not recall ever seeing her in school.

Holena gripped my hand tightly as we entered the dimly lit kitchen. Aneshka crowded close as well, and I couldn't blame her. The smells of dirty laundry and urine were overpowering, and I fought the urge to pinch my nose. At the stove an old woman stirred a pot while a thin, naked toddler pulled on her skirts and whimpered. Dirty dishes were piled on the table, crawling with flies. From the bedroom came the high, sharp wail of a baby.

Glenys said something in Welsh to the old woman at the stove. She smiled toothlessly at us and waved her spoon toward the bedroom. There we met the lady of the house, a woman about the same age as our mother, but far more worn. Her blond hair was streaked with gray. Strands of it had escaped her bun and hung limp in her face, as if even they had given up hope. She was trying to get the fussy baby to nurse, but the baby kept throwing his head back and wailing.

"Nancy, I've brought some girls here to help you out," said Glenys.

The mother frowned. She turned the baby up over her shoulder and started thumping its back.

"I can't afford to hire help," she said.

"This is that Polish — er, sorry — Bohemian lass that gets goods for cheap."

Nancy looked at me again, a bit of hope in her eyes. "Can you now? Can you get me flour, oats, and potatoes to feed me wee ones? I'd be grateful."

"I'm sorry, I can't get food, only dry goods. But I can get shoes or clothes for your children."

"What good are shoes for them if I can't feed them," she said.

I could see her point. "Maybe I could get you flour or oats," I said. Mr. Johnson wouldn't be hurt if we broke that rule just once. "I think it would be about fifteen cents for a sack of flour, and about the same for oats. I have to have the money in advance, though."

Nancy's face fell. "Could you give me credit? Come fall when the mine's back to full production, I could pay you then."

Before I could answer, Aneshka spoke up.

"No credit," she said firmly. "The man who brings it demands his pay in advance."

Nancy bit her lip and shifted the still-crying baby. "We could pay you next week in scrip. Just as soon as my husband and son collect their pay."

I frowned. I was thinking that perhaps we could take scrip, just this once, but Aneshka shook her head and said "Cash only!" before I could respond.

Nancy nodded, her face grimly resigned. "Thank you anyway."

She laid the squalling baby in a worn cradle and limped into the front room of the house, where the old lady was dishing up bowls of thin gruel and handing them to the crowd of children.

Seeing we'd make no sale here, we retreated quickly. We walked in silence up the street with Glenys.

"What's wrong with that baby?" Aneshka asked.

Glenys shrugged and shook her head. "The doctor can't say. He won't nurse proper. He can eat a little gruel made real thin, is all. Poor wee thing." She shook her head again.

"I am sorry," I said. "I wish there was something I could do."

"I don't think you're that sorry, lass," Glenys said. "It's the same with everyone in America. Money first; nothing else matters much here." She turned and walked up the path to her own front door, not saying good-bye to us. I felt a rush of shame.

"Maybe we should give her goods on credit," I said. "Just this once."

Aneshka scowled at me. "If we start giving people things they haven't paid for, how are we going to save enough for a farm?"

"But they will pay later," I said.

Aneshka snorted. "They are never going to have the money. You saw that house."

"I wish there was some way to help them," Holena said quietly, slipping her hand into mine again at the memory of the house.

I wished it too, but I could see Aneshka's point. Since I had surrendered control of the money to her, I would have to convince her otherwise if I wanted to spend any money from the box.

We walked on in silence, crossing the railroad tracks and continuing toward home. There we helped Momma with supper. Aneshka and Holena laid the table while I rolled the dumplings and sliced cucumbers. I was quiet as I worked. I was still thinking of the poor family, but there was more to consider. We had made no sales on our trip across town, and we weren't likely to, even if we went back. Momma had been wrong; my business wasn't going to grow. I was glad now that I hadn't said anything about the money or the new plans for a farm to Mark, glad I hadn't disappointed him for nothing. Glad I had his happiness as a refuge.

Old Jan, Mark, and Martina arrived after supper, just as we finished washing up. We went out onto the porch, where a hint of breeze cooled the sweat on my brow. Mark smiled at me and I smiled back, despite the tangle of feelings inside me. He still had a dream, at least, and I felt lucky that he had made room in it for me. After seeing the poor Llewellyn family, I could see just how lucky we all were, despite our disappointments. I watched my sisters, fed and clothed, settling on the porch at Old Jan's feet, and an idea came to me.

"Old Jan, would you tell us a story?" I said. At once Aneshka and Holena added their voices to the request, as I knew they would.

Old Jan looked at me, his eyebrows raised. "Aren't you getting a little old for stories, Trina? After all, you're nearly a woman."

I smiled back. "We're never too old for the lessons," I said.

Papa smiled. "My Trina's becoming a philosopher," he said.

"What story would you like?" Old Jan said.

"A princess story!" Aneshka said, as she always did.

"I like animals," Holena said.

"How about the one about the boy betrothed to a toad?" I suggested. "It has a princess and animals."

"Ewww!" Aneshka said, and both my sisters giggled. "Who would want to marry a toad?"

"Exactly what the boy thought," Old Jan said, and he began the story.

"That's a fine story," Momma said when he finished.

"And what is the lesson?" Mark asked, smiling at me. "Am I your ugly toad, Trina?"

"Of course not," I said. "The lesson is, goodness will be rewarded. If the boy hadn't been so kind and charitable toward the toads, he would have ended up with nothing. But his charity brought a great reward in the end."

"That is a good lesson, indeed," Old Jan said. "Trina *is* becoming a philosopher."

I glanced at Aneshka. She was chewing on her lip thoughtfully. I took the opportunity to raise an idea to my mother. I told her of our visit that day, of the squalid house, the poor family, and the thin gruel they ate for their dinner.

"May we take them some cucumbers?" I suggested. "I don't think they had anything good to eat. And I was thinking that tomorrow if you don't need the tubs, we could go do some washing for them. With that baby, I don't think the mother has been able to keep up. Plus, she's got the gout."

Momma's eyebrows raised. "And what do you plan to charge them for your help?"

"Nothing. They can't afford it. I just want to be charitable."

Aneshka gave a little "hmph" in her throat, but Momma smiled.

"Of course you may help them. I am glad to see there is charity in your heart, Trina, and not just the desire for money," she said. "You will find that good deeds are their own reward."

"And I'll help," Holena said. "Will you help too, Aneshka?"

Everyone looked at Aneshka. She scowled at me, but agreed.

Old Jan smiled. "And good will come of it, too. Wait and see. Good always comes from good, one way or another."

The next morning, when our chores were finished, we set out once again across the tracks, carrying our washtubs between us.

When we reached the Welsh district, Glenys was outside, sweeping her porch.

"Where are you going with that?" she called out.

I told her of our plan.

"Bless you! Wait a minute," she said, and disappeared into her house. She reappeared a moment later with a tub of her own and a loaf of bread. She accompanied us through the streets, calling out to her neighbors in Welsh when she saw them. By the time we arrived at the Llewellyn house, we had two women with us and others collecting their things to come along.

I had never imagined that laundry could be as fun as it was that day. We built fires and heated tubs of water in the yard behind the house. The women who knew the family best worked together to carry the laundry out of the house. They laughed and joked as they scrubbed and rinsed and hung the clothes in the sunshine. Soon Aneshka, Holena, and I had joined in their jokes, just like family. Nancy's children helped by toting water or keeping their little siblings out from underfoot. We had the laundry done in no time, so we washed the dishes and swept out the house. When the work was finally done and the women were all leaving in chatty groups, I gave Nancy the cucumbers I had picked that morning.

"For your family," I said.

Tears rose in Nancy's eyes. "How can I thank you?" she said.

"No need," I replied.

"And about your order," Aneshka suddenly said, surprising me. "We could do a little on credit. A bag of potatoes, maybe? Or a bag of flour?"

"Potatoes," Nancy said at once. I wrote it down on my pad, feeling so proud of my little sister I thought I'd burst.

I delivered the week's orders to Mr. Torentino, including the sack of potatoes for Nancy. I was nervous that he might not agree to bring them, but I explained the situation to him. My new partner was a good man with a good heart. He agreed to bring the potatoes, suggesting that he might be able to throw in a sack of flour, as well.

I walked home, content in my heart. Momma had been right; good deeds were their own reward.

Chapter 21

I HAD ASKED Old Jan to tell the story of the boy and the toad to convince Aneshka that we should help the poor family we had met. I had not expected a rich reward for doing so. After all, Nancy Llewellyn was a miner's wife, not an enchanted princess. But perhaps the old stories had more magic in them than I realized, or perhaps their wisdom was eternal, because right away good things began to happen.

Good news came just after supper on the very next evening, when Old Jan arrived for his usual visit. Since Mark had been hurt and Karel had married, he was often accompanied by Martina and Mark when he arrived, but this evening, Mark was not with him. Old Jan was grinning from ear to ear, so we did not have to wait long to learn where Mark was.

"Our worries are over!" Old Jan announced. "The steel mill in Pueblo got a contract for a new rail line, and they are firing up the smelters. The mine's going back into full production!"

"Already?" Momma said.

"Several weeks early," Old Jan said. "No more worries about layoffs. They're looking for men to hire. They've already put my Marek on the night shift. He's at work right now. We'll all soon be back on our feet again, and Karel and Martina can get a proper place of their own."

"That is good news," Momma agreed.

"I hope that means they'll be paying with cash again soon," Papa said.

"And that the bachelors will be coming back to the camp too," Momma said with a smile. "With their laundry."

"And their orders," Aneshka said, her eyes glowing with an ambition bordering on greed.

Papa laughed and tousled her hair. "You see? Our worries are over!"

I couldn't quite see it as Papa did, although I knew I should. Hard times were easing up, but it also meant one more person I loved in the mine. In harm's way.

News spread fast through camp, and the very next day, I began to see its effect in another bit of luck. I was in the hot kitchen with a hot iron, trying to press the wrinkles from Papa's collars, when someone knocked on the open kitchen door. I looked up to see Glenys and her friend who had first sent us to the Llewellyn house. They were both smiling.

"How much did you say for a yard of fabric?" Glenys asked.

I told her again, and she pulled money from her pocket at once. "I have two girls in school this year," she said, "and at that price they can both have new dresses."

"Mine too," agreed her companion. "I could use a new coffee-pot. What else do you sell?"

Before they had gone, I had taken down orders and collected money for a long list of goods, and my new customers left chatting cheerfully in Welsh. Half an hour later it happened again — and again. In fact, for an hour or so in the early afternoon, I had a small crowd of women waiting with their money in hand to place their orders. Some of them I had met at the wash party, but many I had not. Word of my good deed or my good prices had spread through the other side of town. Now that the mine had announced more work and, as my father had hoped, cash payment, purse strings were loosening. It was just as Momma had predicted; people had been waiting for better times. With those times in sight, they weren't waiting another minute. They were spending the money they had, knowing more was on the way, and they were getting the things they had been doing without. And because of my good deed in the Welsh district, they were trusting me to get those things for them. By the time I had a break and could empty my pockets into Aneshka's eager hands, my apron was sagging under the weight of the coins I carried. That evening, Aneshka piled the day's earnings on the kitchen table and counted it out as my whole family watched.

"One hundred and twenty-one dollars!" she announced in an awed whisper.

"And twenty-seven cents," Holena added.

We gathered around it, my sisters stroking the coins lovingly. None of us, except perhaps Papa, had seen so much money in one place before.

"That's twelve dollars for us," I said, "in one day!"

"It's a miracle," Momma whispered.

None of us slept well that night. We had tied the money in a sack and placed it under the mattress for safekeeping, but the excitement of it was enough to keep us all awake.

The excitement was not over, however. The next morning, the wife of a Scottish crew foreman appeared on our doorstep with money in hand. Through her husband, who supervised a crew of Italians and Greeks, word spread to the remaining corners of camp. Our house was a hub of activity for the rest of the week. By the following Monday, I had more than eight hundred dollars to give Mr. Torentino, and an answer to my two-week bargain with my wish. One hundred dollars was tucked away at home. A farm of our own seemed possible once again.

My sisters and I were eager to see Mr. Torentino that afternoon, anxious to hand over the large sum of money I had for him. When he arrived at last, I quickly thrust the orders and the money at him.

His eyes grew wide when he saw how much I had. "All this is from this camp?"

I had expected him to be as pleased as I was with all the business, but he looked worried.

"What's wrong?" I asked.

"It's so much. I don't know if I can fit it into my wagon with all that I have to bring to the store. I would have to raise the prices if I had to bring up a second wagon. But never mind." He brightened and smiled at me. "You're quite a salesman. Maybe someday you'll have his job," he said, pointing over his shoulder toward the store. "And believe me, there's none of us who wouldn't be glad to see him go. Now, let's get these things unloaded."

Together we took all the goods from the previous week's order out of the wagon. It was nearly more than we could carry.

"It's too heavy," Aneshka complained as I handed her a crate.

"Well, we have to get it home—we can't leave half of it sitting here to make two trips."

"You better get a plan in place for next week," Mr. Torentino said. "You'll have to have plenty of help for that order!"

He was right, of course, but at the moment I could think only of getting our current load home. We usually cut through an open field of weeds to avoid passing Mr. Johnson's store. But the ground there was uneven and the tangles of tansy and bindweed made tripping easier than walking. Since we had so much to carry, we decided to stay on the road and walk past the store, just this once. And though we had had exceptional luck that summer, it did not seem to be with us then. While we were passing the store, Mr. Johnson stepped out onto his porch. His face registered surprise, then malice when he saw us.

"Where did you get all that?" he demanded.

"It's ours," I said, and picked up the pace.

Mr. Johnson said nothing more, but Holena looked back just before his store disappeared from view. "He's still watching us," she said.

"He can't do anything. Mr. Torentino says everything we're doing is legal." I tried to sound more confident than I actually felt. I did not want to alarm my sisters. I waited until they were out playing that afternoon before I found a better hiding place for our savings. Afterward, I told them it was hidden, but didn't tell them where. The fewer people who knew, the safer it was. I figured if Mr. Johnson could not find our money, he could not hurt us.

Orders were still pouring in that next week, and I turned my attention away from Mr. Johnson and toward the problem of delivering so much. Even if I got the help of my mother and Martina, we could not carry it all up the hill in one load. We could have asked another neighbor, but I was hesitant to introduce more people to Mr. Torentino. I didn't want anyone else to see how the business worked or to negotiate with Mr. Torentino directly. He had called me his partner, but I wasn't sure that he had any particular loyalty to me. If people found out they could buy directly from Mr. Torentino without paying my ten percent, they would surely do so.

I decided the best way to handle the larger delivery of the next week was to ask those who had placed orders to come directly to the field where I unloaded from the wagon, but not until after Mr. Torentino had gone. Then they could each carry their own order up the hill. Aneshka and Holena agreed it was a good plan. We each took a portion of the names on our order list and spread the word to meet us Monday afternoon at the designated place.

By Saturday afternoon, I thought that nothing could ever go wrong again. Our lives seemed charmed at last. I did not hesitate for a minute when Mark asked me to take a walk with him that evening. He said he had something to show me. My heart sang as we set off up the road, hand in hand.

We walked past his house and on toward the edge of town. We were out of the Bohemian area now, into a group of houses occupied almost entirely by Greeks. I was increasingly curious of what he might be planning to show me that required us to come here. At last we came to an empty house on the very edge of the camp, its back door opening out onto a steep, treeless ridge.

"We will rent this," he announced proudly. I looked at the house, then at him. He had an expectant look on his face, as if I was supposed to understand something. I turned back to the house, looking again, trying to see what was special about it. As far as I could tell, it was just like every other house in town.

"Why here?" I said at last.

"Don't you see?" he said, wrapping an arm around my waist

as we looked together at the little house. "There's a whole empty hillside behind it. We could move the chicken coop here and plant a garden twice the size of what you had. When we have the money, we can buy a goat or even a cow. There's plenty of hillside where we can keep it. With his new leg, Papa could take a goat or a cow up the hill each day to pasture. It would be good for him."

"That's a nice idea, Mark, but that's all still years away. I'm not old enough to get married yet, and you don't have the money to do any of this now. This house will be rented to someone else long before we are ready for any of that."

"It doesn't have to be, Trina. We can start before we are married. Karel and Martina want to be on their own anyway, so they are going to stay in our house, and Papa and I are going to move here. We can move the chicken coop and get chickens right away. We can't plant the garden until next spring, but you can come over and help Papa start preparing the ground for the garden patch. We can go by the mine dump on Sundays and look for more fencing, to keep the dogs and the goat out of the garden, but if we can't find any, we can always buy that, too. I've seen it in the Sears and Roebuck catalog. What do you think? I'll go tomorrow to the mine office and rent this place."

"But how are you going to do all this now? You've only been back to work for a week, and you have back rent to pay off first."

"We'll do it with the money you've saved. Everyone knows you've been making money on your deliveries. Why should we wait? This is exactly the opportunity that we need!"

I pulled out of his embrace. "My money! But it's not my money—it's my family's. We can't spend it on this."

"But your mother told me you were setting it aside for us,

for our future. After all, it's your delivery business; you do all the work. Your momma's very proud of you for building such a good dowry."

"Mark, it's not my dowry. It's for —" I stopped myself.

"For what?"

I took a deep breath. "It's for my family. Don't you see? We came to America so my father could own land."

"A farm, you mean," Mark said, his voice hardening.

I nodded. "A farm. And this is the first time we've saved any money at all since we came here. This is our chance to get what we really want — what we came to America for. This is our chance to get out of the coal camp for good!"

"Not we. You. You know I want nothing to do with a farm."

"Aneshka and Holena are counting on a farm," I said.

"And what about me? About us? You made a promise to me, and I've been counting on that."

"I can't crush their dreams, and my father's dreams, by spending that money on anything that would trap us here in the coal camp."

"Is that how you see your promise to me? As a trap?"

I hesitated, unable to look him in the eye.

"You said you would stay forever," he said, his voice full of bitterness.

"I can't, Mark."

"Can't? Or won't?"

I bit my lip. I wasn't sure myself.

"You lied to me," he said.

I shook my head. "I didn't. But when I promised myself to you, I thought there was no chance of a farm. Things have changed."

"Nothing's changed for me."

"Don't you want to get out of here? Come with us! Come help my papa on our farm—a real farm away from here. Your papa can come too!"

"I won't be a farmer."

"Just to get out of here. Then you can go to high school, or get a job in town, or—"

He shook his head. "I've got a job now, a real job, to support *us* like *we* planned, you and me. Like we promised each other."

"Try to understand, Mark. You know this has always been my dream."

"If this has always been your dream, Trina," Mark said, his voice shaking with anger, "what have I been to you?"

I hesitated, trying to sort out the confusion of disappointment, hope, and pain in my heart.

He took another step away, misinterpreting my silence. "Never mind. I think I'd rather not know. Go on, then. Get your farm. Find yourself a nice farm boy." He spat out the last words with such anger that it seemed to scorch the air between us.

"I don't want a farm boy!" I insisted.

"But you sure don't want a coal miner."

I put my hand on his arm, trying to stop the widening gap between us. "But don't you see? You don't have to be a coal miner. I want you, Mark, but I want to get out of here too. This is our chance! What about your dreams?"

At that he jerked back and pulled his arm from my grasp, as if I had been a wasp and stung him. "This is my dream, having all this with you. But you never wanted any of it, did you? You never wanted me. So, I know it's not much more than a piece of trash, but if you'll give me back my ring, I'll be out of your way."

"Mark—"

"My ring, please," he said, holding out his hand.

Tears were stinging my eyes, but I blinked them away angrily and pulled the copper band from my finger. He put it in his pocket and pulled out the smooth pebble I had given him. I refused to take it back, so he dropped it in the dirt before me. I stared at it as he walked away. No longer shining with the creek's water, it looked dull and worthless, just the way I felt.

Chapter 22

I FORCED my thoughts back to the farm that was nearly within reach. That was what I had really wanted all along, I told myself. But inside I felt my heart going as dry and dull as the pebble in the dust.

I did not tell my mother what had happened, but it wasn't long before she knew. Her anger and disappointment were thick in the air at home all the next week as I went about my chores and my orders. By the end of the workweek on Saturday, my sales were nearly equal to the week before. I set off to church on Sunday, hoping to push my total a little higher. Sure enough, women found me in the crowd outside after church, their money in hand. I wanted to keep my attention diverted from Mark, so I paid no attention to anything but the orders. I was surprised by my mother's question at the dinner table a short time later.

"How long has Mr. Johnson been watching you like that, Trina?" she asked.

I stiffened. "Mr. Johnson was watching me?"

"After church, when you were taking orders."

I felt a chill go through me, but I tried to hide it. "Mr. Johnson is afraid of competition," I said. "That is why I have to be careful and only sell dry goods. Most of his business is in food."

Momma frowned. "I don't like it. Don't cross him, Trina. He's trouble."

"I haven't. There's nothing wrong with what I'm doing. It's perfectly legal, and I've been careful to keep away from him."

"You worry too much, Ivana," Papa said to Momma, casting a quick smile to me. "What harm can Mr. Johnson do us? Trina's making so much money now, we'll be out of here in a few months' time. It won't matter one whit what some shopkeeper thinks of her."

I felt a pang of guilt. I wanted to agree with Papa, but I knew that Mr. Johnson could cause us harm, that he had already done so. When dinner was over, I went as soon as I could and checked our hidden money. I would have to be careful no one knew where it was. And I would be more careful to take and deliver orders out of Mr. Johnson's sight.

I didn't have to deliver orders forever. As Papa had said, only a few more months and we would have enough money saved. We could leave here for good, and never worry about Mr. Johnson again. I reminded myself, too, that he had known of my garden and chickens for weeks before he had found a way to destroy them. I had time.

The following day was laundry day, but since we only had our own to do, I carried water from the creek, and we did the job at home. That way, we did not leave the house unguarded. I was hanging the last basket of clothes on the line beside the house when I looked up to see my father approaching, though

214

it was only midmorning. The only reason I knew why a miner would be home so early was because he was hurt—but though my heart skipped a beat at the thought, I knew immediately it could not be true. Papa wasn't even dirty; he didn't appear to have been in the mine at all that day.

Curious, I went in the back door, just as he went in the front.

Momma and my sisters were in the kitchen, kneading bread dough. Momma looked up in alarm when Papa stepped in and set his lunch pail, still full, on the counter by the sink.

"What on earth? Are you hurt?" Momma asked, echoing our constant fear as she hurriedly pulled out a chair for him.

Papa flopped down into the chair. "I've been fired, Ivana," he said quietly.

There was a moment of silence as we all stared open-mouthed at him. Momma shooed my sisters outside to play before she spoke again.

"I thought they were going to full production. I thought they were hiring more men," Momma said.

Papa nodded. "I've been fired. Not laid off, but fired."

"But—why?"

Papa glanced up at me and I knew I had misjudged Mr. Johnson's malice, and his power.

"When I arrived at work this morning the foreman told me the bosses wanted to talk to me. I was to go to the super-intendent's office. The superintendent was waiting for me with two Pinkerton detectives, as well as the mine officials. They asked me all kinds of questions about the union—was I an organizer, had I been talking to the other men? Where were we holding our secret meetings?"

"But you're not involved in any of that!" Momma said.

"I'm not, but I couldn't convince them of that," Papa said. "They said they knew I had been organizing, that I had a gathering after the funerals that they figure was a union meeting. And they said I had organized a network to smuggle goods into camp. They've seen people from all over camp coming in and out of our house, even the Welsh and Scottish from across the tracks. They figure the only reason we would mingle is to unionize. They said they wouldn't tolerate such 'subversive labor practices.' That's when they gave me my back pay and told me I would have to leave."

Momma looked at Papa, then at me, then back at Papa. Papa nodded.

"But what I'm doing isn't illegal!" I insisted again. "They can't do this!"

Papa shook his head. "It doesn't matter whether it's legal or not to them. They can fire or hire as they see fit. They don't have to put up with anyone who does something they don't like."

"But it has nothing to do with the unions or with your job," I said. "This was Mr. Johnson's doing. He's hated me since we bought those plums. He killed my chickens, and now he's lied to get you fired. It's not fair!"

"What do you mean, he killed your chickens?" Papa asked. Shamefaced, I told them everything I knew.

Anger flared in Momma's eyes. "Why didn't you say any of this before, Trina? You knew he could be dangerous. Why haven't you been more careful?"

"She couldn't have known, Ivana. She couldn't know he would go to the superintendent with lies."

"Well, know or not, you still have to make this right, Trina. You will go to the superintendent and apologize to the company.

Tell them your father had nothing to do with it so they will take him back! Promise to stop your little business right here and now!"

"I can't do that," I said. "My biggest order yet is coming this afternoon, and people have already paid for it. I have to pick up and make these deliveries. But Papa, with this week's orders we have nearly one hundred and eighty dollars saved! We don't need their job, right?"

Papa smiled at me, but it was a sad smile. "That's not enough for a farm, Trina. And with autumn already upon us, we wouldn't have a cent left come spring to buy seed, even if we did get a farm for so little. But it is a good cushion while I find other work, and that's a lucky thing. Run on about your business now, and let your momma and me sort out what we are going to do."

My heart was heavy as I walked down the hill with my sisters to meet Mr. Torentino that afternoon. Though Aneshka and Holena didn't know everything, they knew enough to be quiet on our walk. They each walked close, burrowing their hands into mine. At least I would have this one last order to deliver, and maybe Mr. Torentino would know of someplace that would have work for my papa. Or maybe Papa was wrong, and we *could* somehow get a farm with the money that we had. I could not bear the crushing disappointment of failure now, so I pretended to myself that all would become right when I saw Mr. Torentino.

I arrived at our usual meeting place a little early. I wanted to be sure to get there while he was still unloading Mr. Johnson's goods. But when I squinted up the road toward the store, I did not see his wagon. A hint of foreboding stirred within me. Mr. Torentino should have already been there, unloading or wrangling with Mr. Johnson about unkept promises, as he did every week.

Perhaps, because my order was so large this week, Mr. Torentino ran late loading it in Trinidad. Or maybe his team plodded up the hills toward our town more slowly than usual because of the extra weight in the wagon. I looked down the road in the other direction, but saw no sign of him coming. I began to pace nervously.

I was so unnerved by Mr. Torentino's absence that I forgot that I had arranged for the ladies who had placed orders to meet me, until the first of them appeared. I should have been completely unloaded and had their goods waiting for them long since. When I saw them and realized how late it was, hope died in my heart.

"I'm afraid my partner from town is running late today," I said as they gathered around me with questions. What else could I say? "But I'm sure he will be along. He's usually very punctual."

We waited there for another half an hour. With each minute that ticked by, more women arrived, more suspicious comments were whispered, and I grew more desperate. Something was very wrong, and I was going to have to face it alone.

"You haven't cheated us, have you?" said an impatient Welsh woman. Though it was a question, it was stated more as an accusation.

"No, of course not. Perhaps his wagon broke down."

"Or maybe his horse went lame," Aneshka suggested.

"Maybe we should get our money back," came another voice from the crowd.

"Please, you have to believe me. He always comes!"

A stir went through the crowd of women, and their

attention turned away from me. Women at the edges of the crowd scurried away. I turned to look where everyone else was looking. Mr. Johnson was approaching with three men in dark suits. Two of the men carried shotguns and wore badges. I couldn't read the badges, but I didn't have to. I knew they were the Pinkerton detectives my father had mentioned — the private police force of the mining camps. I had heard plenty of rumors about Pinkertons in our year in America, and none of them were good. The sight of the detectives now sent a bolt of fear through me. I whispered to Aneshka to run home with Holena, and I pushed them both away from me. The little girls slipped out of the crowd through the legs of the women. There was no such simple escape for me. I knew it from the look on Mr. Johnson's face when his eyes met mine.

Chapter 23

"WHAT'S GOING on here?" One of the detectives called out as he approached. "Who's in charge here?"

I glanced around at the women, every one of them struggling to get by. None of them could afford trouble with the mine.

"I am, sir," I said, stepping forward on trembling knees.

"You," the man said, surprised.

"She's the one, all right," Mr. Johnson said. "She's been nothing but trouble. She's a union rabble-rouser if there ever was one. Her and her pa, too."

The detective gave Mr. Johnson a doubtful look, and his shotgun sagged a little. "Hardly Mother Jones, is she? She's just a kid!" He looked back at me, a sarcastic smile on his face. "You a union organizer, miss?"

"No, sir," I said, trying to look as young and innocent as possible. "I am only thirteen."

"Then what's going on here?" Mr. Johnson demanded. "What are all these women doing here?"

The crowd had continued to scatter, but there were still women around me who had not been able to slip away. My mind raced for an answer, but I couldn't think of anything that would save us all.

"Sewing circle," said a bold voice behind me. I turned, and was surprised to see Nancy Llewellyn.

"Sewing circle?" asked one of the detectives.

"My oldest girl's getting married," Nancy said, "and we've fallen on hard times, a bit."

"So Trina, here, organized a sewing circle so the lass will have some pretty things to take with her," added Glenys.

"Is that so?" said the second Pinkerton, looking at me. "Friend of yours, is she?"

"Yes, sir," I said, trying to keep my voice steady.

"What's her name, then?"

"Mary." Half the girls in school were named Mary, so it was as good a guess as any. "We're schoolmates."

"So then let's see this sewing you're doing," Mr. Johnson said, trying to trap us in our lie.

I suppressed a smile as all the women around me pulled bits of sewing, mending, knitting, or crocheting from apron pockets. These were the sorts of things women carried with them to fill idle moments.

The detectives looked at each other, their shotguns now hanging casually at their sides. Mr. Johnson shouted at them to arrest me, but they only shook their heads and rolled their eyes. They did not seem to have any better opinion of the storekeeper than anyone else.

"You've got quite an imagination, Johnson," said one of the detectives. He turned back toward the store. The other clapped a hand on Mr. Johnson's shoulder to walk him back the same way, but Mr. Johnson jerked loose. He glared at me, practically purple with rage and humiliation.

"You think you're so clever, pulling the wool over their eyes, missy, but think again. You haven't got any of the things you sold. I'd say you better pay the money back or you could be finding yourself in jail. It's theft to take the money and not deliver the goods." He gave one last nasty smirk in my direction and turned to follow the Pinkertons back to his store.

The women dispersed quickly, but not without giving me looks of warning.

"We've got to have our goods or our money back," Glenys said before slipping away herself. "I'm sorry, lass, but that's just the way it is."

I nodded and fled to the one place I could be alone, the cottonwood by the creek. Once again, my family's hopes and dreams had been snatched away. I did not have the goods or the money to return to the women. Even if I paid them back with the money we had saved, it wasn't nearly enough. And besides, that money was all my family had now.

I simply had to get the goods, but it was impossible. Mr. Torentino must have been run off by the Pinkertons, and I had no way of bringing the delivery up from Trinidad myself. I had lost everything—Mark, our money, my business. And all for having believed once again in a foolish dream. I sunk down in my shady refuge, and gave in to my misery.

I don't know how long I cried beside the pool before Papa found me. Holena was with him, and of course she had known where to look. Papa sat down on the raised root of the tree and gently caressed my hair.

"There now, Trina. Things aren't so bad; you've just had a fright, that's all," he said.

I shook my head. "I'm sorry, Papa. I've ruined us. I didn't mean to." I could not go on. Fresh tears spilled down my cheeks.

"Trina, you are taking this too hard. I will find another job. Come to think of it, this is probably a lucky turn."

"But Papa, there's more that you don't know." Shakily I told him of the delivery that hadn't come. "People want their money or their goods, and I don't have either. Papa, it was eight hundred dollars! We can't even begin to repay them."

Papa's face looked grim and he sat silent for a long moment.

"I'm scared, Papa. What if they send me to jail? Mr. Johnson says—"

"Where does this Mr. Torentino come from?"

Papa's sudden question surprised me. "His store is in Trinidad. I have the address." I pulled the order book from my pocket and showed Papa the first page with the prices. Mr. Torentino had written the name and address of his store across the top.

"Then we will have to go find him. Come on."

"Today? Now?"

"We haven't got time to waste."

We returned home only long enough to tell Momma we were going and to gather a few things for our trip, including a substantial portion of our money. I wasn't sure that Mr. Johnson wouldn't concoct some reason for the Pinkertons to raid our home, and I couldn't bear to lose the money we had to them!

"If anyone comes for their order, tell them there has been a delay and I have gone to town to sort it out," I instructed Aneshka. She nodded seriously, a fierce look on her face, and I knew she was adequate to the task.

Momma frowned. "But Tomas, we are already in enough trouble. Let's just pack and go."

"We can't." Papa said. "Trina and I will be back tomorrow."

We set out on foot, carrying supper in Papa's lunch pail since we could not expect to reach Trinidad before nightfall. A shred of luck remained with us, for we encountered a farmer with a wagon headed to town. We hitched a ride for almost half our journey, but it was still past dark before we arrived in Trinidad, and all the businesses were closed. We walked the main streets, until we found Mr. Torentino's store. It occupied a brick storefront with a large glass window along the front. The words TORENTINO AND SONS MERCANTILE AND EXCHANGE were painted in large gold letters across the window. We stood outside and peered through the glass, looking for all the world like country yokels who had never seen a store before. It looked much like Mr. Johnson's store inside, the narrow interior crammed with everything under the sun. It was dark and silent, and there was no sign of Mr. Torentino.

"We'll come back in the morning," Papa said. We walked on, past the closed businesses around Mr. Torentino's store, pausing briefly in front of the land office, looking at the advertisements pasted on the board just inside the window. Everything cost more money than we had, and once again my hope failed me. Papa, though, smiled and pointed at listings for acres of fruit trees or prime river-bottom land for vegetables, pretending we could afford them. I let out a deep sigh of sadness, but Papa patted my hand where it nestled in his.

"Someday, Trina. You'll see," he said.

Turning from the land office, we crossed the street to the hotel, where we took a room with two narrow, squeaky beds.

Despite my exhaustion, it was hard to sleep in the strange room without my whole family around me. I was worried about Momma and my sisters, alone in our house. I was praying that Mr. Johnson and his Pinkerton detectives would not give them any trouble. I could hear Papa stirring in the next bed, and I knew he could not sleep either.

I squeezed my eyes shut, but a sense of shame washed over me. How had I gotten my family into this? I thought I had learned my lesson when the chickens were killed. How had I gone back to my foolish dreams, and made matters even worse?

"I'm sorry, Papa," I said into the darkness. "I didn't mean for this to happen."

"Nothing's happened yet, Trina. In fact"—Papa paused, but I could hear the mischief that had slipped into his voice—"I think it is just my wish going according to plan."

"Your wish?"

"Remember? I wished for a farm, and I thought it was the garden and chickens, but now I think I was wrong. This must be it—I got fired so I could get my farm."

"Papa, be serious," I said. I appreciated his attempt to make me feel better, but it didn't help. He didn't know that I really had, for a time, believed there was magic in those wishes.

"What good is being serious?" Papa said. "Besides, maybe I am serious. We don't any of us know what's going to happen, do we? So where's the harm in expecting the best instead of the worst?"

"Because it's like Momma says—dreams like that only lead to disappointment."

"And you were disappointed when your chickens died, weren't you."

"Yes," I said, feeling a lump rising again in my throat as I remembered that awful day.

"But was it really the loss of the chickens that hurt you, Trina?"

"No," I admitted. "It was so much more."

"Right. It hurt so much because you lost your dream that day. You gave up on all your hopes and plans."

I lay in silence, surprised that Papa understood all that so well, when I hadn't been able to make Momma understand. "So," I said, "that's my point. Dreams just set you up for disappointment."

"No, *giving up* sets you up for disappointment. That's the big difference," Papa said. "That's why I say we are on our way to getting that farm. I refuse to give up."

His logic was tugging at my heart, tempting me back into the dream. But fear and remembered pain held me back.

"Momma says only a fool believes in dreams," I said.

"Your Momma's afraid," he said quietly. "That is why we have to do her dreaming for her." I heard him shift in the bed. "But for now we had better get on with some real dreaming of our own, don't you think?"

I rolled over onto my side and realized I could sleep now. Papa had made me feel better. "Good night, Papa," I said.

The next morning we were up early. Papa waited patiently at Mr. Torentino's storefront door, but I couldn't hold still. My stomach was knotting with nerves. I paced the length of the block until he arrived to open.

"Mr. Torentino!" I cried from nearly a block away when I saw him putting his key into the lock. Two boys were with him, both somewhat younger than me. I assumed they were the sons referred to on his window.

He turned, looking surprised, then broke into a warm smile. "Miss Trina!"

"Mr. Torentino, I have to have those orders, or else the money back!" I blurted out, without even a "good morning."

226

He unlocked the door and ushered us inside, glancing around nervously as he did. When we were all in the cool, dusty interior of the store, he spoke again. "I am glad to see you safe, Trina. I was worried! Did they give you any trouble?"

"A little," I said. I introduced my father to Mr. Torentino and told him what had happened.

"They accused us of trying to organize a labor union, but I don't think Mr. Johnson really believes that. I think he just wanted to be rid of competition," I said.

Mr. Torentino nodded and smiled at Papa. "Your girl's got quite a head for business. When she first came up with this idea, I didn't think it would amount to much. This week I've gotten more business from her than from the coal company. That's what's got them scared."

"What happened to you?" I said. "Why didn't you come yesterday?"

"Well, I was up at the store at my usual time. My wagon was half-full of produce and canned goods for the store, and half-full of your orders. But I never unloaded a thing. When I stopped my wagon in front of the store, old Johnson steps out with three Pinkertons. One of them had a shotgun. I didn't even get down from my wagon seat before Johnson says, 'You been cheating me right under my nose.' I says, 'I don't know what you're talking about.' And he says, 'You've been supplying them union organizers, haven't you? I've seen all the extra goods that you don't unload here. And then next thing I know, there goes that Greek girl with a load of goods, up to camp. I know what you're up to.'

"And then, two of the Pinkerton men came up to my wagon and started pawing through everything, spoiling the vegetables while they were at it. I couldn't do a thing to stop them, as the one with the gun was keeping his eye on me every minute."

"Did they confiscate your merchandise?" Papa asked.

"Did they hurt you?" I added.

"No, but they made me plenty mad, that's for sure. I guess they were looking for guns or something illegal. I says to them, 'There's no law that says I can't deliver supplies to my customers here.' And old Johnson, he just laughs and says, 'No, but this is private property; this whole town belongs to CF&I. If you come up here again, we'll have you fined for trespassing. And no need to make other deliveries to me, either. I'll be doing business elsewhere.'

"Then his Pinkertons escorted me back down the road to the edge of the company land and told me to go on back home. I hated to leave without letting you know what had happened, Trina, but what else could I do? That man with the shotgun just kept standing in the road watching me. So I kept going, right back here with everything still loaded in my wagon."

"Were you scared?" I asked. Chills were creeping up my spine just listening to him.

"Mostly I was mad, but I'll admit it gave me a prickle on my neck to have that fellow with the shotgun watching at my back. I'd have been a lot more scared if you had been waiting for me. I've been worrying about you ever since. I'm awful sorry to hear what this has done to your family."

Papa nodded. "They say we've got to be out of our house and out of camp by tomorrow. You can see that we have a real problem if Trina doesn't have the money to give back to the people in the camp. They are going to demand it before we go."

"But I don't have it either. It's all in the merchandise on the wagon," Mr. Torentino said, "and I can't take my wagon back up there. If your customers will come to Trinidad, I'll be happy to give them their goods."

I shook my head. "It is fifteen miles or more," I said. "And no one in camp owns a horse or wagon. But—" I paused and thought. An idea was starting to form in my mind. "How much space does the merchandise take up in the wagon?"

"Without the delivery that went to the store, about half the bed."

"So if it was all spread out on the bottom, no one could see it without actually coming up and looking in."

"If you are thinking that I could sneak it in, forget it. I can't go back up there whether I have anything in my wagon or not. I'm sorry, Trina, but it's not worth the risk. The coal companies have so much power around here, they could put me right out of business if they wanted to."

"You can't go back up there, but we can, until tomorrow. In fact, we have to. So, I was wondering if Papa could borrow your wagon for my family to move our household into town," I said with an innocent smile.

Both Papa and Mr. Torentino stared at me.

"If they knew it was his wagon, they still might stop us," Papa said. "They will likely recognize his team."

"But if we wait until this evening to go into camp, after the store is closed we could get by. Besides, they admitted to Mr. Torentino that there was nothing illegal in his deliveries, just trespassing. And until tomorrow, we still live there, so we won't be trespassing."

"I don't know, Trina. There could still be trouble. They pretty much make the law up there," Mr. Torentino said.

"But if we don't do it, all those people will lose their money.

Mr. Johnson said I could be arrested for stealing. Please, Mr. Torentino? Papa?"

Papa nodded slowly. "I'll try it, if Mr. Torentino would be willing to loan us his wagon and team."

"It's the least I can do," Mr. Torentino said.

"Oh, thank you!" I exclaimed, feeling relieved and nervous all at the same time. I had to deliver the orders; I knew that. Still, the thought of getting caught by the Pinkertons sent another shiver along my spine.

"I wish I could do something more," Mr. Torentino said with a kind smile. "If you'll be staying here in town, I could offer Trina a few hours of work here in the store. It wouldn't be much, but I hate to see such a good head for business go to waste."

"What I was hoping is that I might find work on a farm," Papa said. "You know of any that need help?"

"I'm sure there's plenty that need help with the harvest," Mr. Torentino said. "But that won't keep you through the winter."

"We came to America to have a farm," I said. "If I had been able to take orders in camp for just a few more months, we might have been able to buy one."

Mr. Torentino's eyebrows raised. "You mean you have been saving your money all this time for your family?"

I nodded. "But it hasn't been enough."

Mr. Torentino laughed. "I figured you and your sisters were spending it on lemonade and candy and new dresses to impress the boys."

"No, sir."

"I should have known better. Like I said, a good head for business. So how much money have you saved up?"

"Not enough for a farm," I said. "I'll have one hundred and eighty dollars if I could fill this week's order."

"And I collected fifteen from the mine yesterday," Papa said. "They had to pay it all out in cash since they were firing me."

"Well, I have a few connections, but I have to get opened up here first," Mr. Torentino said. "Then, Trina, if you'll stay here with my boys and run the store, your papa and I can go talk to the folks at the land office."

Eagerly I agreed to the arrangement. While Papa and Mr. Torentino were gone, I waited on customers for him. When there were no customers, I gathered the necessary goods for my remaining orders. Mr. Torentino's sons, Antonio and Vincenzo, though younger than me, were very helpful. I better understood his willingness to work with me despite my young age.

When all the goods were gathered, I watched for Papa's return. With each passing hour I felt a little more nervous about my plan, and I knew that Momma must be beside herself with worry by now. Finally I saw Papa and Mr. Torentino approaching. They both looked pleased, which I hoped was good news. I wanted to ask the moment they came through the door, but I didn't get the chance. Before I could say a word, Papa had swept me off my feet and spun me around in a big hug.

"What did I tell you, Trina! Didn't I tell you? We've got a farm!"

I gasped. I couldn't help it; it was too much to believe. "A farm! A real farm?"

"On the Arkansas River," Mr. Torentino said with a smile. "Sixty acres of vegetables and another thirty of apple trees."

I pulled away from Papa. "So much? But we don't have the money for that!"

"Not to buy," Papa said, "but enough to lease. Turns out there's a fellow looking to move into town, but he hasn't been able to sell his farm, so he's willing to lease it."

"Lease it?" Such an idea had never occurred to me before.

Papa nodded, grinning wildly. "The papers are already drawn up. There'll be no real profit this year, since we didn't plant or tend the crops there now. But after that, we can use our profits toward buying it. And I think, Trina, that in just one good year, we could make the money to buy it. What do you think?"

I smiled. Papa was off and dreaming again, and he'd never looked happier. I was feeling pretty happy myself. Who would have thought so much good could come from so much trouble? I stepped back into Papa's embrace and let his big dreams and big arms catch me up.

"Why not, Papa. It's a new country and a whole new century," I said. And it was America — a land for dreamers — where lucky coincidences made those dreams come true. Or at least it had been for me, since I had seen a fish and made a wish.

Chapter 24

ALL THE WAY back to camp in the wagon, Papa was whistling Bohemian folk songs or talking about what we'd plant in the spring. I shared his happiness at first, but as we got closer to camp I felt increasingly nervous. We still had the load of goods to deliver. I had no choice but to deliver it, for Papa had already committed our saved money to the lease of the farm. Refunding so much as a penny to my customers was no longer an option.

One other fact weighed on me as well, marring my happiness. Leaving the mining camp meant saying good-bye to people I loved. Saying good-bye to Mark. The fear and excitement of the previous day had kept me from thinking about him or the little ring of copper wire I had returned to him. I wanted him to come away from the coal camp, but how was I to convince him? He'd made it plenty clear he had no desire to farm.

As we came nearer the camp, Papa's whistling quieted, then stopped altogether. I could see his expression through the dim light and knew that he was worried about trouble too.

"Do you think they'll be waiting for us?" I asked into a silence that was already filled with the question. We could see the mine hoist in the distance now, haloed by the setting sun.

Papa shaded his eyes with his hand. "Well, we'll know soon, won't we?" he said. I shaded my eyes too, and looked where his gaze was fixed. Someone was standing on the road ahead of us, just this side of the store. I felt my chest tighten and I forced in a deep breath. *It might not be anyone connected to us at all*, I reminded myself. But as we drew closer, I could see the man was watching our approach. With the sun behind him, I could not tell who it was, though he could probably recognize us.

"Should we keep going?" I asked uncertainly.

Papa shrugged, but his grip tightened on the reins. "What else can we do?"

We continued forward, now almost to within shouting distance of the man in the road. He could have easily called out a greeting to us, but instead he turned and ran back toward the camp.

"Well!" Papa said. "I do believe that's your Marek."

He was right. We could see Mark's uneven gait. As we watched, he ran past the store, which was closed at this hour, and on up the road until he was out of sight.

I felt relieved, but also confused. Why hadn't he greeted us or waited long enough to tell us whether or not the Pinkertons were watching for us?

"Perhaps he's gone to let Momma know we are coming," Papa said. "She's probably worried sick with us being so late."

"You are probably right," I agreed, but my nerves only tightened.

"Well," Papa said, "he gave no warning, so the road must be clear."

I nodded, but I gripped the seat tightly with both hands as we came into town, passing the company store first. The doors were closed and the lights were out in all the buildings, but I could not keep my eyes from turning toward them as we passed. I saw no movement in any window and no one stepped out any door. Once past the store, we were climbing the hill, passing the houses of our neighbors. Many of them were on their front porches and watched us pass. I looked back and saw several of them, those who had orders to be filled, rise from their chairs and follow us up the road. By the time Papa reined in the team in front of our house, it would have looked like a welcome-home parade if not for their silent, nervous expressions. They wanted their goods, but they didn't want trouble with the mine officials.

Momma was on the front porch, drying her hands on a towel as Papa stopped the wagon and we both jumped down. Papa hurried up the steps and grabbed her in a hug like he had done to me as he announced the good news. Momma gave a quick, girlish squeal of surprise that set both of my sisters giggling, but over the din of it all, Papa was telling Momma of the farm.

I looked around. "Where's Mark?" I asked. He should have been here after the way he had run ahead of us.

Old Jan, who had been sitting on the porch with my sisters, put his arm around my shoulders and walked me back off the porch and toward the wagon, where women were congregating. His face wore a worried, strained expression.

"Do you have those purchases you went for?" he asked.

"I do."

"Then you better get on with your deliveries as quick as you can."

"But where's Mark?" I asked again.

Old Jan glanced around before he spoke in a low voice. "He's at the superintendent's office."

My heart froze. Had Mark been stopped by the Pinkertons when he had run ahead of us?

"He's not going to get fired too, is he?"

"Just get your deliveries taken care of," Old Jan said. "Quickly."

I nodded and climbed up into the wagon, calling Aneshka and Holena to help, and we were soon handing down goods to the women who had followed us. I had expected to be done with that quickly, as only a handful of women had seen our wagon coming into camp, but soon I noticed that the line was not getting any shorter, and I was handing out goods to women who lived several streets away. Word was apparently spreading fast. Within an hour, I had dispersed nearly everything.

Aneshka and Momma set off to deliver the few orders that remained so that Papa and I could eat our supper. We were just walking up the porch steps when someone shouted behind us.

"There they are — and that's Torentino's wagon. I recognize his team! I knew it!"

We turned back to see Mr. Johnson walking toward us, Mark beside him. He didn't look like he had been dragged in by the Pinkertons. No one was forcing him to walk with Mr. Johnson. I threw a questioning glance at him, but he looked away.

"If you've brought contraband goods to this town, I'll have you arrested!" Mr. Johnson shouted, running to the wagon to look inside. When he saw that the bed was empty, he didn't seem to know whether to puff up indignantly or slink away shamefaced.

"We rented the team and wagon to move to town," Papa said. "So we can get out of our house by the deadline."

Mr. Johnson squinted at us, angry he hadn't caught us red-handed. Then he wagged a finger at my father. "You think you're so smart, do you? Well, don't. We know all about you—this boy has told us everything about your secret union meetings."

"But that's a lie!" I said, looking angrily at Mark. "There were no secret meetings here."

Mr. Johnson gave a snorting laugh, his arrogance returning in force. "We know all about you now, and word's gone out to every other mine in the state. You won't find work anywhere. You're finished in the mines. You might as well pack up your bags and go back to where you came from."

Papa and I looked at each other for a brief moment, then Papa burst out laughing.

"You're right, Mr. Johnson," Papa said. "We are finished in the mines. Good-bye."

We went inside and shut the door behind us, but not before seeing Mr. Johnson's shocked expression. My father was still laughing.

I watched through the window to make sure he did no harm to the team or the wagon. It was probably the sort of thing he would gladly have done if he'd thought of it. As it was, he was so surprised by Papa's reaction that he did nothing but walk away. I might have laughed too, but through the gathering darkness, I could see someone else turn away.

Tears sprang to my eyes. I knew Mark was angry with me, but I never thought he would be spiteful toward my whole family. The pain of his betrayal was sinking in now that the confrontation with Mr. Johnson was over. I skipped the supper my papa was piling on a plate for me and went straight to bed, where I cried myself to sleep before my sisters got home.

* * *

The next morning we were all up early. We ate a hasty breakfast of oat porridge and coffee. Momma, who had been up before any of us, packed a cold lunch of bread, pickles, and cheese. When breakfast was done, we cleaned everything in the kitchen and arranged it all in the washtubs or crates, using towels and blankets to cushion the few fine things Momma had brought with her from Bohemia. Packing was not a difficult task; after a year in America we had little more than what we had come with. Yet our hearts and minds were all filled to bursting with the realization of Papa's dream, and that gave a new richness to our labors.

Of our neighbors, only Old Jan and Martina came to help us. She brought plum kolaces for our dinner on the road and stayed to help Momma fold the sheets and blankets so they would come out crisp and ready to use. Old Jan helped lift our goods up into the bed of the wagon. I avoided him, still too angry about his son's lies to want to face him.

When nearly everything was in the wagon, Old Jan and my sisters took the team to the creek to drink and eat a few mouthfuls of grass before we hitched them up. I stayed behind to help Momma with the last few chores. Papa found me out back a short time later, beating the dirt from the last rag rug.

"That will do, Trina. Don't you have any good-byes you want to say before you go?" he said, jabbing his thumb over his shoulder toward Mark's house. "He's working the night shift again, so he should be home."

Bitter anger surged in me again. "He betrayed us, Papa! He lied to the superintendent about you just to get us in trouble. I never want to see him again!"

Papa's eyebrows shot up. "Is that what's been bothering you all this time? Trina, it was a trick."

"A trick?"

"The superintendent and his detectives will listen for hours to anyone willing to squeal on union organizers. Marek knew we were going to need time to unload goods if we had them. When he saw us coming, he ran to the superintendent and told them the kind of stories they wanted to hear so we had time to unload. Old Jan explained it all last night."

"Why did he say you'd had meetings, then?" I said, still angry.

"Well, what harm could the mine do to me? He didn't want to get anyone else in trouble who still needed the job here."

"What about them?" I asked. "If he said he'd been at these meetings, couldn't he have been in trouble too?"

Papa's face grew serious and he nodded. "It was certainly a big risk for him. We can only hope that it doesn't come back to hurt them. He did it for you, Trina. Now go say good-bye."

Tears burned my eyes as I realized the size of my mistake. Mark had risked his own job to help me get a dream, even though that dream stood in the way of what he wanted. I put down my broom and hurried to Mark's house.

He was not home, so I knew where he had to be. If he had things on his mind, he had always gone to the same place I went, so I set off for the creek. At the creek bottom I found the horses tethered in a patch of dry grass where they were chewing contentedly. But my sisters and Old Jan were not with them. It seemed all our paths led to the same place in this last hour before we left the camp for good. That felt right to me. Whether there was any magic in that quiet pool or not, it was forever linked to our dream in America. I was glad to get the chance to say good-bye to Mark and his father there, where so many good things had happened. And I hoped that the spot might have one more bit of magic left for Mark and me.

When I rounded the bend, I saw what I had expected to see. The cottonwood leaves were turning autumn gold, and Old Jan, Mark, and my sisters were all together in their golden shade. I had thought that perhaps my sisters had taken Old Jan there so he could tell them one last story, but the telling seemed to be the other way around. Aneshka was talking up a storm, her hands gesturing wildly. Holena was nodding in agreement and throwing bits of bread into the pool. Mark was sitting by himself a short distance from the others with his back toward them and his shoulders hunched. A painful tug at my heart stilled my breath when I saw him.

Aneshka glanced up from her storytelling and saw me approaching. A huge smile spread across her face and she gave a quick bounce of excitement.

"Trina's here! Now he will come for sure!" she called excitedly. She ran to me and grabbed my hand, to pull me to the tree.

"What? Who will come?" I asked. Everyone I expected to see was already there.

"The magic carp, of course," Aneshka said.

Old Jan smiled up at me from his seat on the tree root. "Your sisters have been telling me the whole story of your wishes, and how they have all come true. They brought me here so I could see the carp and make a wish too."

Holena turned to me. "Please help us find him, Trina. We want Old Jan to get a farm too."

"And he could wish to have his leg back," Aneshka said.

"And Mark could marry you," Holena added quietly.

"Holena!" I said, glancing, mortified, at Mark's back. He gave no sign that he had heard, but I knew he had.

Old Jan laughed. "That's an awful lot to wish for," he said.

"But we got all our wishes," Aneshka pointed out.

"But you have to see the fish first," said Holena, "and we've been down here a long time. I don't think he's going to come."

"Well, never mind, girls," said Old Jan. "Magic carp can be finicky things. They don't show themselves until they're good and ready."

The twinkle of pleasure in his eyes warmed me. "That's true," I agreed. "But Old Jan will still be here, Aneshka. He can come look for it, and sooner or later, he's bound to see it. Then he can make whatever wish he wants to."

"Will you, Old Jan?" asked Aneshka. "Promise you will come down here every day until you see the carp and make your wishes."

"Please?" Holena said.

"Well, I don't know if I can promise every day," said Old Jan, "but I'll try, for you girls."

"Oh, but it's not for us," Aneshka said. "It's for you."

"This is all such nonsense!" Mark said suddenly, jumping to his feet. "Enough of your magic and your wishes and your dreams, Papa! It all comes to nothing!"

"But it hasn't," I said. "My family has their farm, and we are going there right at harvest. Come with us, Mark. Please."

"We've been through this before, Trina."

"But it would just be for a little while. You could look for work in town. Maybe you could even go to high school. You told me once you had planned to do that before your papa's accident."

"It wouldn't make a difference! I'm a coal miner, and I'll always be a coal miner, and that's not good enough for you."

"But what about your dreams for the future?" I begged.

"My dream for the future was you. I don't think I believe in dreams anymore."

241

I stepped forward and took his hand. "Mark, I love you. If you would just try again, I promise I will wait for you, and I'll go anywhere with you."

"Anywhere but here," he said.

Slowly I nodded. "Anywhere but here."

"And with this foot, I can't work anywhere else."

"But you can, if you just try! If you would just believe—"

Mark shook his head and pulled his hand out of mine. "It's all dreams, Trina. And for a while you had me believing, but life isn't like that. Life isn't one of Papa's fairy tales, full of dreams and wishes and magic fish." He paused and took a deep breath. When he spoke again, he was pleading with me, his eyes desperate. "I have something here, Trina. It may not be much, but it's real. Stay with me, like you promised."

"I can't, even if I wanted to. Mr. Johnson would just have you fired too, to get rid of me."

"And, you don't want to."

I dropped my eyes and shook my head again.

"Good-bye, then," he said, bitter and defeated. He stepped out of the shade and walked away without looking back. I wanted to run after him and beg him to change his mind, but I knew it was no use. I sat down on the root, trying to fight back tears, but without success. Holena sat down beside me and slipped her hand into mine.

"He'll change his mind, Trina, when he hears how nice our farm is," she said. "You will write him every day. He'll see how much he misses you, and he'll come join us and marry you, and you'll be happy. Okay?"

Despite my sadness, I couldn't help smiling at her innocent faith. "You are just like Papa," I said, hugging her to me.

She squeezed my hand and nestled against me. "So are you."

"Come on, we're wasting time!" Aneshka said. "Trina, help us make the fish come out."

The pool had shrunk over the summer to little more than a wide spot in the creek. I could see no sign of the fish. I couldn't even be sure it was still there now that the water was so low. With noisy Aneshka there and the water no longer lapping at the roots of the tree, the magical feel of the place was gone. Or maybe the magical feeling was gone because all the wishes had been granted.

I shook my head to clear it of the idea. Though it had only been a few months since I'd first come here, I felt much more grown up. I planned to face the future with a clear head. No more magic fish for me.

"Aneshka," I said, "seeing the fish won't make any difference. Everyone has to do what they will in their own time."

Aneshka stamped her foot. "But it will! The fish is magic! You saw it, and we got three wishes."

"It's true we got our wishes," I said, thinking back over all that had happened that summer, "but we've worked hard for them too, haven't we. The fish didn't send me to the Llewellyns' house to do their washing, or to Mr. Torentino for jars." I laughed at a new thought. "In fact, you might say it was Mr. Johnson who granted our wishes. He's the one who sent away the plums, overcharged me for the jars, and made Papa and me go to Trinidad for the order. Why don't you go ask Mr. Johnson for three more wishes, Aneshka."

She glared at me. "You said you believed, Trina. You said so yourself!"

I nodded. "I did believe, and that's when things really started getting better. I think —" I paused and chose my words carefully, wanting to get it right. "I think the magic was in the believing, and not the other way around."

Aneshka looked confused, but Old Jan smiled and nodded. "Believing can be powerful magic, indeed."

"But if there's no magic fish, what is there to believe in?" Aneshka said.

"Your dreams," I said. "Don't you see? Once we believed we could get our dream, we all started working harder for it and didn't give up. Well, *you* didn't give up, Aneshka, even when I did, and you pulled me back when I strayed. Hard work and believing is what got us our farm."

"That's not true!" Aneshka said. "How do you explain the plums? How do you explain that Mr. Torentino just happened to know someone with a farm for us? That wasn't our hard work; that was magic!"

"Well, let's think about that," Old Jan said slowly, considering. "The plums were certainly lucky. But as for the farm, what does Mr. Torentino do for a living?"

"He owns a store," Aneshka said.

"More than that. He brings all kinds of goods to the mining camps like ours, right? He buys produce from farmers and sells it to Mr. Johnson. He probably knows a hundred farmers, and farming's hard work for low pay. Some of them are bound to be as desperate to get out as you are here. I think opportunities are probably around us all the time, but we have to be looking for them before we see them. What do you think?"

Aneshka frowned, but before she could answer, Papa appeared from upstream with the horses and called to us. Holena and Aneshka both got to their feet. Aneshka gave Old Jan a hug. "I still think it's magic," she insisted before flouncing off to where Papa was waiting.

"Maybe when Mark sees it like Trina does, his dreams will come true too," Holena said to Old Jan as she hugged him.

He patted her cheek and smiled. "Perhaps."

He chuckled as he watched her skip away. "With her wisdom, Holena will always have magic," he said.

"And Aneshka?" I asked. We watched as she took the reins from Papa and started bullying the horses up the path.

"That one won't need magic. She'll make things happen all on her own."

"And Mark?" I asked quietly after a moment. "What about Mark?"

Old Jan sighed. "My little Marek has let magic slip through his fingers, and not for the first time."

"Do you think Holena is right? Do you think he might still change his mind if I write?"

Old Jan gave a sad sigh. "Marek gave up on his dreams when I lost my leg. That was my fault, I suppose, because I quit believing. He tried to revive his dreams this summer, but they are so fragile, Trina. Maybe, when his heart is not so full, he'll find the strength to try again.

"As for me, watching you this summer has me believing again. I think you may be leaving behind just enough magic for the two of us."

I brushed tears from my cheeks and gave Old Jan a hug. "I'll miss you," I said.

"Write when you can, child," he said.

I started back up the path, toward where Papa and my sisters had disappeared around the bend. Just enough magic, he had said, but I was leaving behind more than that. I was leaving behind good people, the hardest thing of all to leave. But just maybe I was leaving behind enough hope for a wish, and of course, there was still the magic carp.

No sooner than I had the thought, I heard the familiar soft

plop in the water. I turned to look back. Ripples were forming on the surface of the pool, and the fish's nose was just breaking the surface as it nibbled on a bit of Holena's bread. Old Jan turned toward it, and I could see his lips move.

Smiling to myself, I turned and climbed the bank to join my family as we set out once again, chasing the dream that had brought us to America.

Author's Note

WHILE I have not specified the coal camp in which this story takes place, I have tried to make the setting of this novel typical of the coal camps of southern Colorado around the year 1900. Though they were called "camps," these were permanent communities where many mining families spent their entire lives. The coal companies owned all the houses, stores, saloons, and gathering places in the towns, and since they were somewhat isolated from other communities, there were few options for residents other than those the coal company provided.

The many nationalities of miners that I have presented are accurate to those found in turn-of-the-century coal camps. Prior to 1900, the Welsh and Scottish were recruited heavily, and they were established in some of the better-paying jobs by the time my story starts. After 1900, the mines recruited heavily from eastern and southern Europe. They believed that by maintaining a large population of diverse foreigners who spoke many different languages, they could keep their labor force from unionizing, since the immigrants could not communicate well.

Of course, the difficulties in communication also led to more accidents in the mines, which increased the distrust among ethnic groups. And mining accidents were common. In 1900, half of all workers' deaths in the United States occurred in two industries: coal mining and railroading.

To create authentic details for the family life of miners, I relied heavily on the book *Coal People: Life in Southern Colorado's Company Towns 1890–1930* by Rick J. Clyne (Colorado Historical

Society, 2000), which not only describes the social life of the camps but contains numerous firsthand accounts of what life was like. Many of the background details of my story are based on the anecdotes recorded in those accounts. I also drew upon visits to the area and historic photos in the Western History Archives of the Denver Public Library, which can be accessed by the general public online at photoswest.org. Prices for goods were taken from newspaper ads of the era, and inflated, as they would have been in the coal company stores.

The Eastern European fairy tales told by Old Jan are all traditional stories, although I allowed Old Jan to tell them in his own style, as all traditional storytellers do. Versions of some of these stories can be found in the Favorite Fairy Tales series, retold by Virginia Haviland and published by Little, Brown and Company. For variety, other versions of the same or similar stories were found on the Internet.

Acknowledgments

I OWE heartfelt thanks to a number of people. My mother Betty and daughter Leah have always been my first and best readers. I have benefited from the advice, encouragement, and at times much needed nagging, from excellent critique partners: Mike, Megan, Kiersten, Jenn, Victoria, Lisa, and Rebecca. My son Greg has been my go-to idea man and keeps me laughing, and I suspect my husband Ken has stayed in bed longer than he really wanted to some Saturday mornings to give me quiet time to write. In addition, thank you to my young beta readers, Holland and Graham, who helped me see it through middle-grade eyes.

Once my little manuscript got past all of them, it benefited from the wisdom, insight, and professionalism of my brilliant agent, Erin Murphy, and my wonderful editor at McElderry, Karen Wojtyla. And to her patient assistant Emily Fabre and all the behind-the-scenes folks at Simon & Schuster who take a stack of pages and turn it into a beautiful book, thank you.